RAVEN'S
PEACE

BOOK 1

PEACEKEEPERS
OF SOL

RAVEN'S PEACE

GLYNN STEWART

FAOLAN'S PEN
PUBLISHING
faolanspen.com

This edition published in 2019 by:

Faolan's Pen Publishing Inc.

22 King St. S, Suite 300

Waterloo, Ontario

N2J 1N8 Canada

ISBN-13: 978-1-988035-93-2 (print)

ISBN-13: 978-1-989674-02-4 (epub)

A record of this book is available from Library and Archives Canada.

Printed in the United States of America

1 2 3 4 5 6 7 8 9 10

First edition

First printing: November 2019

Illustration by Sam Leung

Faolan's Pen Publishing logo is a registered trademark of Faolan's Pen Publishing Inc.

Read more books from Glynn Stewart at faolanspen.com

CHAPTER ONE

THE BATTLECRUISER SHOOK AROUND HIM AND HENRY WONG recognized the dream. It was a familiar nightmare now, which helped rob it of the strength it had had months before.

"We have a grav-shield blowthrough," a seemingly faceless noncom reported across the warship's bridge. "That dreadnought hit us dead-on."

"We're going to get shot to pieces!" That figure had a face. Commander Kveta Vela wasn't *that* pale and sunken-eyed in reality, though. The dream warped Henry's old navigator into a figure of nightmare.

It fit there.

"The shield will hold," Henry heard himself bark. With a moment of practiced effort, he separated himself from the dream-him.

He'd learned he couldn't *stop* the dream, but months of therapy allowed him to disconnect from it.

The man in the center of the bridge of the battlecruiser *Panther* was less warped than the officers and crew around him. Tall and narrow-shouldered, Colonel Henry Wong was a beanpole of a man with short-cropped black hair, dark skin and his father's dark Chinese eyes.

The dream didn't distort him much as his old ship dove through the maelstrom. The figure of dream-Henry was focusing on the set of massive screens giving the bridge a view of the world around the United Planets Space Force battlecruiser.

Henry himself didn't need to look. The arrangement of forces in the Set-Sixteen System was burned into his brain, even asleep. His perception was still pinned to his dream self's, though, and he was dragged to it.

Set-Sixteen was a Kenmiri provincial capital, deep on the far side of the Empire from the United Planets. The Kenmiri hadn't been expecting an attack and their defense fleet was weaker than it should have been. That fleet was still five full dreadnought battle groups and the UPSF's Vesheron allies were getting hammered.

Panther's grav-shields and weapons could turn the tide of that fight—but that wasn't their mission, and the birdlike starship plunged through the Kenmiri lines.

"There," Henry's avatar said sharply. "That ship. Broos, confirm."

Commander Broos Van Agteren wasn't a normal part of *Panther*'s crew. He was from United Planets Intelligence, their handler for Operation Golden Lancelot.

In person, he was a squat and dark-haired man with a ready smile and a brilliant glint to his eyes. In the dream, he was a distorted goblin, every aspect of his features twisted and torn to make him into the monster of Henry's own subconscious.

"Confirmed," Van Agteren told him. "That's the evacuation ship for the Kenmorad. The queen and her consorts will be aboard."

The ship was the size of one of the dreadnoughts pounding the Vesheron ships behind *Panther* but lacked their devastating main guns. The evacuation ship had one purpose and one purpose only: to evacuate the Kenmorad population of Set-Sixteen if they felt the planet was threatened.

A Kenmorad breeding sect could repopulate an entire planet of

Kenmiri drones in a few years. They could create more breeding sects, more drones...more Kenmiri.

The Kenmiri couldn't reproduce *without* the Kenmorad.

"Ser, that's the last one. We *can't* kill her!"

Lieutenant Colonel Emil Tyson had been *Panther's* executive officer, Henry's right-hand man and lubricant who kept a battle-cruiser working in the face of the enemy. The redheaded Irishman hadn't raised any complaints on the day. They hadn't known.

"Stand by all missiles and prep the main gun," Henry's avatar ordered, as if Tyson hadn't spoken. "Vela, get us in hard and fast."

Panther lunged across the void in a quarter of the time she had in real life. Suddenly, it was the moment of truth, the evacuation ship's escorts making a suicide charge at the battlecruiser as *Panther* dove toward her prey.

"She's the last one, ser," Tyson repeated, the avatar of Henry's subconscious. The one that *knew* what he'd done, even if he hadn't then. "If we kill that ship, *we* commit genocide. *We* end a species."

Henry hadn't known the full scope of Golden Lancelot. He wasn't sure if anyone aboard *Panther* had—he knew that Van Agteren *hadn't* known when they fired. He suspected the Intel officer had guessed...but hadn't realized that the breeding sect they were firing on was the last one left.

"Ignore the escorts," dream-Henry barked. "Target the evac ship with *everything*. Fire!"

It had taken dozens of missiles and multiple hits from the main gun to take out the evacuation ship. In his dreams, however, there was only the single gravity-driver round that had finished her off. It flashed across space and detonated, turning itself into a shotgun blast of superheated plasma.

The Kenmorad evacuation ship vanished inside that blast, and Henry released a chunk of unconscious hope. Even separated from the dream as he'd been taught, he still hoped that it would end differently.

"That's it, then," Van Agteren said, the goblin-like appearance of the dream version of the man growing more grotesque by the moment. "The Kenmorad are no more. The Kenmiri will die. We are victorious!"

Henry didn't need to look. He already knew that both the version of him in the dream and the version of him watching the dream had hands covered in blood.

HENRY STARTED awake as the dream ended. He always did. Time and familiarity had eased much of the horror of the dream, along with copious amounts of therapy, but...well. He poked at the metal band wrapped around his left arm.

MedSuite detected nightmares. At this stage in your treatment, MedSuite recommends meditation.

He sighed. The band was linked into his internal network and talking to the implants in his head and elsewhere. He had enough authority over the device now to override it and tell it to give him drugs. If he did that, though, it would probably add days to his medical leave.

Rolling out of bed, Colonel Henry Wong settled himself onto the floor of his bedroom. The apartment wasn't much, but it at least gave him privacy. It was better than the orbital hospital he'd spent the first six weeks of his twelve-week medical leave inside.

"One more appointment," he said aloud. The walls were bare. This wasn't *his* apartment—it belonged to the United Planets Space Force Medical Division. The entire building on Sandoval did.

The ground floor of the building was shops and restaurants, like most of the not-quite-downtown area of New Detroit, Sandoval's capital city. Above that was a floor of UPSF security, then two floors of medical clinics, then fifteen floors of apartments.

If his appointment went well, he'd finally be out of there *today*. Command only knew where he'd go from there—psychological casualties were notorious for being unpredictable in how long it took to return to duty, so *Panther* had a new Captain now.

He focused on the meditation, letting his anger, grief, horror...all of his emotions flow through him. He might have given the order for the final critical shot, but no one had told *him* what Operation Golden Lancelot entailed.

Henry was honest enough to admit that after seventeen years of war, he'd have signed off on Golden Lancelot. He was also honest enough to admit that he understood why the full scale of Lancelot's objectives had been kept under wraps.

It had worked, after all. Henry had gone into psych treatment in a Space Force still on a war footing. He'd be coming out of it into a Space Force on a peacetime footing.

Seventeen years of war.

Henry Wong had started the conflict with a fiancé and a starfighter. He'd ended it a divorcé with a battlecruiser.

He barely *remembered* the all-too-excited younger pilot who'd greeted the news of first contact with joy.

But the world turned and people adapted. He'd adapted to a decades-long, seemingly unwinnable war.

He was pretty sure he could handle peace.

CHAPTER TWO

"WELL, COLONEL?" DR. SCHULT ASKED. THE PSYCHIATRIST HAD spent over an hour grilling Henry on everything from his nightmares to his datanet use over the last few weeks. She was a dark-haired woman wearing the same dark blue UPSF uniform as he was, though hers came with a black headscarf as well.

"Well what, Doctor?" he asked after a moment. After twelve weeks of at *least* daily sessions with Dr. Schult and her colleagues, he still found them brutal. He'd thought he was an introspective man, but the intensive psych rehab that followed being casualtied out of active duty was something else.

"Your mental state has been stable for a solid eight days now," she told him. "You're not quite to where I'd want you to be, to be completely frank, but you may well be as close to fighting fit as I can get you.

"So, I'm looking at one critical question, Colonel Wong. Do *you* feel that you are ready to return to active service?"

Henry breathed a long sigh as he considered the question. He didn't even know what active service was going to entail for him. There weren't *that* many spacegoing commands that needed a full

Colonel—the UPSF's trio of carriers had Commodores in command, their thirty-two destroyers only needed Lieutenant Colonels, and all twenty-three battlecruisers already had captains.

"I…" He paused. "I don't know, Dr. Schult," he admitted. "I know I'm probably reaching the end of how long I can be under supervision in a MedDiv apartment without going nuts, no matter how much freedom I have inside that.

"I don't know if I'm ready to be put back in the command seat of a warship, but I also don't think the UPSF has one for me. I know… I know I need to do *something*, Doctor, and the only thing I know how to be is a combat spacer."

Everything dropped into place and he smiled broadly at the doctor as he leaned back in his chair.

"I don't know if I'm ready," he repeated. "But I know I'm ready to try."

"Good answer," Schult said with an answering smile. "And good enough for me, Colonel Wong." She waved a hand through the haptic interface field above her desk, looked at something in the screen only she could see, and then pressed her thumb down.

"You're released from MedDiv supervision and returned to active duty as of twelve hundred hours GMT today, Colonel," she told him. "That's about one thirty New Detroit time. It takes at least an hour for everything to process through, so I like to give it extra time.

"Standard protocol is for you to report in to the nearest Force Base. There'll be a car waiting for you at one thirty. By the time you make it to Base Skyrim, they'll have visitor quarters ready for you—that's included in the order I just submitted."

She rose and offered a hand to Wong.

"You've been as cooperative a patient as I could ever hope for, Colonel, and I know this was a terrible situation all around," she told him. "My own opinion of the situation that led you here is complicated, but I doubt your own is simple."

"No, Doctor," he confirmed as he shook her hand. "It's not. But we deal with the past and move on. Nothing else we can do, is there?"

"No. So, get your ass back to work, Colonel," Schult told him. "Between you, me and the wall, I had an official request to confirm whether you'd be returning to duty in the next week. I suspect there may be *something* waiting for you."

"Thank you, Dr. Schult," Henry replied. "For everything."

Something waiting for him? That wasn't intimidating at all...but it was definitely the game he'd put on the uniform to play.

THE CAR COULDN'T DELIVER him directly to Base Skyrim, if for no other reason than that Base Skyrim wasn't *on* Sandoval. The massive Force Base had been the anchor for UPSF actions against the Kenmiri Empire, and it orbited Procyon's fourth planet: Rose.

Procyon's government was the one of the UPA's eight member star systems most likely to support UPSF expansion and funding. Part of that was because Base Skyrim was now the largest Space Force base, so Procyon benefited disproportionately from spending by the United Planets Alliance's military.

The other was that Procyon was the closest of those eight star systems to the Kenmiri Empire. The Red Wing Campaign—so named for the near-complete annihilation of the UPSF's starfighter corps over a six-month period—had ended *in* Procyon.

Memories of that battle flashed through Henry's head as the space elevator delivered him to a transfer orbital. He and Peter had been the only survivors of the Red Wing Campaign from their carrier. By the time *Rygel* had gone into the Battle of Procyon, there'd been only four veteran pilots aboard.

The newbies had all died in orbit above this planet. So had half of the surviving vets. Henry and his fiancé had lived blessed lives, but they'd been there to watch the first Kenmiri invasion fleet hit the massed strength of the UPSF and fail.

In some ways, the starfighter corps had never recovered from that campaign. Henry and Peter had both transferred to starship track after that, and they hadn't been the only ones. It was the starfighters that had saved the UPA at the beginning, but it was the battlecruisers that had carried the war after that.

From the orbital, he boarded a UPSF official shuttle, exchanging salutes with the pilot and security as he took his seat.

Senior officers were first on, first off, and there was no one on the small interplanetary craft more senior than a UPSF Colonel. The ship was too small for artificial gravity, too. The generators for that were bulky and fragile things—and since the shuttle would spend its entire trip accelerating and decelerating, thrust would provide what "gravity" was needed—while inertial compensators kept that thrust from crushing the passengers.

"Ser, may I ask a question?"

Henry looked up at the young man sitting across from him. For a second, he thought the younger officer had to be a relatively new recruit. Then his implant highlighted the insignia on the other man's uniform: the paired steel bars of a full Commander, combined with the crossed rifles of the UPSF's Ground Division.

The UPSF was a combined military. A GroundDiv Commander could be in charge of as many as six hundred men, a full strike battalion. The man had to be at least in his thirties, even if modern medicine kept his age from showing at all.

From the grand precipice of fifty, Henry thought the man still looked like a kid.

"The flight lasts four hours, Commander," Henry pointed out. "Colonel Henry Wong. You?"

"Commander Alex Thompson," the Commander replied. He was a solidly built blond and blue-eyed man. He could have stepped out of a recruiting poster.

"Your question, Commander?"

"Your wings," Thompson said, gesturing at the icon pinned to Henry's uniform. "I've never seen that particular version before. Red and gold?"

Henry nodded slowly. He still wore the wings that marked him as qualified to fly a starfighter—these days, he'd probably be better off conning a battlecruiser, but he'd kept up the qualification—but his were done in gold with a red center. Most officers would have a chrome insignia with either a black or gold center, depending on whether they were qualified on shuttles or combat starfighters.

The red center wouldn't have shown up on the other man's implant because it was technically a violation of the uniform code—if one that no one had begrudged its wearers in the last fifteen years.

"You know what red wings mean," he told the younger man. "You're here in Procyon, after all."

"You flew in the Red Wing Campaign?" Thompson asked. "I... didn't think there was anyone left!"

"Not flying starfighters," Henry said with a moment of sadness. "Last I checked, there were eleven of us left."

Four battlecruiser captains. One carrier captain—Henry's ex-husband, Commodore Peter Barrie. One Admiral. Five retired or medically discharged. He'd checked the previous day. He hadn't had much to do *except* research, after all.

"As for the gold," Henry forced a smile. "I'm not surprised you don't know, Commander. It means I made ace, shooting down at least three hostile combat spacecraft from a starfighter."

Thompson looked suitably awed for a moment, then confused.

"I didn't think the Kenmiri had starfighters," he noted. "Bunch of the rocket-jocks I knew kept complaining about it: nobody made ace in the war 'cause there was nothing to shoot down."

Henry chuckled.

"I would be very surprised if I am not significantly older than any rocket-jock you know now, Commander," he pointed out. "I didn't make ace against the Kenmiri. I made it before the war in anti-piracy patrols."

He shook his head. Enough people had died in peacetime anti-piracy actions that he couldn't call them "better days." Gold ace wings had been more common then.

Most of the pilots who'd earned them *during* the war had earned them the same way Henry had. Just because humanity was locked in a desperate struggle for their lives didn't mean the pirates had packed up and gone home.

"Damn." Thompson shook his head. "They say you were there from the beginning to the end, ser, but it's easy to forget what that means!"

"'They,' Commander?" Henry asked. It appeared that introducing himself had been redundant.

"Rumor mill and reputation, ser," Thompson replied. "Not much for them to do these days but chatter about heroes."

"I'm no hero, Commander," the Asian-American Colonel said firmly. "We have a job. We do the job. If we do it right, a lot fewer people die. You get me?"

"I get you, ser," Thompson confirmed. "I've led extraction drops on Kenmiri worlds, ser. The people you pull out of work camps, they think you're a hero...but all you remember is the ones you didn't save."

"Exactly." Henry shook his head. "You being transferred to Skyrim, Commander?"

"Just got the bump to O-4," the younger man told him. "I'm transferring to *Raven*, taking over her onboard ground detachment."

"I've heard good things about the *Corvid*-class ships," the Colonel replied. "I'm sure she's lucky to have you."

"Everyone's paranoid about peace cuts," Thompson said quietly. "I'm just glad to have a billet. Government seems to think the war is over, but I hadn't seen anything saying the Kenmiri agree just yet!"

Henry chuckled, but he didn't argue. The Kenmiri hadn't officially surrendered or given up or...well, anything. But the reports from the Vesheron—the rebels from the many species the Kenmiri had conquered—were that the insects were pulling back. They weren't just pulling occupation garrisons from annexed worlds but evacuating entire colonies.

Millions—probably *billions*—of red insectoids were on the move as the Kenmiri tried to find a path into a future that no longer included their breeding and ruling caste.

He'd seen the wrong end of their fleets and their ground troops too many times to cry crocodile tears for them, but he could still feel sorry for them.

And if he hadn't had that skill, he wasn't sure Dr. Schult would have let him go!

CHAPTER THREE

LARGE CHUNKS OF BASE SKYRIM PREDATED ARTIFICIAL GRAVITY, which meant that the core facilities were built around massive habitation rings. They no longer rotated, but it was easier to refit an old station with gravity generators than to build a new station.

The largest of the rings was the central station. A trio of UPSF SF-122 Dragoon starfighters orbited above it, a cautious reminder that the station's weapons had proven far harder to update. Two battlecruisers were docked to the station at opposite sides.

One at least looked familiar to Henry: one of the *Jaguar*-class battlecruisers that had carried the weight of the war against the Kenmiri. She carried a three-hundred-and-sixty-meter-long gravity driver as the main weapon, matching the length of the core hull. Thirty meters wide and tall with eighty-meter-long wings, each carrying four missile launchers.

He knew the *Jaguar* class like the back of his hand. The ship on the far side of the station from the *Jaguar*—this one was *Leopard*, he picked out as the shuttle swooped over it—was both similar and very different.

His implant told him that this one was only three hundred meters long—which dredged the rest of the details from his memories and databases. Her core hull was forty-five meters wide and tall, and her wings stretched a hundred meters out from her hull. A *Corvid*-class battlecruiser, she was in every sense a superior ship to the old *Jaguar* class.

"That's *Raven*," Commander Thompson told him. "Hell of a ship, right?"

"I have my biases," Henry admitted with a smile. "I commanded a *Jaguar* for six years, Commander. They're damn fine ships. But I have to admit, you can't argue with the upgrades for the *Corvid*s."

"I'm mostly partial to the expanded ground detachment myself," Thompson admitted. "A short battalion instead of a double company. Double the size."

"And a full Commander's slot instead of a Lieutenant Commander's?" Henry asked. "So, a command that lets you stay in space?"

The younger man chuckled.

"Only three carriers in the fleet," he agreed genially. "Unless you have strings to pull, you're not getting one of those slots as a GroundDiv officer. Doesn't take much promotion to get yourself kicked to a desk as a ground-pounder, ser."

"A desk" was an exaggeration for the senior ranks in the Space Force's ground contingents...but not much of one. In seventeen years of war, Henry wasn't sure there'd been fifteen ground deployments larger than a battalion. There definitely hadn't been twenty.

"So, the *Corvid*s having larger detachments is good for GroundDiv careers, huh?" Henry asked. "I wonder if that was the reason."

He heard Thompson swallow hard as the shuttle swung into its final docking bay.

"I don't believe so, ser, but I wouldn't know," he admitted.

"Neither would I," Henry agreed. "Though I can tell you there were a few times during the war when I wished my *Panther* had another company or two of GroundDiv troopers. Ground-pounders or not, you always managed to make yourself useful."

"We do try, ser."

The shuttle settled down into the artificial gravity field with an almost unfelt impact. The pilot was *good.*

"And it seems we have finally reached Base Skyrim," Henry said aloud, rising and stretching. "It's been a pleasure, Commander Thompson. Perhaps we'll meet again."

"I'll buy you a beer if we have the chance, Colonel," Thompson replied. "Less rank in the mess, after all."

"That there is," Henry agreed. The shuttle hatch slid open and he gave the GroundDiv officer a salute. "Good luck, Commander. I suspect *Raven* is lucky to get you."

HENRY WONG DIDN'T KNOW Skyrim Central as well as he'd known *Panther*, but his ship had been based there for most of the six years he'd commanded her. It only took him a moment to reorient himself and look up his destination.

It had been all of those six years since he'd needed Visiting Officers Administration, after all! The area was located close by, thankfully, near most of the shuttle bays that people would arrive on the station through.

Declining an offer of assistance from the NCO of the deck for the landing bay, he shouldered his duffle bag and set off. The steel oak leaf of his rank would get him a human donkey if he needed, but he was perfectly capable of hauling the duffle himself.

It might have been over ten years since he'd been on Earth and almost twenty since he'd visited the United States, but he'd still been raised a self-sufficient Montana boy. His father might have looked like he'd escaped a Hong Kong action movie about rogue cops, but *he'd* been born in Montana too.

And the old man would have laughed his ass off at his son needing someone to haul the duffle bag for him.

Visiting Officers Administration had a small reception area in front of two large desks. The chairs looked reasonably comfortable, and both of the Chief Petty Officers holding down the desks themselves were attentive and awake.

The black Chief in the desk on the right was free and gestured for Henry to come over.

"Chief Petty Officer Andrew Adebayo," he said in a sharp accent distinctive to the main colony in Keid, known as 40 Eridani until people actually lived there. "Scan in, please, Colonel."

Adebayo flipped a reader field across the haptic interface of his desk, and Henry placed his hand on it. The field ran over his hand for a second, a mild tingling sensation as it scanned his handprint and linked to his network, then vanished in a green halo around his hand.

"Colonel Henry Wong, correct?" Adebayo asked. "I have your appointment listed in the system as being in just over an hour on Deck One. You should be able to grab a transit pod and make it there in plenty of time."

Henry blinked.

"That might be a mistake," he admitted. "I'm supposed to be checking into Visitors' Quarters and notifying Command of my location as I stand by for assignment."

"Let me check," the noncom replied. His hands flickered across the desk, but the system projected whatever he was looking for directly into his eyes. Henry couldn't see anything.

"Yes, I see that," he finally said. "That request was filed at eleven hundred GMT this morning. You were flagged as assigned and the request for housing was canceled at fourteen hundred GMT."

"I was an on interplanetary shuttle in deep space at fourteen hundred hours, Chief," Henry pointed out. "Assigned where?"

"That information hasn't been released to the general system yet," Adebayo told him. "It usually isn't until the officer has been informed by their superiors or received a physical writ, in the case of a proper command."

Henry couldn't help himself. He fingered the rocket insignia that declared him a member of Space Division—the portion of the Space Force that *actually* contained starships.

He'd held two of the archaic paper writs declaring him captain of a UPSF starship in his life, but he hadn't realized that no one was advised of the assignment until the captain held that writ.

"You don't know anything, Chief?" he asked. "That's fair, but it leaves me swinging in the dark."

"I know you have an appointment at eighteen hundred hours on Deck One," Adebayo said with a brilliantly white grin. "Office one-six-six-eight." He paused. "That's the visitor office in the Admirals' box, ser. Security on the Deck One Command Center, then more security for the Admiralty Annex. Might take you more time to get in than you think."

There were seven Admirals in Base Skyrim, but Henry felt a sinking sensation in his chest as he realized that, with his luck, it could only be one of them.

"I need somewhere to change and store my duffle," he told Adebayo. He'd traveled to Base Skyrim in a duty uniform—dark blue slacks and a turtleneck with his insignia.

He was *not* meeting an Admiral in that!

ONE DRESS UNIFORM, one transit pod, and two extremely thorough security checks later, Henry had entered the Admiralty Annex on Deck One. Part of him wanted to go right to Office 1668 without checking who the room was assigned to.

The rest of him was too much a tactician to go into battle without knowing the ground. Stepping over to the wall just inside the door, a gesture into the haptic interface field brought up the directory.

Confidentiality and habit might keep the identity of the occupant of the visitor's office in the Annex quiet outside this space, but efficiency required the directory there, inside all of the security, to be complete.

Henry was unsurprised by the name: Vice Admiral Sonia Hamilton. She wasn't officially assigned to Base Skyrim—officially, she commanded the United Planets Fifth Fleet—but her command was notorious for being sliced up into single-ship detachments scattered across known space.

It was Fifth Fleet's battlecruisers that had carried out the long-distance strikes of Operation Golden Lancelot, including *Panther* under Henry's command.

Hamilton was also the woman who'd ordered him declared a psychological casualty. She'd probably saved his life...but she'd done so after he'd had what he now recognized as a PTSD attack and sworn at her.

Staring at the name, he pulled out a flimsy. Unrolling the thin display, he gave it instructions via his network and checked his current status in the system.

As Chief Adebayo had noted, his new assignment hadn't been released yet. What *was* in the system, however, was that while he'd been transferred off *Panther,* he had never been reassigned from Fifth Fleet.

An Admiral's orders always had priority. In this case, though, not only was Vice Admiral Sonia Hamilton an Admiral, she was also his direct superior officer.

There was no way to avoid what he suspected was going to be an awkward conversation at best. Concealing a sigh, Henry rolled up the flimsy and returned it to the pocket inside his jacket. Another gesture flipped the directory to a mirror, and he double-checked the uniform.

Class Two Undress Uniform was basically the same dark blue slacks and turtleneck as a duty uniform—though lacking the safety features that would turn a duty uniform into an emergency vac-suit—with a black jacket overtop carrying his full medals and decorations.

After seventeen years of war and twenty-seven years of active service, Henry Wong had enough of those that his uniform jacket could probably be used as a bludgeoning weapon.

Its perfect alignment, an unconscious arrangement borne of practice, wasn't going to give him an excuse to delay. With a deep breath he concealed from the Commander holding down the Annex's front desk, he turned.

Giving the young man at that desk a firm nod, he set off for Office 1668.

CHAPTER FOUR

Arriving at Admiral Hamilton's office several minutes early despite everything, Henry parked himself on the wall across from the door and prepared to wait.

He was rudely disabused of that notion when the door slid open and Hamilton's familiar bark echoed out.

"Get your ass in here, Henry," she ordered. "They gave me an adorable security camera and I don't have anything *else* scheduled for the next hour."

"Yes, ser."

Removing himself from the wall before he even managed to get comfortable, he entered the office. Coming to attention, he saluted the white-haired woman sitting behind the desk.

"When, in the twenty years you have known me and been under my command, have you known me to want that mickey mouse shit, Colonel?" Hamilton asked. "Sit. Down."

"Yes, ser," he responded, echoing his earlier words as he obeyed.

Then–Colonel Sonia Hamilton had been the captain of the support carrier *Rygel* when the war had started. Henry had spent two years under her command as one of her Fighter-Div pilots, the aptly-nicknamed rocket-jocks, but had lost track of her when he'd transferred to SpaceDiv.

They'd met again when she was the battle group commander when he'd served as executive officer on a destroyer, and she'd been his first battle group commander when he commanded his own destroyer.

She'd received Fifth Fleet around the same time he'd received *Panther*. Age had whitened the Admiral's hair, and she'd gone from wearing it in a long braid to shaving it into a tight white cap. It certainly hadn't *softened* her.

"Let's get one thing out of the way, since I know you're going to have a stick up your ass about it," Hamilton said calmly. "You told me, and I quote, that you 'didn't have a fucking clue where your ship was and didn't give a flying fuck.'"

Henry winced.

"That was followed by a stream of gibberish that I believe *may* have included the phrases 'tin-pot dictator' and 'ironclad bitch,'" she continued. "Do I have that roughly correct, Colonel?"

"I don't remember the details that well," he admitted. "But roughly correct, yes."

"I got the report from the medics I sent to your office, but would you like to tell me what was on your desk when we had that *memorable* conversation?" Hamilton asked him, her voice suddenly soft and gentle.

That he was never going to forget.

"My insignia, a bottle of rum, and a loaded nine-millimeter pistol," Henry said flatly.

"You are aware, I assume, that being a psych casualty is recorded on your record merely as being wounded?" she asked. "While we all believe ourselves to be modern souls, people are people and make dumb choices. It is never officially revealed that you were stood down for psychiatric reasons.

"So far as I'm concerned, Colonel, you bled on me," she told him. "I no more hold it against you than if you'd lost an arm and physically leaked on me. You were injured and that was how you showed it. We got you the help you needed. End of story, yes?"

"If you insist, ser," Henry conceded.

"I do insist," Hamilton said as she pulled a pair of glasses and a bottle of rum from under the table. "Not least because *I'm* quoting what Admiral Sasaki told *me* when I returned to duty after the Battle of Procyon."

"Ser?"

"I was psych-casualtied after Procyon, yes," she confirmed. "And *I* told Admiral Sasaki to go stick their iron pipe up their ass."

Henry had met Admiral Jun Sasaki once. The legendary admiral had died with their flagship in the fifth year of the war, in the daring offensive that had led to humanity's first contact with the Vesheron. Sasaki had been a notoriously strict taskmaster with, as Hamilton was suggesting, a reputation for having an iron stick up their ass.

"I did not know that," he admitted.

"And that's how much people will know about your own incident," Hamilton told him. "PTSD is a sneaky evil bitch, but we *can* treat it. You're going to be okay."

"So I'm told," Henry replied. "Dr. Schult cleared me for active duty, and it seems Base Skyrim's systems say I'm assigned somewhere. I'm guessing that's why I'm here?"

"Of course it's why you're here," Hamilton snapped. "I've had a fucking Fabergé egg of a project dropped in my lap: fragile, critical... and no one in Command seems to give a shit. You get to haul it for me."

Henry took a moment to process that, then felt a smile spread over his face. There was only one meaning to that: he was getting another ship.

"What's the mission?" he asked.

"The war is over," Hamilton noted. "That's the part Command and the General Assembly are paying attention to. So far as we can tell, there isn't a Kenmiri within a hundred light-years of UPA space.

They've abandoned occupied planets, garrisons, outposts...even the provincial capital at Ra-7."

"I'd heard the reports," he said. "I didn't think it was that complete."

"Right now, it appears that the Kenmiri Conclave of Warriors is in charge," she said. "That's the eldest and best of their Warrior drones. I'm guessing there's a lot of push and pull between the Warriors and the Artisans, with the Workers stuck in the middle."

She made a throwaway gesture.

"Their problem, not ours."

Henry nodded his agreement. The three-way split of the sterile Kenmiri drones had always weirded him out, but if the Conclave of Warriors was in charge, Hamilton's assessment was probably right.

All of the drones were easily of human-level intelligence with genetic memories, but each caste was physically and mentally tailored to their purpose. Warriors were bigger, stronger and faster, their minds and bodies programmed for war. Artisans were smaller and smarter, their minds and bodies programmed for delicate construction and technology.

Workers fell somewhere in between, with the catch that *they* only had a life expectancy of about fifteen years to a Warrior or Artisan's seventy. During the Empire, they'd been supported in turn by vast numbers of non-Kenmiri slaves from the occupied worlds.

"So we're, what, looting?" he asked. The UPA had been lucky in that their gravity technology was well ahead of the Kenmiri, but the *rest* of their tech was still behind. Gravity shields had rendered Terran warships nearly invulnerable, allowing them to close with Kenmiri warships that were faster and armed with longer-ranged weapons.

"I wish," Hamilton replied. "No. Diplomacy, Colonel. The Vesheron have called a Great Gathering, with all of the people who fought the Kenmiri to meet and discuss the future of the galaxy."

"Which Vesheron?" Henry asked carefully. "I mean, hell, technically *we're* Vesheron."

Vesheron basically just meant *rebel*. All of the groups that had fought the Kenmiri were Vesheron, and that included at least twenty species and twice that many factions.

"El-Vesheron," the Admiral corrected. "We were outside the Empire, so we're El-Vesheron. Like the Londu or the Terzan."

"And we have no idea which Vesheron, which I find bloody fascinating," she concluded. "Given the nature of that fragmented collection of factions, I'm surprised the call was broad enough to prevent us pinpointing a source.

"But that's what it looks like we've got."

Henry nodded slowly. The Vesheron had always been interesting to work with. They'd mostly been equipped with stolen Kenmiri ships, usually the lighter warships, but they'd refitted them to be disturbingly effective.

The word *Vesheron* itself, though, was in the Kenmiri trade language, Kem. Kem was the only language the Vesheron factions had in common with each other, let alone the El-Vesheron outsiders who'd joined their fight.

Plus, well, three-quarters of the species included in the Vesheron could pass for human at a distance—as could the Londu, one of the other two El-Vesheron species. *That* was a headache that was driving biologists nuts but was thankfully outside of Henry's area of expertise.

"It probably came out of the Restan initially," he said slowly. "They were probably the single most organized of the factions, basically a government in exile."

"I'd agree. Not least because the Gathering is going to take *place* at Resta," Hamilton told him. "But that could just as easily be because they were the first faction to really reestablish themselves in a position of authority. They're firmly back in control of their system and even building ships."

She waved a hand through the desk's interface field and threw a hologram of the region into the air. UPA space was blue. Londu space was orange. The old Kenmiri Empire was marked in translucent red.

Resta flashed purple inside that translucent red. Well into Kenmiri space, it was also almost exactly halfway between Londu and UPA space.

"I wonder if they're worrying about us and the Londu," he murmured.

"I would in their place, though I know damn well they don't need to worry about us," Hamilton replied. "Half of the General Assembly wants to pull in all of our connections and pretend the rest of the galaxy doesn't exist. Deal with our own problems.

"The other half is in shock at what we did to the Kenmorad." She shook her head. "Nobody wants to conquer anybody. We're going to be watching our own planets and claimed stars."

Henry's gaze focused on the blue area claimed by the United Planets Alliance. Eight member systems, the colonies with tens of millions of people or more. Three dozen outposts or claimed systems, none with more than a couple of million souls and half of them empty.

There were entire inhabitable worlds inside the zone the UPA had claimed. They had more than enough to keep them busy.

"But the Resta are right in the middle of everything and feeling threatened," he concluded. "So, they get a puppet or six to set this Gathering in motion to set up rules and plans going forward."

"That's Intel's read," Hamilton confirmed. "You'll have a briefing waiting for you when you get to your ship, but that's most of it. The two key things you need to know are that we don't want to get dragged into anything. We want peace and trade deals, but not enough to want to commit ships or troops."

He nodded.

"And the second?" he asked.

"Intel is one hundred percent certain the Londu are going to take advantage of the opportunity to press for territorial gains," she told him. "They've already got two near-human species in their space, and they're not going to blink at integrating a few more if it gets them a few dozen inhabitable worlds and a hundred or so stars."

That would probably be more than the Londu could digest, Henry figured, but it would also still only be a fraction of the space up for grabs. The Kenmiri had ruled ten thousand stars, and it looked like they'd already abandoned half of that.

At least.

"I see what you mean about *Fabergé egg*, ser," he told Hamilton. "It's going to be a game of intimidation and diplomacy, and I can't do much of either on my own. I'm assuming there's going to be a diplomat?"

"We're meeting her for dinner in thirty minutes," the Admiral said calmly. "And the intimidation is going to be a matter of everyone waving their dicks around and saying 'mine's bigger.' We're the UPA. They know what we bring to the table."

"So, how much 'dick' am I going to have to swing?" Henry asked bluntly.

"If some folks had their way, we'd have been sending your ex's carrier with a full support group," Hamilton told him. "The Assembly nixed anything more than a single ship—and specifically said no carriers, too."

Henry swallowed a snort of amusement at that. The UPA's carriers weren't designed for independent deployment, not really, but the four-hundred-meter-long starships definitely made for a solid argument of "mine's bigger."

"Instead, I'm sending the nastiest hunk of metal I've got, with a Captain whose name they all know. The man who landed the final blow: Colonel Henry Wong."

"I'm...not entirely comfortable leaning on that particular reputation, ser," he admitted.

"Get comfortable, Colonel," she told him. "You paid for it. Just like I paid for the reputation of being an ice-cold bitch who'd feed starfighters into the grinder without blinking. If you've already bought it, you may as well use it.

"But most important for now..."

She pulled two things out from under the desk and slid them across the desk.

He'd been expecting them both, but they still sent shivers down his spine. The first was the writ, the archaic paper document giving him command of a United Planets Space Force starship.

The second *looked* simple. It was simply a piece of white fabric, a wrap that would velcro onto the neck of his uniform sweater. Only one type of person in the entire UPSF wore a turtleneck with a differently colored collar.

That white collar declared the wearer the Captain of a UPSF starship.

"We're giving you *Raven*," she told him. "Shiniest and nastiest of the *Corvid*-class battlecruisers. She isn't *Panther*—and believe me, I know that hurts—but she's the sharpest sword I have to give to the sharpest Captain I have."

Henry stared at the writ and the collar for several silent seconds.

"Well, Colonel? Is it *Captain* again...or do I need to find another officer for this mission?"

He grabbed both items and met Sonia Hamilton's gaze.

"Captain Wong, reporting for duty, ser."

CHAPTER FIVE

The collar and the writ both went into an inner pocket of Henry's uniform jacket. He was allowed to wear the collar now— as a former starship Captain, he still had uniform turtlenecks with the white collar as part of the garment instead of an add-on—but he wouldn't feel entitled to it until he'd actually taken command of *Raven*.

Admiral Hamilton clearly felt that was lower priority than meeting his passenger and led the way into a private transit pod that whipped them through the station.

With a gesture in the air, she flipped a three-dimensional image from her internal network to him. It was hard to judge size from a hologram, but he guessed the woman to be tall and slim, a sharp-faced individual with shoulder-length blond hair and a piercing gaze.

"Piercing" looked like a good descriptor of her in general, and he suspected that was at least partially intentional.

"This is Em Sylvia Todorovich," Hamilton told him. "UPA Diplomatic Corps. For this mission, she's acting as our plenipoten-tiary Ambassador."

With the name and the face, Henry's internal network easily

pulled Em Todorovich's official record. Ten years younger than him, she'd entered the diplomatic corps directly from university—on the exact day, in fact, that he and Hamilton had watched the rest of *Rygel*'s fighter complement die at Procyon.

"She's from Epsilon Eridani," Hamilton told him. "Long tradition of service in the Eridani government and in the Novaya Imperiya before that."

Henry snorted.

"I can't blame anyone for that," he pointed out. "My great-grandfather dropped on Tau Ceti with the USMC."

"And my also-American great-grandmother led the relief fleet for the EU under a Canadian nationality everyone knew was a lie," Hamilton said dryly. "If we're going to hold the Unity War against people, we'll be here all day."

He chuckled as Todorovich's record unspooled in front of him. She'd served as an aide to the Eridani General Assembly Member during the early years of the war against the Kenmiri. Then a junior negotiator on several trade missions through the UPA. And then...

"Wait, she was part of the Vesheron missions?" he asked.

"The junior-most of four negotiators on the second delegation," Hamilton told him. "She spent five years in Kenmiri space working to help keep the Vesheron factions pointed at the same enemy—and if you haven't made it that far, she was then joint Ambassador to the Londu with Em Karl Rembrandt.

"Rembrandt's retired, which means she's the only diplomat we've got that knows the Londu and she's probably the best we've got that knows the Vesheron. Todorovich is probably more critical to this mission than you are, Captain Wong."

Henry shook his head at the memory of Em Karl Rembrandt. *Panther* had been one of four battlecruisers on the extraction mission after the Ambassador had been captured by the Kenmiri. They'd got him out...but he'd left both legs behind.

He'd have taken Rembrandt over anyone else in the UPA's diplomatic corps, but he could understand why the old man had retired.

"I figured that from the beginning, ser," he pointed out. "I didn't know she'd worked with Rembrandt." He paused, pulling up the data. "Sorry, *joint* Ambassadors alongside Rembrandt?"

Rembrandt was almost twice Todorovich's age and had been *the* star diplomat of the UPA. If he'd accepted the woman as his equal, she was going to be one tough lady.

"Bingo. So, don't shove your foot in it, Captain. If Em Todorovich decides she wants a different driver, well..." Hamilton chuckled. "Well, it's too late for that, but she can damn well make your life miserable."

Henry smiled thinly.

He couldn't say, after all, that the Admiral was the more likely of the two of them to shove a foot in it.

THE RESTAURANT on deck two had clearly been expecting them. While technically a civilian establishment, Maya's was also one of the top five eating establishments on a military base with a hundred thousand spacers and officers.

They were quite familiar with the concept of "Admiral's priority," and a white-suited host retrieved them from the end of the already-short line within seconds of their arrival.

"Admiral Hamilton, Colonel Wong," the androgynous, shaven-headed host said with a small bow. "Welcome, welcome. Your table is waiting for you."

The host led them in, past others waiting for their own reservations—but they saw Hamilton's stars, and no one complained.

"The Ambassador's staff just updated us via the datanet that she's running slightly late and will be here in just over five minutes," the host told the two officers as they led the way through the restaurant. A mix of red and gold silk fabrics created decorative cubicles around the tables, and the sound of running water permeated the place.

There was only one fountain in the middle of the main space, though. The rest of the water sound in the restaurant was artificial—a subtler and more pleasing form of white-noise generator, Henry suspected.

They were ushered into an end table with more solid-looking walls than the rest of the dining cubicles as a strong smell of mixed spices wafted out from the kitchen.

"I'll have a server bring you water to start," the host told them as they seated the pair. "I'll be waiting for Em Todorovich myself. She won't go astray."

"Thank you," Hamilton told their guide.

The host disappeared before either of them could say more. Henry shook his head as he inspected the table. Wood wasn't cheap on a space station, but there were vast plantations of both local and Terran trees on Sandoval to supply the system's needs.

This table, though. He poked at one of the small burn marks, and his internal network cheerfully assessed it as having been varnished over. Repeatedly. Most of the varnish on the table would have been removed, but the pockmark from the burn kept the layers.

"This table is older than I am," he observed. "I think it might be older than Skyrim."

"The first Chef Maya apparently brought the tables from her mother's restaurant in India," Hamilton told him. "That restaurant had been around since the twenty-second century. At least some of the tables are over two hundred years old."

She rapped the table. "Solid enough."

Their water materialized a moment later, and Henry barely had time to take a sip before their guest arrived.

The impression of sharpness he'd picked up from Sylvia Todorovich's image was an underestimate. She was at least ten centimeters taller than he was but probably weighed twenty kilograms less. Everything about her face and body was sharp, nearly gaunt in the hard lines of her bones and her gaze as she met his eyes.

"So, this is your captain, Admiral Hamilton?" Todorovich asked, her words as swift and sharp as her movements.

"Colonel Henry Wong, meet Em Sylvia Todorovich," Hamilton replied. "Ambassador plenipotentiary for the United Planets Alliance to the Vesheron factions."

"It's just the Vesheron," Todorovich corrected as she took a seat. "The word includes an equivalent to 'factions' in its meaning. Calling them the Vesheron factions is like calling us the UPA Alliance."

"Fair." The Admiral gestured her concession. "I am not a linguist, Ambassador. Neither is the Colonel."

"I speak Kem," Henry pointed out. "The use of the extra word is to clarify to English speakers a meaning they may not pick up from the Kem word. Clarity is often a more important part of communication than the correct use of language."

The Ambassador laughed, a crisp and precise sound.

"*Teta*," she told him. The Kem word meant "struck" and served much the same purpose in formal combat contests for the Kenmiri warrior caste as *touché* did in Terran fencing.

"Only a quarter of officers serving alongside the Vesheron bothered to learn Kem," she continued after a moment. "That always struck me as unwise. Translation software is powerful and fast...but far from perfect."

"Most officers in the area of operations didn't have time to pick up a new language alongside their duties," Henry replied. "We were there to fight a war. So long as some of us could validate the translation and talk to people face to face, most of our officers could communicate by computer and their actions.

"It was more important that we fought by their side than that we could engage in cross-lingual punning."

Todorovich leaned back in her chair, studying him in silence with those piercing eyes.

"He'll do, Admiral," she said. "Where *did* you find him?"

"Rembrandt liked him. I figured you could tolerate him," Hamilton concluded. "Now, I know *you* two seem ready to verbally spar until Maya's throws you out, but *I* am hungry and would prefer to be eating this restaurant's vindaloo while I watch you do so.

"Shall we order?"

V

"YOUR JOB, Colonel, is going to be to sit in orbit and be a pointed reminder to the Vesheron that their massed fleet couldn't reliably penetrate your shields," Todorovich noted as they sipped hot milk tea after the meal.

"I know it's not going to be that simple," she continued as he opened his mouth to argue, "but at least your mission is going to be the same on a day-to-day basis. I'm not so sure of my own."

She grimaced.

"The Assembly is that bad?" Hamilton asked. "I thought we had a pretty solid idea of what we wanted."

"To be left alone?" Todorovich replied. "Yeah. Basically. But there's a lot of variation in what qualifies as an isolationist foreign policy, Admiral. The Monroe Doctrine, after all, was technically an isolationist policy—and it committed the United States to challenging the great powers of the day if they came near areas that weren't American territory."

"Is the Assembly likely to jog your elbow that much?" Henry asked. "I know we have subspace coms and all that, but that seems contrary to even your job title."

The Ambassador sighed.

"The days of radio and telephone undermined the meaning of *plenipotentiary*," she noted. "Subspace communication brings us back to that situation. When the Assembly can update my orders daily—*hourly*, if they really want to be a pain in the ass—or even have a live conversation with me, the question of how much plenipotentiary authority I have is an open one.

"My orders are to do all within our power to create a situation where the general population of the UPA does not expect their governments to ask the UPSF to intervene," she concluded. "There are certain red lines the UPA General Assembly will probably act on their own about, but in the main, they're more worried about popular opinion.

"War weariness is one thing. News and pictures of atrocities and chaos out of the former Kenmiri Empire is another. If the member systems face populations that demand intervention, then the UPA will have to intervene.

"We don't want to do that and neither do the member system governments. So, we want a stable, self-sustaining and self-policing replacement entity or entities." She shrugged. "While, at the same time, keeping enough counterbalances in place that we aren't *threatened*. There's a lot of stars and planets between us and the old border —and a lot *more* if we decide to run our colonization efforts in the other direction."

"I don't envy you your job, Ambassador," Henry admitted. "At least mine is always straightforward once the shooting starts."

The hard part was deciding *when* the shooting should start.

DINNER WRAPPED up and the three of them left the restaurant. Pausing just around the corner, Hamilton stretched exaggeratedly.

"I've got twenty years on either of you," she noted. "And my inbox is going to explode overnight, as per usual. I'm going to bed. You two should probably get better acquainted, given your mission."

And with that strange advice, Hamilton traded salutes with Henry and took off.

He checked his own internal network for the time. At twenty hundred hours, it wasn't the best time for him to report aboard a starship and take command. On the other hand, that made for a perfect opportunity to see how his new crew and officers responded to the Captain showing up without warning at an awkward time.

"Barring alternate needs, I think it's time for me to head to my ship," he told Todorovich. She gave him an oddly sharp glance.

"What kind of alternate needs do you think are going to come up,

Colonel?" she snapped. "I hardly need to tell you that is going to remain an utterly professional relationship—and I dislike the suggestion that it might not be!"

Henry blinked, reconsidered what he'd said, then sighed.

"Poor phrasing, perhaps," he said slowly. "I apologize. I was unsure if you were intending to brief me further tonight or if there were other plans discussed between you and the Admiral that I was unaware of.

"I certainly did not intend to make any kind of advance." He chuckled. "No offense, Em Todorovich, but you're not my type."

He'd never seen an eyebrow arch into *quite* so perfectly neat an angle before. That probably took practice and particularly careful grooming, too.

"I see," she replied. Her tone was still cold, but it had warmed a bit. "I have had...averse interactions with SpaceDiv Captains before, Colonel. In men especially, that collar seems to cut off blood flow to parts of the brain."

"My experience is that fighter pilots are the worst, but in that case, I think it's the helmets cutting off higher circulation," he told her.

"I haven't met many pilots, I'll admit," she said. "I'll keep that in mind. In any case, Colonel, I believe I should let you get to your ship before I embarrass either of us further."

He chuckled.

"Em Todorovich...I *was* a starfighter pilot. A minor misunderstanding is far from the most embarrassing thing I've dealt with." He gave her a precise salute. "Do you know when you'll report aboard *Raven*? My understanding is that we have less than seventy-two hours remaining before we'll need to be on our way."

"I have a few items to deal with here still, but I should be able to report aboard around nineteen hundred hours tomorrow," she told him. "An additional twenty-four hours would be optimal, but if we're in a hurry..."

"Let's plan for a hurry, Ambassador," Henry suggested. "It's your call, of course, but it's a long trip with multiple potential delays. From the Vesheron I've dealt with, we'll want to make sure we aren't the last ones there."

"Which is a vast difference from making sure we aren't late," she noted. "I'll bring my staff aboard tomorrow night, then, Colonel. Good luck with your ship."

"It's appreciated, but I doubt I'll need it," he said with a firm smile. "It's not the first time I've taken command of a battlecruiser, after all."

CHAPTER SIX

A QUICK VISIT BACK TO VISITING OFFICERS ADMINISTRATION reclaimed Henry's duffle bag from the desk and produced an eager young Spacer Second Class to carry the bag for him. Self-sufficiency was secondary to appearances when taking command of a new starship.

That young woman followed him onto the docks as he approached the tube connected to *Raven*. The area was quiet right now, with both the station and the ship running on GMT from Earth. There would still be activity outside as supplies were loaded onto the battlecruiser, but the UPSF tried to keep personnel movements during the ship's "day" where possible.

Admiral Hamilton had clearly not cared about that particular tradition, and Henry had every intention of abusing that choice. He approached the entryway at a brisk pace, watching to see how quickly the two black-armored GroundDiv troopers standing guard spotted him.

They clearly *spotted* him at least ten meters away. The pair moved slightly, one shifting toward Henry as the other one pulled back. It wasn't much of an adjustment, but it was enough to put one of them mostly out of any potential line of fire.

"This area is restricted," the closer guard stated as Henry approached more closely. "There's no one on the schedule supposed to be coming through here. What's your business?"

"She's with me," Henry said, gesturing at the young Spacer behind him. "As for my business, well..."

He slowly and carefully drew the archaic paper out of his uniform jacket. Slow and careful was necessary, since the paper was *inside* the jacket and the guards were being properly paranoid.

Their watchfulness was calibrated just about perfectly, and he made a note to get their names and pass that on to Commander Thompson. His companion on the shuttle to Base Skyrim was now going to be *his* GroundDiv commander, after all.

"I'm here to take command of *Raven*," he told the two guards. "Now, I suggest we continue on as we've started and you check my ID and orders before you take me at my word."

The closer Spacer chuckled and held out his hand.

"Orders and ident scan, please, ser," he told Henry. "We received notification of your assignment earlier today, Colonel Wong, but I'll admit we were expecting you tomorrow."

One guard made a point of reviewing the writ, but the real test was the physical handshake between Henry and the other guard. That linked their networks and allowed the security trooper to check that Henry was who he said he was—and to compare the orders on Henry's internal network against both Base Skyrim's and *Raven*'s networks.

"Everything is clear, ser."

"Good. Your names, Spacer?" Henry asked.

"I'm Spacer First Class Reginald Osprey and this is Spacer Second Class Carol Hammond," the GroundDiv trooper told him. "It's a pleasure to be the first to welcome you to *Raven*, Captain Wong."

The title sent a shiver down his spine and he inclined his head to the trooper.

"Please send a ping ahead to the XO," he told the man. "Command didn't see fit to assign me quarters aboard Skyrim, so I imagine I won't make his evening *too* hectic...but I will be taking command first."

"Yes, ser!"

"PARTY TO ATTENTION!"

Either the boarding tunnel was longer than Henry thought it was, or the guards at the door had been exaggerating the expectation that he'd arrive tomorrow.

The welcoming party of saluting spacers were all SpaceDiv, so maybe neither. It looked exactly, in fact, like an on-the-ball Chief had grabbed everyone within a minute's walk of the personnel dock to form a party.

He returned the salute as his internal network scanned the spacers. Not a single GroundDiv or FighterDiv spacer among them, and they were in duty fatigues. Some of them looked like they'd barely managed to doff their toolbelts.

Plus, there wasn't a single commissioned officer present. Out of twenty spacers, there were two Petty Officers...and one Chief. Whenever something went more right than expected, Henry's experience said to always look for the Chief.

"Thank you, Chief, POs, Spacers," he told them. "Anyone got an ETA on the XO?"

"Chief Wang Xi," the CPO introduced herself. "Lieutenant Colonel Tatanka Iyotake should be here...now."

The man in question rounded the corner as Chief Wang finished the name-dropping. A perfect piece of timing and theater on the Chief's part, and Henry made a mental note to keep an eye on her.

"Reporting, ser," Iyotake said crisply as he came to a halt in front of Henry and saluted. If he'd been on the bridge, the dark-skinned man must have started running when the guard called in Henry's approach, but he showed no signs of it.

Iyotake was a Native American man with broad shoulders and shoulder-length black hair tied into a neat braid. He radiated solid reliability, but Henry had seen men who managed to radiate that but snapped under pressure.

Most of them didn't make Lieutenant Colonel in the United Planets Space Force, let alone become the executive officer of a battlecruiser.

He returned Iyotake's salute.

"Colonel Henry Wong, here to assume command," he told the junior officer. "Everyone's doing a damn fine job dealing with my unexpected arrival so far, so I'll admit I'm impressed.

"Shall we proceed to the bridge, Colonel Iyotake?"

"Yes, Captain Wong."

"Not yet," Henry said softly. "Not quite. Lead the way."

The entire point of removing *Captain* from the rank structure, after all, was to avoid the confusion about who was in command of a ship. Several people had given him the title so far today, but Wong hadn't been a Captain since surrendering command of *Panther*—and was not yet a Captain until he read himself in on *Raven*'s bridge.

IT WAS PROBABLY a good thing for Henry's calm that *Raven*'s bridge looked very little like *Panther*'s. The *Corvid*-class ship might be sixty meters shorter than her older sibling, but she was actually a bigger ship in terms of volume and mass.

The bridge was six meters wide and eleven long, an absolutely immense two-level space designed to allow a dozen officers and three dozen crew to handle every aspect of a three-hundred-meter-long warship that massed two million tons fully loaded.

Right now, there was only a station-keeping watch on the bridge.

Two Petty Officers and five Spacers were holding down consoles on the second-level balcony, running sensors and communications.

Two-sided screens marked the edge of the balcony and divided the pit from the center of the bridge on the main level as well, surrounding the command crew with the information their people were working on. From the seat at the center of the space, the Captain could orient themselves with any department and see what was going on at a glance.

Communications.

Navigation.

Sensors.

Weapons.

Engineering.

Five major sections, each intended to have an officer and three to six enlisted at their consoles. Engineering had the smallest bridge section; Weapons had the largest. There was a spot for a junior officer of the watch and two observers inside the central bubble alongside the Captain.

Henry wasn't the largest fan of how the design separated the Captain from his bridge crew, but he had to admit he could still see and hear his people through the screens and it put all of the information easily in the Captain's line of sight.

A civilian ship would have used holoprojectors, but those were fragile things, more vulnerable to battle damage than the time-tested screens that filled *Raven*'s bridge.

Henry looked around, taking it all in as he approached the seat at the center of the entire space, with its own set of additional screens in case the Captain needed something that wasn't on the big displays around them.

He stopped next to it and glanced over at Lieutenant Colonel Iyotake.

"It's my watch," the XO confirmed. "But it's your chair, ser."

"Not yet," Henry echoed his earlier comment. He pulled the writ out of his suit jacket and studied the command seat for a few seconds.

They hadn't changed it *that* much from the *Jaguar* class, and he opened an all-hands channel with practiced ease.

"All hands, attention to orders," he snapped. No one aboard the battlecruiser would be sleeping yet. He might wake them up if they were, but that was unavoidable.

"I am Colonel Henry Wong and I am in possession of a writ of authority from UPSF Command," he said formally. "Tradition requires I read those orders into the record with you all as witnesses. So, I repeat myself: attention to orders.

"To: Colonel Henry Wong. From: Admiral Lee Saren, United Planets Space Force Command, Base Halo, Sol.

"You are hereby ordered to proceed aboard the United Planets Space Vessel BC-Zero-Six-One *Raven* and assume command of said vessel in the joint defense of our member systems. You are charged to carry the duties and responsibilities of Captain and commander of UPSV *Raven* to the highest and best standards and traditions of the United Planets Space Force.

"We charge you with the memory of those who came before and the fate of those yet to come.

"Signed: Admiral Lee Saren. Personnel Division. United Planets Space Force."

Henry paused, letting the formal words hang on the channel for several moments.

"I assume command of this vessel. You'll hear from me again before we leave, I promise you that, but twenty-one hundred hours two days before we set out is not the time for me to be keeping you all awake. Good luck, spacers."

He closed the channel and turned his attention back to Iyotake.

"I assume command," he repeated to the junior officer.

"I stand relieved," Iyotake confirmed. "Not least to *have* a Captain, ser. Even yesterday, all I was being told was that there would be *someone* in that chair before we launched for Kenmiri space!"

"I can see that being intimidating," Henry conceded. "Many would have hoped for the chair themselves."

"I just made Lieutenant Colonel after a three-year stint as XO on a destroyer, ser," his new XO replied. "I'd take command on a destroyer if the Admiralty ordered it, but I'm not ready to command this ship, ser."

"A wise man knows both his limits and when to push past them," Henry said. "I was never great at the second part." He gestured around at the bridge. "Normally, this is the point where I ask you for a tour, XO, but in truth? This morning, I didn't know if I was getting released from medical leave today.

"It's been a whirlwind and I need a solid eight hours. I assume the Captain's cabin is ready?"

"I had the stewards in it as soon as they told me you were coming. Your bag should have made it there already." Iyotake paused. "Chief Wang asked if there would be more effects coming that she should be watching for."

"Not...today, XO," Henry said slowly. His effects from his quarters on *Panther* were in storage on Sandoval. He had expected to have more than an hour's warning of his next command. He didn't think he could get his stuff out of storage in less than two days, anyway.

"I'll want that tour and a full briefing on our status at oh six hundred hours in the morning," Henry told the other man. "Any problems?"

"I'll make sure the stewards check the coffee machine in your office," Iyotake told him. "It should work, it's brand-new, but I don't think anyone's touched it yet—and if oh six hundred is your time of day, we're both going to need it!"

CHAPTER SEVEN

The Captain's office on Raven was identical to the one on *Panther*. That gave Henry a moment of twitchiness, but he was able to push past it with ease. Probably because his *office* didn't feature in his nightmares of the battle in Set-Sixteen.

The desk with its built-in screens and haptic interfaces was the same. The walls with their concealed projectors for holograms were the same. The low-slung cabinets that concealed collapsing chairs and a coffee machine instead of paper files and folders, the same.

The biggest difference was the back wall, which would be behind the Captain as they sat at their desk. On *Panther* that had had the name of the ship emblazoned across it, below the eight-star half-circle seal of the United Planets Alliance.

All of that was present, but the UPA seal shared space with the commissioning seal of *Raven* herself: a sideview of a bird in flight holding a quill pen.

The same circular seal was embroidered into the patch one of the stewards had added to his duty uniform's shoulder overnight. The turtleneck of this uniform was one of the ones he'd worn as Captain of *Panther* and already had the white collar, but when he'd dropped his duffle off with Chief Wang's people, there'd been a clear blank spot on the shoulder where *Panther*'s seal had sat.

When he'd opened his closest to retrieve a shirt that morning, all six of the sweaters had been updated with the new shoulder flash. Everything he'd seen so far suggested that Lieutenant Colonel Iyotake and the rest of the crew had been doing a good job without him.

Five minutes before his meeting with the XO, however, he started trying to get the coffee machine to work. At oh six hundred hours, Iyotake entered the room to him *still* trying to get the machine working.

"Ser?" the XO asked quietly.

"Water connection is broken," Henry concluded, stepping back from the machine and gesturing to it. "Bean hopper's empty too, but there are at least beans *here*. I am capable of filling a box on my own," he said with a smile as he shook his head, "but water fittings are a *bit* outside my expertise."

Iyotake looked over his shoulder and sighed.

"There was a work ticket to make sure your coffee machine was functioning," he said as he poked at the fitting. "Yeah. Install job was slightly off, shifted under acceleration. Easy fix with the right tools."

"My mostly forgotten degree that came with my commission is in astrophysics, Lieutenant Colonel," Henry pointed out. "Plumbing is...not my forte."

"Nor mine. My degree was mechanical engineering, though, so I can at least see the problem," Iyotake replied. "I'll ping a steward to bring us coffee and make sure the work ticket is postponed till later today."

Henry took his seat and gestured for the XO to take the chair across from him.

"So, is this typical?" he asked. "Was there something more critical taking up time, or did the ticket just slip?"

"I should have tasked one of the chiefs with it personally, ser," Iyotake admitted.

"We have an automated ticketing system for noncritical repairs for a reason," Henry pointed out gently. "Are we having problems with it?"

"No." The XO sighed. "What we have, ser, is an engineering department of a hundred and forty-two brand-new graduates and two hundred and thirty spacers, chiefs, and officers pulled from every other ship in the Space Force. The new blood is following their petty officers' leads, and their POs are following the practices from their old ship."

"Ouch," Henry conceded. "If we've got people from every ship in the UPSF, that's a lot of penny packets of crew."

"Average transfer was thirteen people," Iyotake told him. "That gave us just over six hundred hands. We pulled a hundred from Base Skyrim and three hundred brand-spanking-new Spacer Third Classes from the Procyon UPSF Training School."

Henry whistled quietly. That was every battlecruiser, every carrier and a good chunk of the destroyers being raided for people. *Raven*'s name was going to be *ash* with a significant portion of his fellow Captains for a while.

He had a thousand SpaceDiv and FighterDiv crew aboard the battlecruiser, plus four hundred GroundDiv troopers.

Although...

"How many did we get from *Scorpius*?" he asked.

"She was the closest carrier. Captain Barrie sent a contingent of thirty-six, I believe, and we got our starfighters and their pilots from her. Why, ser?"

Henry snorted.

"I'll want to keep an eye on them," he said. "Peter Barrie is my ex-husband, XO. I...*probably* trust him not to intentionally hand me problem cases, but it's not like we talk anymore unless duty requires it."

"Ah." Iyotake looked like he wanted to vanish out of that particular conflict before it splashed on him. Which was entirely fair.

"How many problem cases do we actually have?" Henry asked. "We got their disciplinary records, after all."

"Less than I was afraid of when they told me how *Raven*'s crew had been put together. More than I'd like, though," the XO admitted. "Commander O'Flannagain is potentially going to be a problem. She's your starfighter group leader, and while I can't get anyone to *tell* me anything, I have grounds to believe she's already had one fistfight with an engineering Chief."

Henry closed his eyes.

"Please tell me that's a joke," he said slowly as he brought the image of the redheaded officer up in his internal network. There were a *lot* of red flags in her record for someone who'd never—*quite*—been busted a rank or cashiered.

It was telling that she'd spent twelve years as a combat pilot and was still only a Commander. That took *effort*.

"No, ser. I wish. Commander Samira O'Flannagain is *theoretically* Irish via Ophiuchi. She's so determinedly stereotypical I suspect her family has to actually be Belgian or something similarly innocuous."

"I know rocket-jocks," Henry said. "I'll find a way to deal with her. Her record suggests she knows just where to sit with regards to the line—but she has to realize that won't fly for long without a war going on."

"I hope so, ser," Iyotake agreed. "She's probably our biggest problem-child officer. We've got a few issues scattered through the crew, but most of them can probably be handled by the Chiefs. Where we can trust the Chiefs."

"If we can't trust the Chiefs, XO, this ship is *fucked*," the older Colonel reported. A gesture vanished O'Flannagain's record and brought up a holographic projection of *Raven*. "And we can't be fucked, to be blunt.

"This ship is supposed to be able to reliably take on *two* Kenmiri dreadnoughts and win," he continued. "The old *Jaguars* were only supposed to do that with one."

Both statements were either impressive or arrogant, depending on your point of view. A Kenmiri dreadnought was an eight-hundred-meter-long war machine forged out of a conveniently sized asteroid. With energy screens, super-heavy plasma cannon, and an arsenal of terrifyingly smart missiles, they had been the premier warships of the galaxy before the UPA broke onto the scene.

"That assumption requires that everything is running at full efficiency," Henry continued. "Most especially the gravity shield, but if the lasers, the grav-driver, or our missiles are underperforming, we can very easily end up dead."

"All it takes is one blowthrough in the wrong spot," Iyotake agreed. "Too many of our people think we're invulnerable."

Henry shivered as the discussion brought up a spark of remembered nightmare, but managed to shrug it aside.

"We're not," he confirmed. "Enough of our people have seen the elephant that I think that message has got through. But we're going back into Kenmiri space. It might be a diplomatic mission, but we're back in the Empire and I doubt the Empire is dying in as neat and organized a fashion as it sounds in the briefings.

"Our job is going to be to back up the Ambassador and to look mean and intimidating," Henry concluded. "I suspect we're going to be shooting at *somebody* before this is done. So, tell me, XO, are we fucked?"

"I don't think we're fucked," Iyotake told him. "Our Chiefs are solid, but they're not used to working together and they all have their ways that they expect things to work. We've got POs working for Chiefs from different ships, running crews pulled together from four other ships.

"It'll sort itself out in time, but it's going to be a rough few weeks."

"We have a three-week trip to Resta," Henry said. "My orders say we have sixty hours to get underway. I'd *like* to be underway in thirty-six. Is that going to happen, XO?"

"Yes," the younger man said without hesitation. "I don't know if we'll even have the officers lined up and moving in the same direction at that point, though."

"I'll settle for everyone moving in the same direction." He smiled grimly. "*My* direction. They'll learn the rest if they can follow orders for now—and if they can't, I *will* break them out of the Space Force.

"We're a peacetime fleet now, after all. The Powers That Be *want* to bring down headcount."

CHAPTER EIGHT

A SINGLE FOURTEEN-HOUR WORKING DAY WASN'T ENOUGH TO break the fourteen-hundred-person crew of a modern battlecruiser to a single man's will, but Henry was feeling cautiously optimistic as he made his way back to the docking port to the station.

He'd met his senior SpaceDiv officers and most of his bridge crew, and then taken a quick tour of almost the entire ship. The starfighter deck had been the last on his list and had been delayed when he'd received the notice that Ambassador Todorovich was coming aboard.

Commander Thompson and Lieutenant Colonel Iyotake met him in the boarding area, along with an honor guard of twelve GroundDiv troopers. Both gave him crisp salutes and he nodded to Commander Thompson.

"It's a pleasure to meet you again, Commander," he told the younger man. "It appears the Captain lucky enough to have you is me."

"So I see, ser," Thompson replied brightly. "Remind me not to play poker with you, Captain. Your poker face is perfect."

"I didn't know I was taking command of *Raven* when we spoke,

Commander," Henry admitted. "But I'd still suggest not playing poker with me. XO,"—he turned to Iyotake—"what's the Ambassador's ETA?"

"Em Todorovich's chief of staff advised they'd left their quarters on station twenty-five minutes ago," Iyotake told him. "Barring traffic, they should be..."

He paused, the telltale mid-sentence break of someone receiving a message to their internal network.

"They just arrived at the outer door," he noted. "Thompson's troopers are checking their IDs."

"How many people are we getting?" Henry asked.

"Fourteen. The Ambassador travels with a small staff," the XO said. "We're putting them on the flag deck for now, though we've locked off the actual flag *bridge*, of course."

"Of course," the Captain murmured. The "flag deck" was the section of quarters and offices around the flag bridge—*also* often called the flag deck—where an Admiral and their staff would be set up.

Raven was equipped to act as a flagship, and since she wasn't currently acting as one, it was a perfect place to stick a cargo of diplomats.

"They've cleared the security check," Thompson reported. "Honor guard, attention!"

The GroundDiv soldiers snapped to attention, forming a neat double file around the airlock as it slid open.

Todorovich was the first through, her staff following in her wake in an only semi-confused crowd.

Henry smiled and offered his hand to the woman.

"Welcome aboard *Raven*, Em Todorovich," he greeted her. "I appreciate you moving your schedule up to be aboard for an early departure."

"The last thing I want to be, Colonel Wong, is late for the Gathering," Todorovich told him, her voice just as perfectly precise as the previous day.

"Captain Wong now," he corrected gently. "The commander of a starship is always Captain, regardless of their regular rank."

"Right," she replied, eyeing the soldiers lined up. "We have luggage coming aboard via the cargo transfer system, but otherwise, this is my team." She gestured behind her at a broad-featured man with close-shaved black hair and a perfectly maintained beard. "Felix Leitz, my chief of staff, will be taking care of most of our interactions with your crew."

"Lieutenant Colonel Tatanka Iyotake will be our main point of contact from our side," Henry replied, indicating his XO. "We will be leaving Base Skyrim at twelve hundred hours tomorrow. If your people have anything to take care of in Procyon, I suggest you do so before we depart the base.

"It will be some hours after before we engage the skip drive and leave the system, but if you need to get back on the station or to have a guaranteed real-time conversation with anyone, you're better off doing it before we get moving."

Raven might not be a Kenmiri escort or gunship, but at half a kilometer per second squared, she could get to the skip lines fast enough for any purpose except *chasing* a Kenmiri escort or gunship.

"My own immediate situation has been resolved quite satisfactorily," Todorovich told him. She glanced back at her staff. "All that should be left for you lot is personal affairs. Make sure they're sorted.

"Subspace communication on a warship is more restricted that you think," she continued. "Don't rely on having it."

Henry nodded his thanks. He'd given several groups of passengers a very similar speech in the past. It was good that Todorovich, at least, understood the restrictions in place.

"Colonel Iyotake will show you and your people to your quarters," he told the Ambassador. "I would be honored if you and Em Leitz would join myself and my senior officers for dinner tomorrow. Nineteen hundred hours. We won't have skipped yet."

"I'll make sure to clear my schedule," Todorovich replied. "Till then, Captain. I imagine we both have work to do to make sure this mission goes smoothly."

AFTER THREE MONTHS in various medical facilities, Henry was torn between pacing himself to make sure he didn't overdo it—and a burning need to *do* something. Anything. He'd meant to leave the starfighter bays for the next day, but he found himself down there instead of at his quarters after welcoming Todorovich aboard.

The space aboard *Raven* for the starfighters was larger than it had been aboard *Panther*, but the new ship carried eight fighters to his old one's six. It was still tiny compared to *Rygel*, let alone a modern carrier like *Scorpius*.

His ex-husband's command carried a hundred starfighters: eight twelve-ship squadrons and four specialty support craft.

There were none of the latter in *Raven*'s fighter bay. From the entrance, Henry's practiced gaze picked out his parasite complement of eight SF-122 Dragoon starfighters, primarily missile platforms with a secondary laser armament.

They were deadly little ships with a modular armament. If he needed it, FighterDiv could exchange their missiles for additional laser modules and augment *Raven*'s point defense. Their main purpose, though, was to deliver a thirty-two-missile alpha strike to augment *Raven*'s own opening salvo.

"Hey! This is a starfighter bay, not a fucking zoo," a female voice with an Ophiuchi accent barked. "If you're not supposed to be here, stop ogling."

Henry didn't even need to *guess* who the speaker was. He ignored her and stepped over to the nearest starfighter. The Dragoon was a flat-based sphere, with visible divots around the "waist" where missiles or modular lasers would go. There was no visible cockpit—the pilot flew the ship from a liquid-filled acceleration tank in the exact center of the spaceship, their entire view of the world electronically relayed to their helmet and internal network.

He'd flown the SF-119 Vulture in his time, but none of those had been deployed after the Red Wing Campaign. The SF-120 Wolverine had replaced them, a process accelerated by the Campaign seeing basically the entire inventory of Vultures destroyed in bombing runs on the Kenmiri.

"Are you fucking deaf?" the voice snapped. "Get the hell off my flight deck."

"I rather think, Commander O'Flannagain, that this is *my* flight deck," he observed softly without turning. "Did you ever fly the Vulture? They still had some as training craft when you went through Flight Academy, right?"

The voice was silent for several seconds.

"Captain Wong?" she finally asked, stepping up behind him. "What the fuck are you doing on the fighter deck?"

"Asking a question," he noted. "Do I need to repeat myself, Commander?"

"Nah. Yeah, I flew a Vulture in the Academy," she conceded. He could just barely see her out of the corner of his eye as he studied the starfighter. "Only got stick time on the Wolverine at the Academy, too. Got assigned to a Liberator squadron right out of the Academy."

"Top marks at the Academy would get you that," he agreed. The SF-121 Liberator had been the fighter before the Dragoon. Just as obsolete as the Vulture or the Wolverine now. That was how war worked when you had the industrial and research capacity of the UPA and had started the war terrified for your survival.

Three entirely new generations of starfighter had been developed and deployed over seventeen years.

"Of course, most people who graduated in the top three of their Academy class have more...successful careers than you," he continued. "Still Commander at thirty-five?"

"Is this 'shame the CAG day' or something I missed the memo over?" O'Flannagain asked, his new Commander, Air Group sounding more aggravated than anything else. "What do you want, ser?"

"How does the Dragoon stack up against the Vulture?" he asked instead of answering her question. "I get about fifty real space flight hours a year to keep up my certification, but that doesn't answer the real question, does it?"

"No. It doesn't." Her voice was calmer now. "It's all about the turn with this girl. A KPS-squared and a half lets you change velocity fast. Grav-shield will protect you from most mistakes, but you're always better off never getting hit in the first place.

"You're always most vulnerable when you launch. Ports open and a straight-line flight for three-quarters of a second. If you have them confused before that, you can squeeze it in more safely. Kind of sad the Kenmiri never did have fighters."

"They thought the grav-shields were the only thing that made them worthwhile," Henry told her. "Even with the grav-shields, well...we lost a lot of birds and rocket-jocks."

He finally turned, looking away from the orb-like starfighter to study his Commander, Air Group.

As Iyotake had suggested, Commander Samira O'Flannagain looked so stereotypically Irish, it had to be intentional. She was a gawky woman with red hair in a tight circular braid on top of her head. Even now, she wore a flight suit instead of a uniform, though her wings and the two steel bars of her rank remained visible.

"Is there a *point* to this, ser?" she finally asked.

"Perhaps. Perhaps not," he said. "Perhaps I'm meeting the woman who commands my only truly long-range strike option—or perhaps I'm meeting the only officer who has managed to get into a fistfight on a ship that's only been in commission for two weeks."

She hadn't been expecting that and visibly flushed.

"That did—"

"Please, Commander. Just because the Chief didn't sell you out didn't mean that your superior officers are *idiots*," he pointed out. "I don't need to prove it for administrative punishment, either. Do you understand me?"

"Ser."

"I get rocket-jocks," he told her. "I get the friction between the starfighter deck and engineering. What I *also* get, however, is that it is *your* job, as CAG, to reduce that friction and make sure that relationship flows smoothly.

"Not aggravate it by throwing punches."

She was silent.

"Since the Chief involved is apparently willing to let things go, I will too. *This time.* But if things don't improve..." He shrugged. "We're a peacetime military now, Commander. In another time, I might end up going for charges of conduct unbecoming an officer. Right now?"

He turned and met her gaze, and his smile was gentle...and utterly without mercy.

"Right now, O'Flannagain, if you don't shape up, I will beach you," he told her. "A reserve commission with no flight hours, no duties. Just a tiny stipend in case we end up going back to war in the next ten years.

"Do you understand me, Commander?" he asked.

"Yes, ser," she ground out.

"Good. Because I've seen your record, Commander O'Flannagain, and it would be a damn shame to ground one of the half dozen or so best pilots I've ever seen—even if my ex-husband *did* think you'd be a great headache to hand me!"

CHAPTER NINE

"ALL DEPARTMENTS, REPORT READY FOR DEPARTURE," HENRY ordered.

His command seat's repeater screens told him they were ready. His internal network was interfaced with *Raven*'s computers, which told him the departments were ready. He was surrounded by the two-sided screens that showed him what all of his bridge crew were doing —which showed him those departments were ready.

The Book still called for verbal acknowledgement and he agreed with it. There were times to rush, to cut corners and do things as fast as possible.

Leaving a safe port at the start of a mission that could not last less than six weeks even if they turned around the moment they reached Resta was not that time. There were problems that wouldn't show up in the automated checks that could still need to be addressed before they went beyond the reach of help.

"Tactical department is standing by," Commander Okafor Ihejirika reported. *Raven*'s tactical officer was a short and stocky black man. Like Henry himself, Ihejirika was from Earth itself. The homeworld still accounted for roughly forty percent of all humans

—the entire Sol System accounted for just under fifty percent in total—but Earth natives made up less than twenty percent of the UPSF.

"All weapons report green and are safed for transit," Ihejirika continued. "Sensors are green and live. We are ready to go."

"Communications is green." Lieutenant Commander Lauren Moon was from Mars, tall from growing up in low gravity but heavily fleshed out despite living in a full gee aboard UPSF warships. "Radios are all checking green. Lasers and tightbeams are checking green. Subspace network link is stable. We are ready to go."

"Engineering reports all reactors are up to thirty percent," Lieutenant Mariann Henriksson reported. The blonde young woman was the bridge officer for Engineering, a job that nine times out of ten just required repeating what the Chief Engineer—Lieutenant Colonel Anna Song aboard *Raven*—told her.

The other ten percent of the time, it required collating reports from across the ship and providing the summaries the Captain needed when the Chief Engineer was too busy making sure the ship didn't fall apart to answer questions.

"Feed lines to the engines all report clear and operational," Henriksson continued. "Engineering is go for departure."

"Helm?" Henry asked, directing his attention to the currently most critical department on the ship.

Commander Iida Bazzoli looked about as mixed ethnically as her Finnish and Italian name suggested. Her skin was the same vague shade of brown as Henry's own, but she had brilliant green eyes and blond hair so pale as to be almost white.

She was also the woman of the hour and in full control of *Raven*'s engines, inertial dampeners and skip drives.

"Course is plotted all the way to Resta, ser," she reported. "Base Skyrim has provided initial clearance and is standing by to retract the docking arm. Navigation and helm are good to go on your order, Captain."

"Well, then. Let's not keep the stars waiting, shall we?" he replied. "Moon, inform Skyrim we are ready to depart and request docking port and clamp retraction. Bazzoli...you have the ship."

"Understood."

Most of the screens were showing *Raven* at this point, with the clamps and docking tubes lit up in orange. First, the docking tube moved away from the hull, the highlight changing to green once it had cleared the safety zone.

Then, one by one, the docking clamps holding the battlecruiser safely against the space station released and switched to green. Once the last of them was a safe distance away, the highlights vanished. The connectors were no longer relevant except as part of Base Skyrim.

"Base Skyrim confirms we are clear of all connections, and they have sent us clearance all the way out," Moon reported. "I've forwarded the clearance to Commander Bazzoli."

Bazzoli paused for several seconds, hopefully to make sure the clearance aligned with the course she'd submitted and was planning on taking *Raven* along.

"Course is cleared. Bringing up the maneuvering jets," she finally said.

There was no detectable change aboard *Raven*. Inertial compensation designed to absorb half a kilometer per second squared of acceleration—over fifty times Earth's gravity—wasn't going to blip at five *meters* per second squared.

Raven's icon drifted clear of the space station. More maneuvering thrusters came online as the distance opened, bringing the ship up to thirty meters per second squared.

That was as much as the secondary thrusters could manage. Pure ion engines were extremely *efficient*, but didn't have a lot of power. That efficiency and lack of power, however, meant that they were a far lesser danger to anything around the battlecruiser than her main drives.

"Shutting down maneuvering thrusters," Bazzoli noted aloud. "Course calls for thirty seconds of ballistic drift."

No one responded. There was no need. The Book called for the report, but it was the navigator's *next* report that actually mattered.

"Bringing engines up at ten percent in ten seconds," she finally stated. "Stand by. Engines online."

Notification lights flickered across a dozen screens. *Raven*'s four reactors crept up from thirty percent utilization to thirty-five, and the numbers representing her acceleration and velocity started changing rapidly.

Ten percent was point one kilometer per second squared. "Full acceleration" would only be fifty percent of the actual maximum acceleration *Raven* was capable of—but anything above point five kilometers per second squared couldn't be fully compensated for by the artificial gravity and inertial compensation systems.

For every meter per second squared they went over their listed maximum, the crew would experience point four meters per second squared of acceleration. Point six KPS^2 would put roughly four point one gravities on the crew.

A full KPS^2, *Raven*'s actual top acceleration, would put twenty point four gravities on the human crew. They had a dozen systems they could use to make that *survivable*, but it still required special preparation to not be suicide.

It took the same threefold authorization to take *Raven* to maximum acceleration as it did to turn her fusion cores into a thermonuclear self-destruct.

"Bringing the engines up to forty percent and holding," Bazzoli finally concluded. "We are lined up with the Zion skip line and will reach the entrance velocity vector in eleven hours. Enjoy your flight, people. Life gets icky at midnight."

Henry Wong had met many people who insisted that humans could get used to the sensation of skip-drive travel.

He had never met *one* who said that they had done so themselves.

CHAPTER TEN

THE CAPTAIN'S DINING ROOM ABOARD *RAVEN* WASN'T LARGE
enough to host all of Henry's officers. If he needed to do that, he'd
have to take over the officers' mess, which *was* large enough for all
sixty-plus of those people.

His dining room was listed as big enough to host himself and all
seven of his senior officers plus up to six guests. With only Ambassador Todorovich and Felix Leitz there beyond his senior officers,
there was extra space. Not that anyone could ever tell. Putting
another four people in the room would have been doable...but Henry
was left with the conclusion that the fourteen-person capacity of his
dining room was an exaggeration.

"Have you and your people had any problems getting settled?" he
asked Todorovich.

"Nothing serious," the Ambassador told him. "We've got one
analyst who hasn't been aboard a warship before. He's having some
adjustment pains, but he'll get over them."

Henry chuckled.

"They always do, don't they?" he murmured. "I haven't spent

much time hauling diplomats around, but I've made sure a few contact teams made it to their destinations with the Vesheron."

The Vesheron hadn't had anything resembling a combined leadership until the last three years of the war. Even that had only been the result of a combined stance from the UPA and the Londu that they needed *someone* to coordinate with.

The other two El-Vesheron powers had seen the Kenmiri coming. The UPA had just had the red insectoids show up on their doorstep and start trying to take systems over. It had been years before they'd even known the Vesheron existed.

The UPA and the Londu showing a united front had forced the rebels into a more formal alliance and joint command, one that Henry was pretty sure had been critical to ending the war.

He wanted to blame someone other than UPSF Command for Golden Lancelot, but he was too honest with himself. "Exterminate the leadership caste and leave the rest to swing" was far too present a concept in human science fiction for him to believe it hadn't occurred to his superiors.

"You were there at the end, weren't you?" Leitz asked. "Golden Lancelot?"

"I was," Henry confirmed, glancing down the table. He'd checked his people's records, and most of them had been involved in the support operations. Ihejirika was the only other person in the room who had been involved in a Golden Lancelot strike mission.

The tactical officer's face had grown noticeably more shadowed at the mention of the operation name. Hopefully, Henry was doing a better job of hiding his emotions than his subordinate was.

"Right at the end," he continued after a moment of silence that probably stretched too long. "Intelligence confirmed after the fact that the Kenmorad breeding sect *Panther* took out was the last one."

He raised a hand before Leitz could ask any more questions.

"I would strongly recommend against asking too many questions about Lancelot of the people who served in it," he told the chief of staff gently. "Golden Lancelot was a tactical genocide. The officers and crew who served in that didn't know that at the time, but we know it now.

"We have to live with that. I don't think the officers who drew up the plan realized how bad it was going to be for us to do that, though I doubt *they're* sleeping easy at night either. Leave the wound be, Em Leitz. Your curiosity isn't worth it."

He realized the entire table had gone silent and was hanging on his words. Hopefully, none of them saw his shivers or realized how much the simple statement he'd made was threatening his calm.

"I understand, Captain Wong," Leitz said. "I apologize; I did not think through the...consequences of what happened."

"You should have access to the official reports," Henry said gently. "They may not be as useful as first-person encounters, but you're at least not tearing wounds wide open."

The room was silent for several more seconds, then Leitz coughed.

"I understand you were one of the ships that pulled Ambassador Rembrandt out?" he asked. "I never had the pleasure of meeting him myself. What was he like?"

Henry glanced over at Todorovich—who had known Rembrandt for *far* longer than he had—and chuckled.

"I think Em Todorovich might have more to say about him than me," he noted. "But yes. *Panther* was part of the task group that went into Apophis-Six after the Kenmiri caught him. I doubt I saw him at his best—he'd been in the hands of one of the more *imaginative* Kenmorad queens.

"They'd been playing mind games on him—trying to turn him, I think—for at least two weeks by the time we got there. It didn't work, so they decided that they'd rather him dead than rescued. My GroundDiv teams got in without much trouble, but the Kenmiri threw everything they had at us to stop us getting him out.

"The Ambassador lost his legs to a round that went low," Henry concluded. They'd also lost over two hundred GroundDiv troopers, but they'd *wrecked* Apophis-Six's defenses and the maximum-security prison itself. The follow-up attack by the Vesheron had liberated the system and rescued about a hundred thousand Vesheron fighters of different races and factions.

"He took the loss of his limbs with surprising grace, but from the conversations I had with him, he took it as a sign it was time to retire." He shook his head. "He seemed smart, capable and surprisingly lucid, given the pain meds he was on!"

"If there was anything Rembrandt was, it was smart and capable," Todorovich agreed. "Never saw him face a situation he seemed perturbed by. He was one of the first diplomats we sent to the Vesheron, which meant he was the first one to meet a near-human face to face."

Even once the UPSF had found the Vesheron, communication had been via text messages through a Kenmiri channel they both knew. No one had realized that a good three-quarters of the species in the Kenmiri Empire could pass for human until the delegations had met on neutral ground.

Henry hadn't been there for that, but he remembered the first time *he'd* met a member of another of what the Kenmiri called the Ashall: the Seeded Races. She'd at least had head-tentacles to help remind him that she *wasn't* human.

"Don't call them near-humans around anyone but us, either," Henry noted. "They don't like it any more than we'd like being called near-Londu."

"Which *is* the approximate translation of the Londu term for us," Todorovich agreed. "Some day, we might find out what the Kenmiri know about why half the sentient species in the galaxy could pass for each other under a hood."

"The whole name of *Seeded Races* implies they know *something*."

"The Kenmiri didn't talk to us much *before* we...ended the war," Henry pointed out, choosing his phrasing carefully. "Somehow, I don't think we're getting access to their archives."

"They may have left something behind on the worlds they abandoned," Leitz pointed out. "Maybe that's something we should be negotiating for at the Gathering."

"You know our negotiating goals," Todorovich pointed out. "The biggest objective for all of us, including the Space Force, is to get out of this without getting ourselves trapped in any major commitments."

"We'll try not to start any blood feuds," Henry said with a chuckle. "Outside of that, I think most of the not-making-promises falls on you, Ambassador."

"Oh, believe me, Captain Wong, I learned how to not make promises from the *best*."

The only two people in the room who'd ever met Karl Rembrandt met each other's gazes again, and Henry nodded his understanding to Todorovich. The old man had been many things, but in another age, he'd have been buying land from Native Americans with shiny glass beads.

Henry didn't *like* the terms that the UPA wanted to walk away from the Vesheron Gathering with...but it wasn't his call. And, thankfully, it wasn't his job to sit in a negotiation and tell people that, either.

CHAPTER ELEVEN

"WE ARE APPROACHING THE TARGET VECTOR AND LOCATION now," Bazzoli said calmly.

The bridge wasn't usually full at midnight ship's time. The first skip of a journey always seemed to bring everyone out, even when only one watch was supposed to be on duty.

Not that Henry had a problem with that. *He* was supposed to be on duty only because he'd told Iyotake to make sure he was. Rank hath its privileges—but he'd also shown up for the first skip when he wasn't on duty, too.

As he was thinking that, Iyotake sent him a silent ping telling him to check the door. The XO was currently holding down the tactical station—Ihejirika had the next watch and was doing the sensible thing and sleeping.

Turning around slightly in his seat, Henry was only mildly surprised to see Sylvia Todorovich standing in the door. He gestured her over to him.

"There are observer seats on the bridge for a reason, Em Todorovich," he told her as she reached him. "I presume you have seen a skip before?"

"A few times," she conceded. "It seems to be a tradition to watch the first one with the Force, though, doesn't it?"

"Helps you know when to expect the hit," Henry said. She took the nearest observer seat, and he glanced back at the screens to make sure everything was going according to plan. "Right now, even I'm an observer unless something comes out to make us abort the skip. Commander Bazzoli has control of the ship."

"Entrance vector achieved. Shutting down main engines and diverting power to icosaspace impulse generators," the navigator announced, as if she'd heard her name. "We'll reach entry location in one hundred seconds from...now."

"Icosaspace," Todorovich repeated. "Twenty dimensional, right?"

"Exactly. To skip, we're bouncing through seventeen dimensions you and I can't perceive," he confirmed.

"I've never been clear on the name," she admitted. "I see a lot of documents referring to *Icosaspace Traversal System*."

Henry barely managed to keep his laugh to a soft chuckle.

"I don't think I've seen the full name spelled out anywhere in years," he admitted. "ITS or skip drive, that's all I see. The military isn't going to call it by its full name, and everyone else started calling it the skip drive based on the metaphor Dr. Tsao used to explain it."

"Skipping...rocks, right?"

"You ever done it?" Henry asked. "You throw a rock, a three-dimensional object and vector, at a river or lake, a two-dimensional surface. You bounce, and the two-dee surface doesn't see it until it lands again.

"We're doing the same thing...but with a *twenty*-dimensional vector and a three-dimensional surface." He gestured at the screen showing him what Bazzoli was doing.

"Why the specific location, then?" she asked. "I mostly get the drive, or at least how it *works*, but if we're bouncing off realspace in icosaspace, why do we need to line up with stars?"

"If you skip a rock, it loses energy velocity with each skip," Henry told her. "Similarly, if we just skip in a random spot, there's a bit of expansion due to the icosaspace factor, but we only get one skip and it doesn't go very far.

"To mangle the metaphor, we need a current. By hitting the direct vector between two stars, we use their icosaspatial gravity to propel ourselves along. The closer and larger the stars, the faster we go. The skip from Sol to Alpha Centauri takes just over twelve hours. If we were to try and directly skip along the line from Procyon to Resta..."

He snorted.

"I haven't done the math, but I think we'd be looking at two or three years," he told her. "And that would probably kill us."

"All hands, this is your final skip alert. Entrance in ten seconds," Bazzoli barked aloud, her voice going out over the PA system. "If you *aren't* strapped in, *get* strapped in now!"

Henry fell silent, bracing himself for the impact. He'd lost count of the number of skips he'd made in his life, but that didn't make it any easier. Zion was a giant star on the edge of what the UPA claimed as their space, nine light-years from Procyon.

Size helped, meaning they were only looking at a twenty-hour skip to cross those nine light-years.

That was still cutting close to the edge of the twenty-four-hour limit the UPSF was prepared to accept for anything other than an emergency.

"Skip...*now*."

After a lifetime of service in the UPSF, Henry had a pretty good idea of what a skipped rock felt like in the moment of impact. Without the same inertial compensators that allowed *Raven* to accelerate at over fifty gravities, the initial hit could easily be fatal.

Even with the compensators, the angle and force of the hit were so unpredictable, the impacts couldn't be completely stopped.

The ship *fell*...sideways. Then up. Then backward. Each shift was sharp enough to send Henry's stomach reeling.

None were enough to do more than dislodge small random objects, when all was said and done, but the rapid sequence of changing gravity vectors played ugly games with the human inner ear.

It lasted just over twenty seconds, and then he heard Bazzoli breathe a sigh of relief.

"All hands, hear this," she said into the PA. "Skip insertion complete. Initial skip complete. First secondary skip will be in three hours, twenty-seven minutes. Set your alarms. No one wants to clean up after you."

Henry exhaled heavily. Gravity on the ship still felt *wrong*. *Raven's* systems were keeping his sense of *down* firmly pointed in the right direction, but there was still a slowly swirling sense of gravity in other directions.

"And there is why everyone wants to *watch* the skip," Todorovich noted, her gaze focused on the screens around them.

Raven was no longer in the same three-dimensional space she'd started in. What, exactly, a ship was in during the "flight" portion of the skip had defied the astrophysicists who'd taught Henry when he'd earned his degree.

Nothing had changed in the last thirty years. One thing was certain, though: the strangely warped view of the universe available to a ship in mid-skip was beautiful.

Strange colors and shapes swirled around *Raven*, her cameras and sensors faithfully reporting the utter garbage they were receiving as data. It was a whirlpool of light and color, one you could easily get lost in if you let yourself.

"I'm not sure the view is worth the dizziness," Henry admitted. "My balance is messed up enough if I keep my eyes closed. Adding *that*"—he gestured to the screens—"leaves my network working overtime to prevent nausea."

"I doubt I'm any better," Todorovich conceded. "But it's damn pretty, Captain Wong. You have to give the universe that."

CHAPTER TWELVE

TWENTY YEARS BEFORE, ZION HAD BEEN AN ARCHETYPAL example of the outpost systems—star systems claimed by the United Planets Alliance that didn't have an inhabitable world. Originally colonized by a joint Jewish-Mormon-Muslim expedition fleeing the tender mercies of the United States Colonial Administration, there'd been about a quarter-million people in the system, living in asteroids and space stations, when the war started.

It had been a quiet place, a determinedly self-sufficient society that had only hesitantly accepted UPA authority. Henry had visited the system once aboard *Rygel* before everything went wrong.

It looked *very* different now. Five years of Kenmiri occupation had seen the system repurposed as a logistics base for operations against the UPA. When the Terrans had finally retaken the system, they'd taken the logistics base intact.

Only half of the quarter-million inhabitants of the system remained. Many had died. Others had been hauled off deeper into the Kenmiri Empire for interrogation or to work on higher-value tasks.

The logistics base had been repurposed and expanded, and now

Base Fallout was on the outer perimeter of the UPA, the main base from which the war against the Kenmiri had been waged. Repairs and leave had sent ships back to Procyon, but refueling and resupply had taken place here.

"Base Fallout confirms receipt of our subspace IFF," Lieutenant Commander Moon told Henry. "They don't have us on lightspeed yet. Rear Admiral Zhao's staff wants to know if we need anything before we take off 'into the deep black yonder.'"

Henry smiled, but there was an odd sense of strangeness to it.

Zhao Xinyi had been a fixture at Base Fallout for ten years, but she'd never commanded it. The woman had spent a decade making sure that every ship that went out had everything they needed, and anyone who'd taken her soft appearance as weakness had learned otherwise the hard way.

But she'd risen from Colonel to merely Rear Admiral over that decade, and when Henry Wong had taken *Panther* through the system for Golden Lancelot, Base Fallout had been a *Vice* Admiral's command.

"We just left Procyon; I think we're fine," Henry said aloud. "What are we looking at at the base? When I last came through here, *Aeryn* was still holding down the fort with her battle group."

Lieutenant Saule Rao, one of Ihejirika's two assistant tactical officers, was already combing through the data, according to the screen Henry could see.

"It looks like *Jaguar* and three *Tyrannosaur*-class destroyers," she finally reported. "IFFs mark them as *Megaraptor*, *Albertosaurus* and *Labocania*." She paused. "It looks like some of the exterior forts are shut down as well. For maintenance, I guess?"

Henry nodded slowly as the codes crossed his screen and concealed a sigh.

From a carrier, two battlecruisers and *six* destroyers to a single battlecruiser and three destroyers. No wonder Base Fallout had been downgraded from a Vice Admiral's command—the UPSF had clearly already been raiding it for personnel and ships.

Most of the base defenses were automated, but the sphere of sixteen forts that provided her inner defenses had a crew of two hundred apiece. The icons he could see said that four of them had been completely shut down.

Potentially it *was* just maintenance, but he doubted it. The UPA was already determined to claim a "peace dividend" from the "victory" over the Kenmiri. Their cash flows were intentionally restricted, after all, and funding the expansion of the UPSF had required special agreements with the member systems.

Those agreements would need to be renewed in another year or so, but until they ran out, the UPA had wartime funding...and since their enemy was reacting roughly as expected to the annihilation of their future, they didn't have a war to spend it on.

"Commander Moon, send my regards to both Rear Admiral Zhao and to Colonel Tyson aboard *Jaguar*," he ordered. "We won't be in need of anything, and we won't be stopping in Zion. Give Zhao our updated timeline for our next skip."

"Yes, ser."

His bridge crew set to work and Henry leaned back in his chair. It would take them a little over thirty hours to establish the vector for their next jump—*not* a twenty-hour endurance run this time—but once they hit that jump, they were truly on their way.

Zion, after all, was twenty light-years away from Sol on a direct line toward the Kenmiri Empire. This *was* the border, where the UPA's claim and reach ended.

From here on out, they were no longer in friendly stars.

WHILE THE UPSF eschewed holograms at combat stations, there was an impressive setup in the Captain's office that could easily rival the ones in *Raven's* conference rooms. Henry was using it to review their course when there was a knock on his door.

"Enter," he ordered.

He hadn't been expecting Ambassador Todorovich, and he raised a questioning eyebrow at the diplomat.

"How may I assist you, Ambassador?" he asked politely.

"I'm sorry; am I interrupting?" she asked, gesturing to the hologram.

"Not really. Going over our course," Henry told her.

She stood across his desk for a few more seconds, looking at the hologram.

"We're here?" she asked, tapping the green icon of *Raven*. It was in a *very* symbolic orbit of Zion, given that it was almost as large as the star in the display.

"That's right," he confirmed. "And we're heading here." He tapped the gold icon marking the Resta System. "Resta, also known as Geb-Nine before we actually met the inhabitants. One of the major industrial worlds of the Kenmiri province we designated Geb."

"And the homeworld of one of the three largest Vesherons," Todorovich noted. "Even acting as a government in exile, the Restan managed to access far more of their homeworld's resources than I would have expected.

"Weren't they still building their own warships?"

"I don't know where the ships were being built," Henry admitted. "I know they were one of only two 'true' Vesheron factions with capital ships that weren't stolen Kenmiri dreadnoughts."

There hadn't been many of the latter, either. Kenmiri escorts and gunships had been easy enough for the various Vesheron factions to acquire, relatively speaking. Dreadnoughts had been almost impossible.

Most of the heavy ships in the Vesheron fleets had been refitted freighters that no UPSF officer or analyst had ever dignified with the descriptor of *capital ship*.

"And now the war is at least mostly over, they just moved back home and set up shop," she said. "With surprisingly little difficulty, according to our people on the scene. Disturbingly organized people, the Restan."

"They're Ashall," Henry pointed out. Most Ashall looked related to each other as opposed to the same species, but the Restan specifically could pass for human without even trying. "They think a lot like we do—and they knew the Kenmiri were coming before they arrived."

"We'd have spent the effort fighting them, I think," Todorovich said.

"They did. They also applied a very Chinese methodology to losing," Henry said, thinking back to his own ancestors' reaction to the Mongols. "Yes, ser, we work for you now, ser, this is how things work here, ser, we'll just drop you into the Emperor's role now..."

It wouldn't have worked forever with the Kenmiri, he suspected, but it had bought three Restan worlds enough calm and autonomy that they'd secretly built an entire fleet.

"I'll admit, Colonel Wong, that my familiarity with Earth history prior to the twentieth century isn't what it should be," Todorovich told him. "My own focuses of study were mostly on post-space travel politics. The USCA and the Novaya Imperiya, primarily."

He made a throwaway gesture. Both the United States Colonial Administration and the Russian New Empire had been very...*patriotic* in their objectives.

"Resta's a long way away," he said. "Almost a hundred light-years from Zion, even. We'll pass through unclaimed space, the Ra Province and the Apophis Province before we reach Geb."

Todorovich nodded, tracing the pale green line through the three-dimensional map.

"I can see the line," she told him. "How do I read the icons?"

He chuckled and stepped over to her.

"The entire map is at five millimeters to the light-year," he told her. "So, the length of a line will tell you how far we're skipping. If you tap the line"—he did so for the skip from Zion—"it will give you numbers."

Directly beneath the line, small text appeared. Seven light-years, ten hours. They were jumping between two *big* stars this time.

"Twenty more days," he said. "Eighteen more skips. We'll be averaging five point four light-years per skip and just under eleven hours."

"So, we're jumping from giants to giants most of the way?" Todorovich asked. "Bigger stars give us more of a speed boost, right?"

"Exactly. The rest of the trip is spent lining ourselves up for the next skip in each system," he told her. "We're at our most vulnerable in that time period. The Kenmiri used to patrol the stars most easily used for rapid transit. So did the Vesheron."

"It's a long trip," the Ambassador noted. "I've been on a few longer, but not many."

"Each way to the Set Province was five weeks," Henry said. "We were out there for six months before Lancelot."

They'd still been three weeks from home when the news that they'd been the ones to strike the final blow and finish off the Kenmorad had arrived. It was a *slow* genocide that they'd inflicted, but it was *Panther* and Colonel Henry Wong that had inflicted it.

He doubted anyone aboard his ship had been in a great mental state by the time they'd made it back to Procyon. He wasn't the only one who'd ended up a psych casualty out of *that* realization.

"We spent a year with the Londu," she told him. "It was about the same to get there, I think."

She shook herself.

"Sorry, Captain, I got distracted by the map and forgot why I was here," Todorovich said with a small smile. "With the section of the ship you gave us, it turns out that I have a dining room of my own. While I'm well aware that we're eating food you're providing for us, I *do* have a chef with me.

"I'd like to invite you and your executive officer to join my senior staff and me for dinner tonight. Preferably *before* we skip again." Her smile sharpened. "I don't think any of us are up for eating when our sensation of *down* keeps changing!"

Socialization and politics were an inevitable part of Henry's job, if not his favorite. For a moment, he considered trying to just send Iyotake.

But no. This was Todorovich's mission. He was just the driver, which meant he needed to know which way she was planning to go.

"We'd be delighted."

CHAPTER THIRTEEN

"Exit in five. Four. Three. Two. One. *Exit*."

Raven lurched in a direction that Henry Wong could never describe, and they were suddenly back in reality.

"Welcome to the Apophis-Four System and Apophis Province of the Kenmiri Empire," Bazzoli announced aloud. "For those of you who lost your brochure for our little tour, that puts us just over two-thirds of the way to Resta. Four more skips to Geb Province, and then two more to take us all the way there."

Henry shook his head, but he didn't rebuke the navigator for her exuberance. Getting back into real space hit people differently—but for a not-insignificant portion of the population, the feeling was akin to a few minutes of mania or a drug high.

"Ihejirika," he addressed his tactical officer instead. "How's Apophis-Four looking?"

"Like a red giant about twenty-five million years from nova," the broad-shouldered black man replied. "Looks like the Kenmiri fueling station has been abandoned. I've located it, but I'm not picking up any energy signatures."

They'd been in Kenmiri space for over a week now, and that was the story everywhere. The systems they'd traveled through had never been heavily populated, but they'd been useful to the Kenmiri for the same reasons *Raven* was traveling through them.

What infrastructure had existed was abandoned or just gone. It was one thing to hear that the Kenmiri had been withdrawing toward their core worlds.

It was another to pass through what was still, at least theoretically, civilized space and see *nothing*.

A chilly guilt was nestled at the base of Henry's spine, and it hadn't moved in three days.

"Should be a nice, quiet fourteen-hour vector adjustment, then," he said aloud. "Keep our eyes open. This isn't unclaimed space and the degree of quiet we're seeing is making me uncomfortable."

"Feels like there's no one left, doesn't it?" his tactical officer asked. "I guess it's more there's no *ships* left. If the Kenmiri took their ships with them, there's not many worlds that can build a skip drive."

"And five months is barely enough time to establish a new government, let alone start up trade again," Henry conceded. Of course, that had another downside: the Kenmiri had a bad habit of setting up slave worlds full of factories and mines that intentionally lacked a sufficient local food supply.

Somehow, he was grimly certain the insectoids hadn't moved those people before they'd abandoned them. Some of them would have found ways to survive—if nothing else, most of the industrial worlds *could* build skip drives—but others wouldn't.

Which was more blood on Henry Wong's hands, if rather indirectly.

He didn't even need the alert that buzzed in the back of his internal network to realize *that* wasn't a productive thought chain to follow.

"Not much we can do either way," Ihejirika noted. "Though I thought trade was part of what the Ambassador was supposed to negotiate. Did that get mentioned at dinner? Or were things too busy?"

He might not have *meant* it the way it had come out, but the the innuendo was blatant. Henry made a *cut off* gesture that shut his tactical officer up.

"Watch your suggestions, Commander," he warned. He and the Ambassador, plus various members of their staffs, had been trading dinner invites back and forth every few days for the entire trip. It was a good way to make sure he knew her mind, after all.

"Apologies, ser," the other man said, his gaze suddenly fixed on his console. He paused. "Did the Ambassador say anything about trade treaties, though?"

"It's been mentioned," Henry confirmed, letting his tone stay cool. "We'll see how the Gathering goes.

"For now, I suggest we keep our eyes on the scopes. The Kenmiri might have retreated, but we should still be treating this as hostile territory."

WHILE HENRY WOULD NEVER ADMIT it to his people, the warning to treat Kenmiri space as hostile territory was becoming a formality for him, too. Intelligence suggested that the Kenmiri had withdrawn into the core six provinces around their home world.

The nearest system of those provinces was almost sixty light-years away from Apophis-Four. The only people who were likely to be running around out here now were Vesheron, and the Vesheron were allies.

Weird, disorganized, barely-functional-at-times allies...but allies.

He was going over what he'd completed of his dissertation—an occasional hobby that rarely resulted in much. He'd earned his master's in astrophysics by UPSF correspondence shortly after the war started.

He'd been working on his PhD for fifteen years. Even though he was in a correspondence program designed for UPSF officers during wartime, he suspected his advisers never expected to receive a completed document.

Henry wasn't sure he expected to ever give them one, either, but it gave him something to focus on when he didn't have other distractions...which was rare enough as a starship captain.

His internal network interrupted him with a notice that he was getting a priority com from the bridge. Surprised, he flicked the call from his network to his office and answered it.

"Wong."

"Ser, this is Commander Ihejirika," his tactical officer said.

"So I presumed, what with you being the officer of the watch and all," Henry pointed out. "What's going on?"

"I'm transferring a visual pickup to your feed," the other man said in answer. The image that showed up was of one of Apophis-Four's gas giants. The closest one, Henry noted.

"Ninety seconds ago, we saw this."

A series of sparks lit up across the rings of the gas giant. They sparkled for a moment, then went away. It repeated a few seconds later. Then again.

"I was going to say that looked like reflections to me, but it isn't, is it?" Henry asked.

"I've picked up multiple pulses so far," the tactical officer replied. "I *think* they don't think we can see them. We have a pretty significant pickup-and-processing upgrade over the *Jaguar*'s, and most of our sensors are still telling me there's nothing there."

"So, what *is* there, Commander?" Henry asked.

Ihejirika paused.

"At least six ships. They're using short medium-power pulses to launch themselves into a slingshot course around the gas giant. I'd guess their intent is to build up as much velocity as they can before they emerge from behind cover and come out at us."

Henry studied the image and tapped some commands of his own.

"I'm not seeing anything big enough for a capital ship, so let's guess Kenmiri escort-sized ships," he noted. "If they *are* Kenmiri

escorts, they can pull one point two KPS squared. Coming around
the gas giant won't give them that much extra velocity."

"It converts what velocity they've got into a vector toward us,
though," Ihejirika replied. "They'll emerge on an intercept course at
just over two hundred KPS. They'll have just over two million kilometers to close, but it's not like *we* have much that can hit them at
that range."

The tactical officer wasn't wrong. The gravity driver fired a round
at seven percent of lightspeed. That was enough to be deadly at
reasonable combat ranges, but it limited those ranges to about a quarter-million kilometers.

Most people's lasers had a focusing distance of around that as
well. The two heavy lasers flanking *Raven*'s grav-driver were at their
most effective within a hundred thousand kilometers, but their
targets would know they'd been touched at a quarter-million.

Their *missiles* could get to two million kilometers...if they spent
most of the flight ballistic. They only had five minutes of fuel aboard.
Their powered range was only about three-quarters of a million
kilometers.

"You're assuming they're hostile," Henry pointed out. "They're
almost certainly Vesheron, not Kenmiri."

"They're maneuvering like they're hostile."

Raven's Captain sighed.

"You're right," he allowed. "Your estimate of engagement time?"

"Assuming Kenmiri escorts? They'll come out from behind the
gas giant in about two hours. If they bring their drives up at full
immediately, they'll reach laser range for Kenmiri escorts twenty-five
minutes after that unless we do something."

"Take the ship to readiness one," Henry ordered. "Get O'Flannagain's birds into space and held in a defensive patrol. I'll be on the
bridge before FighterDiv is in vacuum."

⁜

ON THE BRIDGE, Ihejirika had highlighted what information they had on the big displays as the alpha crew started making their way in. Readiness one called for two shifts on duty and one shift off, with all bridge officers at their station.

New icons started appearing on the tactical plot as Henry took his seat in the center of the room: O'Flannagain's Dragoons.

"Four birds in space, assuming escort formation," Iyotake reported from his station in the combat information center / auxiliary bridge. "Second flight prepping for launch."

"This is O'Flannagain," the pilot's voice interjected into the channel. "If they want to play games, let's play games. Permission to go buzz them."

"Permission denied, Commander," Henry said with a chuckle. "At least, don't buzz them *yet*. This may all be some unfortunate misunderstanding."

The FighterDiv commander's snort made her opinion of *that* suggestion clear.

"Lieutenant Commander Moon, let's ping them with the Vesheron ID codes. Subspace and radio, if you please," he ordered.

"As for assuming this a misunderstanding...I don't truly think so. Colonel Song? Bring the reactors to full and initialize the gravity shield."

"Yes, ser."

Icons on the relay screen lit up as the reactors came fully online. *Raven* carried four fusion reactors, each capable of providing enough power for her normal maneuvers and operation on their own. Two were required to enter skip drive, assuming they had a lot of time to charge the capacitors.

The gravity shield consumed the full output of a reactor, plus whatever extra it could steal from the rest. With it online, only the gravity driver and missile launchers were fully energized. The lasers, both defensive and offensive, were feeding from capacitors that would take several minutes to recharge from the power that could be spared.

The use of those capacitors and power distribution in general were critical to the successful operation of a battlecruiser. Nine times out of ten, the capacitors would be refilled fast enough that it wouldn't matter.

That tenth time was when you learned just how good your engineers actually were.

"We're receiving no response on any channels to the Vesheron recognition signals," Moon reported. "I'm eighty percent sure they're receiving us, but they're not talking."

"Bazzoli, maintain course for now but bring us up to five hundred MPS squared," Henry ordered calmly. That extra tenth-KPS^2 wouldn't change much in terms of their course—if they'd been at full acceleration from the beginning, maybe, but with only a few hours at most in play...

"I've got live engines in the gas giant rings," Ihejirika reported. "They're going through with the slingshot, but they're actively accelerating. Move that contact window up to forty-five minutes.

"Velocity at optimum weapons range will be two thousand KPS."

"If their engines are live, we should know who we're looking at," Henry replied. "Get me IDs, Tactical. If that's six dreadnoughts over there, we need to be doing something very different than I'm planning right now!"

If it was six dreadnoughts, they needed to run.

If it was the six escorts he was expecting, though...they were going to learn why it had been the United Planets Space Force that had carried the bulk of Operation Golden Lancelot!

CHAPTER FOURTEEN

"Ser, if you want IDs, that's what my birds are for," O'Flannagain interrupted as CIC crunched their data.

"Commander, please," Henry told her. "If it's what I think is over there, I have far better use for you than as scouts. And if we're in more trouble than we think we are, sending your people in would be suicide. Check your people's grav-shields and stand by for orders."

The pilot shut up again, and Henry couldn't conceal the smirk that hit his face.

Rocket-jocks. But better to restrain the eager lion than whip the reluctant donkey.

"Ihejirika? Iyotake?" he addressed the two men running his data. "They're behind that gas giant now. Some data on what I'm looking at would be nice."

"It's not a dreadnought group, if that helps," Iyotake told him. "My people confirm our first assessment: six ships, escort- or gunship-sized."

"I'd love it if you could tell me there were no gunships over there," Henry replied. A Kenmiri escort vessel packed a collection of lasers, including four primary beams that easily rivaled *Raven's* two heavy lasers. Escorts were dangerous opponents, moreso to Henry's fighters than to his battlecruiser, but they were deadliest in numbers.

Gunships, on the other hand, were what happened when you took the heavy plasma-cannon turret from a Kenmiri dreadnought and strapped engines and a life support plant to it. *Raven's* gravity shield could deflect any attack, but there was always a chance that something could still hit the ship.

Plasma cannon were energetic enough that even a tiny sliver of the original plasma blast could strip away heat radiators and sensors. A full blowthrough from a plasma cannon was one of the few things that could kill *Raven* in one shot.

"I can't tell you from what we saw," Ihejirika told him. "Engine signatures for a gunship and an escort are pretty similar; a gunship is only about ten percent bigger."

Henry exhaled sharply, studying the tactical plot. The Kenmiri ships would round the gas giant in just under fifty minutes and lunge toward him at two hundred KPS with an acceleration *Raven* couldn't match.

"Order the ship secured for acceleration," he ordered. "Ambassador Todorovich and her people are to report to acceleration tanks. The rest of the crew is to prepare for up to five gravities of subjective acceleration and report to battle stations."

"Understood. We'll pass the notices."

Henry turned his attention back to the icons. They were Kenmiri ships...but that didn't mean as much as it might. Only the El-Vesheron powers like the UPA had brought fleets of only their own ships to the battle. Even the Resta, with hidden shipyards and their own technology base, had used large numbers of stolen Kenmiri ships.

If nothing else, the Kenmiri wouldn't have picked a fight with a UPSF battlecruiser without a dreadnought. The insectoids calculated every probability before they committed to action, and always tried to tilt the odds in their favor.

Most likely, he was facing Vesheron...but *these* Vesheron didn't seem to be heading to the Gathering.

"Commander O'Flannagain," he addressed his fighter commander. "Set your course to intercept as the enemy clears the gas giant. You will salvo all of your missiles and get clear of their range. No heroics, no laser pass. Shoot to disable, prioritize any gunships present. Understood?"

"Yes, ser!"

Several seconds of silence passed and then the Dragoons leapt away from *Raven*. They had the same inertial compensators as *Raven* did, but with the pilots strapped into dedicated acceleration tanks and suits, they could manage 1.5 KPS^2.

"That doesn't leave us much of a chance to challenge them before we fire," Iyotake pointed out.

"That's what the shoot-to-disable order is about," Henry confirmed. "They're maneuvering to intercept us and they aren't answering the damn phone, XO. Our job is to protect the Ambassador...and if anyone wants to get sticky about it, I have every grounds to believe those are Kenmiri warships."

ICONS STREAMED across the displays around Henry Wong as his crew reported in to their battle stations. From readiness one to full battle stations was supposed to be a matter of a couple of minutes at the worst of times. His order to secure the ship for acceleration didn't help, but it was still concerning that it took almost four minutes for the last station to report in.

"We're going to have to run more emergency drills," he murmured to Iyotake. "Most of the securing for acceleration should be part of battle stations already. It should never take this long from readiness one."

"No," the XO agreed. "I'll be on it as soon as this is over."

"*Raven* is the newest and shiniest battlecruiser in the fleet," Henry said. "Let's make sure we live up to that."

"Yes, ser."

That was all that needed to be said for now, and *Raven*'s Captain turned his attention to his starfighters. After ten minutes, they were only about a third of the way to the gas giant but accelerating *fast*.

He projected their vector and grunted in approval. They didn't know for sure where the Kenmiri ships would come around the gas giant, but assuming they'd followed the slingshot maneuver they'd gone behind the big planet on, there were a limited number of angles they could emerge at.

The starfighters would be in perfect position to volley their missiles at the escorts as they did so—and then vanish around the other side of the gas giant themselves before the enemy could return fire.

The missiles aboard the fighters were smaller than the ones in *Raven*'s magazines, with identical warheads but half the fuel. They also lacked the initial velocity imparted by *Raven*'s missile launchers, which meant they only had the starfighters' velocity to fling them forward.

"Should we divert *Raven* toward the enemy?" Bazzoli asked.

"Negative. Stay on course for now," Henry ordered. "Let them come to us. Initiate evasive maneuvers once they're clear of the gas giant."

Seconds continued to tick away. A gesture threw a timer of the hostiles' estimated emergence time on the screen closest to Henry. Five minutes and counting.

"Thejirika, are the guns ready?" he asked calmly.

"Solid shot in the main gun. Laser capacitors charged. Launchers loaded, conversion warheads." The tactical officer nodded firmly, as much to himself as to his Captain. "All weapons are ready for action."

"Song? Is the shield ready?" Henry continued.

"All shield systems are online and in the green. Sensors confirm a fifteen-thousand-gravity shear zone surrounding the ship."

Very little in existence could handle going from microgravity to fifteen thousand gravities. Even less could handle going *back* seventeen centimeters later. Any physical projectile was shredded by tidal forces. Even lasers were badly distorted, rarely hitting the target they were aimed at.

With her shield up, it was difficult for anyone outside it to even locate *Raven.* They could easily detect the shield itself, though, and the Kenmiri, at least, had learned that the ship was always at the exact center of the spherical shield bubble.

Their own projectiles suffered the same problems, but they could open "gunports" in the shear zone to let beams, missiles and grav-driver slugs through.

"Emergence estimate in sixty seconds," Ihejirika reported. "I hope they're not too far off. O'Flannagain will lose line of sight behind the gas giant in eighty-two seconds."

"For once, I hope they are Kenmiri," Henry told his people with a forced chuckle. "If there's one thing you can count on the bugs to be, it's *punctual.*"

He got the answering chuckles he had hoped for...and then it was time. The flashing red icon showing the projected location of the Kenmiri squadron went solid as O'Flannagain's fighters picked up their targets.

Six light-seconds wasn't enough to *require* using the starfighters' subspace communications for decently timed data, but it made a noticeable difference. Even with live communication to the starfighters, Henry's preference was to let the strike commander make the call.

He'd authorized her to engage and given her the target parameters. Everything after that was the FighterDiv Commander's call—and with only twelve seconds to make the shot, lightspeed coms wouldn't have been fast enough.

Even subspace coms wouldn't have, not really. In those twelve seconds, someone had to make the call, someone had to give the order, and eight UPSF starfighter pilots had to acquire targets and launch their missiles.

It wasn't much time—but it was *enough* time and thirty-two new icons appeared on his screen.

And then froze.

"We've lost real-time data," Ihejirika reported. "Dragoons are behind the planet; they did not come under fire."

The lightspeed delay caught up—and showed that the fighters' safety had been entirely a question of timing, as a salvo of laser fire cut through empty space and into the surface of the gas giant. O'Flannagain's timing had been perfect.

"Missile flight time is forty-five seconds," the tactical officer continued. "We have confirmed two, I repeat, *two*, gunships in the enemy line."

"O'Flannagain targeted the closer one with everything, I presume?" Henry asked.

"Yes, ser," the junior man confirmed. "Will that be enough?"

Henry didn't answer. They'd know in less than thirty seconds and he had his suspicions. It might have been sixteen years since he'd flown fighter strikes against Kenmiri warships, but thirty-two missiles would have been iffy then.

And the Kenmiri might be fielding the same classes—and in some cases, even the same ships—as at the beginning of the war, but those ships had been upgraded and updated over the last seventeen years too.

Missiles were too small for subspace communicators. There was no space to spare in a weapon that needed to accelerate at ten KPS^2 for 150 seconds and do something useful at the end of that.

"Kenmiri defenses engaging."

"They're slow," Henry murmured. "Missile defense should have been online already when they came around the planet. We could have been stacking time-on-target salvos for ten minutes of the time they were behind it."

If he'd had the logistics of an actual combat campaign, he'd have considered it. Right now, though, the only missiles he had for this entire mission were in *Raven*'s magazines. It wasn't *supposed* to be a combat mission.

The reason the thought occurred to him, though, was because he'd seen *Kenmiri* commanders use it.

"They're efficient enough," Ihejirika replied. Starfighter missiles came in slowly at the best of times, and these had been fired from close range. The same forty-five-second flight time that was giving them any advantage of surprise at all meant they were vulnerable to the enemy defenses.

"We're down twenty missiles alrea—warhead conversion!"

The missiles exploded ten thousand kilometers short of their targets. Carefully designed magnetic fields shaped a ten-megaton fusion warhead, converting the entire mass of the missile and its remaining fuel into a ball of coherent plasma that completed the rest of its trip in a tenth of a second.

The UPA couldn't build plasma cannon like the Kenmiri yet, but their conversion warheads were pretty close to the same final effect at impact.

Ten missiles survived long enough to convert and three still missed outright, sending balls of plasma off into deep space, where they would dissipate into harmlessness in under a minute.

Seven blasts, each about half as powerful as the plasma cannon the ship was built around, hammered into the Kenmiri gunship. Henry had seen the results from close up in the past and shivered at the memories.

Armor plating would be vaporizing and splintering. Holes would be torn deep into the ship, where the plasma would disperse itself through the ship's atmosphere, turning entire sections of the vessel into a subdivision of hell.

Seven hits wouldn't be enough to destroy a Kenmiri gunship, but...

"Target is falling out of formation and leaking atmosphere," Ihejirika reported. "Power signature is flickering. I'd say she's lost multiple reactors and… There go her engines. She's dead in the water, ser."

Henry paused, his gaze fixed on the gunship. Two million kilometers would be a ninety-five-second flight for his main gun, but an un-maneuvering target…"dead in the water" was "blood in the water" for a ship with an artificial gravity railgun.

"Flag her as disabled and ignore her for now," he ordered. He could see his people clearly through the screens surrounding him, and that had *not* been the order Ihejirika had been expecting.

"They're not Kenmiri, Commander," Henry told the other man. "They're bandits. They might have been Vesheron. They might *call* themselves Vesheron still, but they're bandits.

"And while I'll shoot down bandits and I'll *kill* bandits, we're not at war with bandits."

He smiled grimly and studied the remaining ships.

"Having said that, the rest of them seem to think that they're going to try and capture a gravity shield out of this. Let's disabuse them of that notion. Commander Bazzoli!"

"Ser!"

They hadn't crossed the half-KPS^2 line that would actually leak thrust into the ship and Henry didn't see any reason to change that.

"Bring us about. Direct course toward the enemy, combat acceleration. Commander Ihejirika, engage the remaining gunship with missiles once you have the range. *Only* the gunship, if you please."

Their missiles would come in far faster than the starfighter missiles had. On the other hand, they were a lot more expensive and *Raven* only had so many missiles.

"If the escorts still want to pick a fight after both of the gunships are down, we'll engage with the grav-driver and the lasers. We don't know what else this mission is going to bring us. Let's keep our missiles for later if we can."

THE BANDITS WERE SURPRISINGLY silent for having lost one of their most powerful ships. They were also still determinedly coming on, and Henry mentally saluted their bravery. They were *dumb*, but brave.

"What was their plan?" Iyotake asked on their private channel. "I mean, six escorts with a dreadnought would be about an even fight, but just six escort-tier ships on their own?"

"Their plan was to only run their engines on the other side of the gas giant," Henry replied. "They'd have come around the planet with about two hundred KPS of velocity and the gas giant's heat signature behind them as they approached us. Against a *Jaguar*, they probably could have made it all the way to a light-second or even closer before we could pick them out from the background radiation if they were careful."

At a light-second, without the grav-shield up, the escorts could potentially have knocked out the battlecruiser's engines and weapons —or even just the power generators. That would have allowed them to board and capture a UPSF warship.

It wouldn't have worked out that easily for them, even against the older battlecruiser whoever was in charge had been anticipating. Even if they'd managed to board, Thompson's people would have massacred them in the close fighting to follow.

"So, their plan has been blown from the beginning?" the XO asked.

"From the moment Ihejirika picked them up," Henry confirmed. "Assuming, of course, that your team in CIC is sweeping to make sure no one *else* is trying to sneak up on us."

Iyotake couldn't make an actual rude noise without the CIC crew hearing him, but the intent carried across the channel quite handily.

"I've got sensor drones spread out now to get different angles on the approaches from the gas giants and the star," he confirmed. "Recalling them will be a pain, but no one is sneaking up on us."

"Then yeah." Henry shook his head. "The commander over there is familiar with the *Jaguar*-class and misjudged us. Now, though, they're committed to their course."

"If they're *that* familiar, though, you'd think they'd know they can't fight us."

"They know," Henry said softly. "And I wouldn't expect a group of bandits to be this determined. They should have broken off behind the gas giant. Without an active threat, we wouldn't have pursued.

"Now, though...now we've punched them in the nose and they're angry."

"Or there's something else going on," his XO replied.

"The only thing I can think of is that someone is *damned* determined to make sure we don't make it to the Gathering," Henry admitted. "And...well. That gunship is still a pretty hefty threat, XO. And there's definitely people out there who will pay through the nose for UPSF ship parts."

That was why *Raven*'s fusion reactors could be overloaded as a self-destruct, after all. The UPA had sacrificed a *lot* to make sure that their gravity technology stayed out of Kenmiri and Vesheron hands.

Henry sure as hell wasn't handing it over to an unknown new player...assuming that was what he was looking at.

If the attackers had been waiting for him, after all, then they'd known about the Gathering.

CHAPTER FIFTEEN

"Missile range in twenty seconds," Ihejirika reported. "Permission to engage as specified?"

Henry chuckled.

"Engage the enemy, Commander," he ordered. It was an unnecessary exchange, but the situation *could* have changed since he'd given the original orders.

Instead, the enemy had stayed on their course directly for him. They'd ignored Moon's attempts to communicate the entire time and seemed undaunted by *Raven* coming about to meet them.

The growing relative velocity extended the range of his missiles in a way it really didn't for his gravity driver or lasers. They'd have eight minutes in missile range before anything else entered weapons range.

"Enemy missile launch," Iyotake reported from CIC. "Standard dispersal pattern, standard acceleration. Estimate ninety missiles inbound."

Henry exhaled and nodded, watching as twelve green icons added themselves to his displays as *Raven*'s missiles fired. That was what he'd expected. A Kenmiri escort had twenty missile launchers. A gunship had ten.

Those missiles weren't really a threat. Close detonation outside the shield could cause *Raven* minor trouble, but the gravity shield would tear missiles apart. *He* had special warheads for his own missiles that would punch right through a grav-shield. The UPA had never encountered gravity shields on somebody else's ships, but that was only a matter of time.

"Permission to engage missiles with defensive lasers?" Ihejirika asked.

"Delegate it to your assistants," Henry ordered. Probably redundant, but this crew was still too green for his taste. "But yes."

Just because no one had demonstrated penetrator warheads *yet* didn't mean they didn't have them. Some kind of surprise would go a long way to explaining why the bandits were picking a fight like this.

New icons flickered across his displays as more heat radiators deployed out from the hull, these specific to the missile-defense lasers arrayed along *Raven*'s wings. A handful of seconds later, the missiles entered *Raven*'s outer defense perimeter and the lasers opened fire.

The Kenmiri-built ships' defenses had opened fire a good ten seconds earlier. The Kenmiri had *always* had better lasers than the UPA.

They didn't have better missiles...mostly because the UPSF had acquired *lots* of samples of intact Kenmiri weapons over the years. Functionally, *Raven*'s missiles were identical to her opponents'.

"Direct hit!" Ihejirika barked. "Two missiles converted, one missed, one hit. Target appears...materially intact."

That was why they'd send six salvos flashing across space in the five minutes it had taken the first salvo to arrive.

"Hold fire on missiles," Henry ordered. "At this point, they'll be in range of the main gun before anything we fire hits them."

Two missiles through the defenses of five ships was impressive. The Kenmiri had shot down ten of their missiles—and *Raven*'s crew had handled eighteen of theirs. That had still left over seventy.

Enough of them exploded into conversion warheads that he didn't immediately realize they hadn't *all* exploded.

"Ser, I need you to take a look at this," Song cut into his feed.

"Show me," he ordered, turning his chair to look at the screen showing him engineering's data.

"Seventy-two missiles made it past the defenses. Forty-five were conversion warheads. We didn't have a blowthrough, not a surprise with the power level involved.

"The other twenty-seven were either conventional warheads or kinetic-kill vehicles. They hit the shield."

"We're still here, so I'm guessing they're scattered in pieces across a few thousand cubic kilometers," Henry pointed out. "What did you see, Colonel Song?"

"We had some *weird* resonance bursts in the shield metrics as they hit," Song told him grimly. "Strained the emitters pretty badly, actually. We've got secondary emitters if we lose any, but I don't have the power available to keep them *all* up."

"Wait, are you telling me they could bring the shield down?" Henry demanded.

"I'm not sure," she admitted. "We didn't use resonance when we built our penetrator warheads, but the theory was discussed. They're certainly straining our system with these things. With *enough* of them…"

"How many is enough, Colonel Song?" he asked as the second salvo hit home. He could see it on the display now, sectors of the shield emitters flashing orange warning colors.

"They've hit us with sixty of the things in the last minute and we're still here, so I'll say more than that," Song said sharply. "I'm going to start swapping over emitters after each hit. That should spread the strain without risking burnout anywhere.

"These aren't going to bring the shield down, Captain…but someone has been *very* clever."

"Not clever enough," Henry replied. "But enough, I suspect, to have convinced our friends out there that they *did* have something that worked."

He smiled.

"Unfortunately for them, it didn't. Commander Ihejirika!"

"Sixty seconds to grav-driver range," the tactical officer replied instantly as a third salvo tore itself to death on the shields. "We've hit the gunship half a dozen times. She's bleeding air and she's bleeding power, but my scans say she's still got a charge in the gun."

"That's not great, Commander," Henry pointed out. The plasma cannon wasn't a lightspeed weapon like the lasers, but it *was* a lot closer to it than the gravity driver was.

"Target her at three-fifty with the main gun and fire a conversion round," he ordered. "Let's see if we can breach that chamber before she shoots us with it!"

At three hundred and fifty thousand kilometers, the slug would have a fifteen-second flight time. Hits weren't likely...but they weren't impossible, either. Not with a conversion round with a fifteen-thousand-kilometer kill zone!

"On your order," the tactical officer replied. "Firing...*now.*"

There were very few things that a Captain could *feel* through the hull of his spaceship. Inertial compensators and a battlecruiser's massively powerful engines combined to protect the crew from almost any exterior or interior force except for the skip drive itself.

Firing a gravitational linear accelerator that took a projectile from zero to 0.07 cee in a quarter-second still shook the ship. There was no recoil created by the focused gravitational field, but even the shields wrapped around the gun didn't prevent the gravity field itself rippling as the projectile flashed by underneath their feet.

"Impact in fourteen seconds," Ihejirika said calmly. "Round is tracking on target. If we miss, that's it, ser. She's in range for the plasma gun a few seconds after that."

And the plasma cannon was the last thing on the board that Henry was actually worried about. The lasers *might* hurt *Raven.* The plasma cannon *could* hurt *Raven*. Battered as that gunship was, she was the only thing in the system that threatened him.

"Target is evading. Projectile thrusters are active." The tactical officer continued his litany. "Thrusters expended. Five seconds. Four. Two...conversion."

Every laser in the Kenmiri fleet had been focused on the projectile, but seven percent of lightspeed was enough to cause serious problems with their tracking. They'd probably even hit it, but the weapon was surrounded by a layer of ablative armor for just that circumstance.

Conversion on a grav-driver slug was even more impressive than on a missile warhead. The two weapons were roughly the same size, after all, and the slug didn't need to worry about engines.

What hit the gunship was a plasma burst *more* powerful than its main gun could generate. But even as parts of the ship blasted away into space, Henry could tell that they'd failed at the main objective.

They'd hit the gunship in the rear third of the ship, gutting her engines and killing her acceleration...but she was already moving fast enough to bring the big gun into range.

"She's firing," he said softly. No one would report that when it happened—at 0.8 cee, there'd be no time.

The plasma bolt held coherence for just under three hundred thousand kilometers—twenty times as long as any plasma weapon the UPA had ever built—and *Raven* didn't have time to dodge. It hit the gravity shield dead-on, a perfectly angled shot that maximized their chance of blowthrough.

And they got it.

"*Blowthrough*," an NCO snapped, and warnings flashed across the bridge. Then...nothing.

"Report," Henry demanded as the alerts on his screens faded.

"It breached the shield but missed the hull," Song reported after several seconds of silence. "I repeat, we have blowthrough, but we do *not* have impact."

"And she's not getting a second chance," Ihejirika said. "Her casing chamber just shattered. She can't charge a second shot."

Henry glanced across his screens and displays, taking in the situation. In a few seconds, the lasers would start...but the bandits had already lost. They had to know that.

"Moon, send a surrender demand," he ordered. "Their surprise failed and their gunships are gone. Let's see if we can end this without any more bloodshed."

"Do we hold fire?" Ihejirika asked.

For a moment, Henry was tempted...but much as he wanted to dismiss the escorts, the truth was that each of them carried four beams powerful enough to wreck *Raven* if they made it through the shield.

He couldn't take the risk.

"No," he told his tactical officer. "If a ship stops shooting, we stop shooting at it...but so long as they're firing, keep pounding them."

"Range in ten seconds." There was a pause. "Do we wait for them to fire first?"

"Unless they've stopped shooting missiles and I didn't notice it, no," Henry said dryly.

"Firing!"

Raven shivered again as the main gun fired. This time, the lasers joined in. They'd be more effective at closer ranges, but no one was going to enjoy being tapped at a quarter-million klicks.

"Laser strikes across the shield and they're continuing to pound us with missiles," Iyotake noted. "Recommend ceasing antimissile engagement to preserve power for the main beams."

"Agreed," Henry replied. "Pull them in, XO."

At this range, the missiles had the same problem as the starfighter missiles had had earlier. They didn't have time to build up velocity, but they also didn't have nearly as far to go—and shipboard missiles were launching with a base velocity of a thousand kilometers a second.

"Direct hit," Ihejirika reported. "Conversion round amidships, hit multiple times with both lasers...target has lost engine power and ceased fire. Switching to target two."

Henry checked the screens and nodded. His crew might not be as smooth a machine as he'd like, but they knew what they were doing. *Raven's* lasers walked their way across their new target as the three remaining escorts threw everything they had at her.

"Good news?" Iyotake said quietly. "They've run out of whatever the hell those missiles they had earlier were. All we're seeing now is conversion warheads."

Those could be bad enough, but Henry could safely ignore them as their second target managed to dance out of the way of the plasma beam from their second main-gun round. The grav-driver took a *lot* longer to cycle than the Kenmiri lasers...and the escorts weren't running their guns from capacitors.

Raven's were running dry. If they had to charge between each shot, their cycle would go from seven seconds to *seventy*...and as Henry watched, the capacitor indicators clicked to zero.

"*Got him!*" Ihejirika exclaimed. "Target two's engines are down and she is spinning. She might have guns, but they aren't pointed at us anymore! Switching to target—"

"Receiving radio transmission on Vesheron protocols," Moon cut in. "They're surrendering. They're ceasing fire and surrendering."

"Tactical—confirm that!" Henry snapped.

"Enemy fire has ceased," Ihejirika confirmed a moment later. "I'm still seeing capacitor charge across all three ships, though."

"Moon, order them to discharge their capacitors and cut their engines," Henry said. "Inform Commander Thompson that his people get to practice boarding ops."

He shook his head.

"I have a sinking feeling about why these guys were here. I want to know who sent them...and I want to know who sold them those resonance warheads!"

CHAPTER SIXTEEN

"WELL, THEY'RE NOT KENMIRI," THOMPSON'S PROJECTED IMAGE said on *Raven*'s bridge. "I'm not familiar with the particular race in play, but they're one of the Ashall."

"Do you have a picture?" Todorovich asked. The Ambassador had arrived on the bridge just as the GroundDiv commander reported in. What was visible of her hair was still glistening with moisture from the gel of the acceleration tank, but she'd wrapped it in a simple black headwrap to keep it out of the way and returned to work.

"Yeah, hold on," the GroundDiv officer confirmed. A moment later, the feed from the captured escort warship split in two. Thompson's image slid to the left and a new picture appeared on the right.

"This is Attallis, the Captain of this particular ship and the one who ordered the surrender," he noted.

Henry studied the image. Assuming they were at the same scale, the alien was *tall*: at least two meters, probably more. She—clearly visible breasts were generally a solid sign of sex across Ashall species —was gaunt by human standards, her limbs looking like her bones were thin and fragile.

Her skin was a pale shade of purple and she had what looked like an armor plate instead of hair, but her facial features were human enough. Ashall, a Seeded Race. She looked like a human in a costume.

"She's Drex," Todorovich noted. "They're from Osiris-Six, in the inner Provinces."

"Where the Kenmiri are still in control," Henry concluded. "Commander, are they all Drex?"

"I'd say ninety percent," Thompson replied. "The rest are mostly other Ashall. We've secured all three nearby ships. There was no resistance. Attallis apparently made her surrender order stick."

"So, she's in command of this little fleet?" the Captain asked, looking away from the image of his GroundDiv commander to study the tactical plot. He snorted as he spotted O'Flannagain's starfighters.

The eight of them were now in a formation around the crippled gunship they'd nuked earlier. Tow cables—super-strong and super-light kilometer-long streams of monofilament—connected the Dragoons to their victim, and they were carefully burning toward *Raven*.

Bringing the wrecked ship with them.

"She wasn't in command before," Thompson told him, unaware of what Henry was seeing. "The three Captains left are apparently equals. The three *dead* Captains were the senior ones—the original commanders for this batch of merry thieves."

"She'll know as much as anyone," Henry said. "We'll need to keep people aboard the ships until we sort out what we're doing with them. Keep the officers and non-coms isolated. The last thing I want is for your people to get stabbed in the back."

"We'll work through the doctrine," the GroundDiv Commander replied. Most board-and-captures carried out by the UPSF had been of Kenmiri ships, which required quite different handling.

Not least because they'd usually been crippled before GroundDiv could get anywhere near them. Kenmiri Warriors did *not* surrender outside of truly extraordinary circumstances.

"And, Commander?" Henry interrupted Thompson before he dropped the channel.

"Ser?"

"Send Attallis back to *Raven*." Henry glanced over at Todorovich. "I want to have a conversation with her and see if we can sort out some bloody answers."

HENRY WASN'T PARTICULARLY surprised when Todorovich followed him into his office after ending the call with the GroundDiv Commander.

"How are you holding up, Ambassador?" he asked her after the door slid closed. "I know *I* wasn't expecting to go into combat on this mission."

"I'm fine," she said shortly. "My chief of staff thinks throwing us into the tanks was some kind of sick joke since you never went past standard acceleration. Fair warning."

"If I order it, my crew is in the tanks in under thirty seconds," Henry pointed out. He had a lot of concerns with how slowly *Raven*'s crew had reported to their stations, but he still suspected the base competence of his people was quite high.

It was getting them to work *together* that was giving him a headache.

"I can't rely on civilians to move as quickly."

"I know that," Todorovich agreed. "Felix is...wet and grumpy. He'll probably get over it."

"I hope so." Henry shook his head as he threw the tactical plot onto his office hologram. "We now find ourselves with two intact Vesheron escorts, a damaged Vesheron escort, a crippled gunship... and two hulks that Thompson's people are doing search-and-rescue on, not boarding ops."

"Not exactly an easy trip to the Gathering," the Ambassador noted. "What do we do with them?"

"Engaging them and forcing their surrender was a military situation," Henry replied. "What we do with them is a *political* situation. Which means it's in your court."

She grimaced.

"Dragging them to the Gathering wouldn't help us," she noted. "At the same time, I don't really want to leave a bandit force in play here. It seems...unneighbourly."

"That's one word for it," Henry agreed. "The dangerous part to all of this, Ambassador, is that they were carrying some kind of specialty weapon designed to take down a gravity shield. It wasn't good enough, but it was definitely moving in the right kind of direction to be a serious threat.

"Our 'allies' are working on ways to undermine our best advantage over them," he concluded. "I'm not *surprised*, but it certainly wasn't my best-case scenario."

"Or mine," she agreed. "I think I need to talk to this Attallis before I make a decision, Captain Wong. If you'll permit?"

"I command this ship, Ambassador Todorovich, but this is your mission," Henry conceded. "Right now, I'm planning a conversation with the woman, not an interrogation. It's a different situation, I suppose, if this was a targeted assassination attempt as opposed to general banditry."

"For me, that might be worse," Todorovich noted dryly. She pulled an image of Attallis up on the hologram and studied the alien.

"She's attractive to human eyes, even with the head-plate," she said. "That's always the oddity of the Ashall, isn't it?"

"According to my old XO, they may *look* like us and are reliably mammalian...but that doesn't mean everything's compatible downstairs," Henry pointed out. "My own experience doesn't stretch that far. Captain Attallis here isn't my type."

"What *is* your type?" Todorovich asked, then laughed. "Sorry, that's inappropriate. Do you have a plan for dealing with her?"

"Right now, I need to look her in the eyes and ask her what the hell her boss was thinking, picking a fight with a UPSF battlecruiser," he replied, her humor bringing a smile to his face. "Once I know the answer to *that*, I think everything else is going to fall into place."

The sharp-edged woman standing across from him nodded.

"We can't wait here for long, but I think we need to deal with this situation before we move on, Captain. The sooner we get answers from this Attallis, the better."

"Well, that's her shuttle." He tapped an icon on the display marking one of his spacecraft leaving the captured escort. "Give us ten minutes to get her aboard and into an interview room."

"Will the rest be secure?" Todorovich asked, looking at the other ships.

"Only two of them can fly under their own power right now," Henry pointed out. "One *might* be repairable here if they cannibalize the wrecks. Two are hulks, basically collections of debris. The gunship O'Flannagain is towing back toward us would probably be salvageable at a shipyard, but I wouldn't count on it being fixed here."

He studied the icons for a long few seconds, letting the memories of being aboard wrecked ships dominate his thoughts for a few seconds as they spiked into his brain. *Let it flow through and be done...*

"Captain?" Todorovich asked.

"Sorry. As I said, only two of them could be a threat, which is why those two have most of our GroundDiv troopers aboard. Hopefully, the people we're pulling out of the wrecks are feeling grateful for the rescue!"

"It wouldn't be the first time if they weren't," the Ambassador pointed out. "I presume your people are being careful?"

"That's the plan," he confirmed. "Thompson seems a competent sort, and while his battalion is assembled from scratch like the rest of the crew, *he* got complete companies to do the assembling with."

"Anything I should know for the interview?" Todorovich asked.

"Let's try not to talk over each other?" Henry said with a chuckle. "This conversation won't be *easy*, but it's not an interrogation."

His smile thinned.

"If it comes down to an actual interrogation, I have people for that."

✦✦
✦✦✦

TWO GROUNDDIV TROOPERS, in mottled gray medium combat armor, escorted Attallis into the room where Henry and Todorovich were waiting.

The room would probably have been recognizable to anyone who'd served on any starship or wet-navy ship of the last half-millennium. A metal box with a single door, a visible camera—and at least five invisible ones—and some plain lights.

The metal table bolted to the floor was standard too. There was nothing in the room the prisoner could pick up and use as a weapon. Even if there were, Attallis's hands were cuffed behind her back.

"Release the cuffs and wait outside," Henry ordered. "She doesn't *leave* unrestrained, but we'll be safe enough in here."

"Are you sure, ser?" the guard asked, glancing over the Captain and the Ambassador—both unarmed. "Should one of us stay in here?"

Henry considered it for a moment, but a look at Attallis made up his mind for him. The woman's body language was utterly crushed. She could be faking it, but even if she *was,* what was she going to do? Injuring or killing him or the Ambassador would just guarantee her death the moment the door opened.

"We'll be fine, PO," he told the GroundDiv noncom. "Thank you."

Attallis let herself be guided to the chair and uncuffed. She rubbed her wrists as the guards withdrew, looking around with the careful eyes of a caged animal that didn't understand what was being said around her.

Henry took a moment to mentally recalibrate. It was easier to *speak* a different language if you were thinking in that language, and with the internal network, it was easier to force that switchover than it would have been without it.

Opening his eyes, he was thinking in Kem and addressed Attallis in the same language.

"My soldiers tell me your name is Attallis," he said. "You were in command?"

He could *see* the moment she registered that he was speaking a language she understood. She still looked defeated but not quite as terrified.

"I was in command of my ship, *Dancing Sister*," she answered. "I did not command the fleet. That was First Warlord Deearan. They commanded the fleet and chose our targets."

"And you were Vesheron once?" Henry asked.

"We are Vesheron still!" she snapped proudly.

"We called on all Vesheron channels," he pointed out. "We tried to communicate. You ignored us."

Attallis was silent.

"We are also Vesheron. Why did you attack us?" Henry demanded.

She was silent for several more seconds, then bowed her head.

"Because First Warlord Deearan commanded it," she admitted. "As they commanded other attacks. We are Vesheron still...but we are not what we were. We have attacked others. Transports. At first, Deearan claimed they were Kenmiri.

"After a while, they stopped pretending."

"But you knew we could not be Kenmiri," Henry pointed out. "Why did you attack us?"

"Because the First Warlord commanded it," she repeated. "And because the last three Captains to defy their orders are dead, spaced without trial. Deearan said we could never go home. No one would ever help us go home.

"We had to make our way here."

Henry concealed a grimace. This "First Warlord" wasn't wrong there. The Drex had been conquered and enslaved by the Kenmiri a *long* time ago. Not only had Attalis never seen her homeworld free, but if she was this far out it was quite possibly she'd never see it at all.

Worse, the Osiris Province was one of the four the insectoids hadn't given up, which meant that Attallis's homeworld was still under Kenmiri control.

And with Kenmiri expansion halted, the El-Vesheron like the Terrans and the Londu weren't going to wage war deep into the Empire to liberate the still-occupied worlds. It would be years—decades, probably—before any of the Vesheron managed to build fleets able to wage those campaigns alone.

The alliance hadn't officially broken down yet, but the Drex among the Vesheron couldn't bring together enough factions to liberate Osiris-Six.

"So, you turned to piracy." Todorovich inserted herself into the conversation in Henry's silence. "Theft. Murder. The traditions of *our* people say your crimes warrant death, Captain Attallis. Why should we spare any of you?"

Henry reminded himself never to get on the Ambassador's bad side. The sharp and cold tone of her voice carried through the alien language *perfectly*. She wasn't wrong, either. UPSF military law called for him to turn pirates over to local authorities if they were present, but in situations like this?

He was entirely within his authority to execute every survivor of Warlord Deearan's crews. It wasn't an option he'd be *comfortable* taking, but…he wasn't sure it was worse than leaving two active pirate ships behind him.

"I am *not* a pirate!" Attallis snapped. A flush of darker purple crossed her face and she was suddenly straighter in her chair. "I am Vesheron, a warrior of the Drex, an escaped slave who carved the path I must to survive. I followed the commands of my Warlord. I am not a pirate."

"Your actions define you, Captain Attallis, not your words," Todorovich replied. "If we left you behind us, you would continue as you have. Innocents would die."

"I am not Deearan," the Drex woman insisted. "I followed my Warlord's orders because I had no choice. With my Warlord dead, the choice is mine."

"Convince me to trust you, Captain," Henry said gently. "Right now, I see a woman we captured attacking this ship who has admitted to acting as a pirate. Why should I see anything else?"

She started to snarl at him...and then stopped herself. She closed her eyes and several seconds passed in silence.

"I can speak for the other Captains that remain," she noted, slowly and with forced calm in her tone. "We were the replacements for the officers Deearan spaced. The other Captains were Deearan's people from long ago. We knew we would die if we defied the Warlord.

"But Deearan is dead. Killed aboard their ship when you wrecked her. The Captains who willingly followed them into piracy are dead. We will not repeat the mistakes of the past. I swear this."

"Even if I am willing to believe you, I need more proof than your word," Henry told her. "Tell me everything, Captain Attallis. You fired new missiles at my ship. Where did they come from?"

"New missiles?" she stared at him, and then slammed a hand onto the table in frustration. "That monster. I understand now, I think."

"Explain, Captain Attallis," Todorovich ordered.

"We met with a Drifter Convoy some weeks ago. Not in this star system but another," she told them. "We traded our stolen goods for supplies...including missiles. We had expended most of those we stole with the ships against the Kenmiri when we were truly Vesheron.

"We acquired more missiles than I had expected, but...one did not question the First Warlord. They must have cut a deal."

That made a lot of sense to Henry. The Drifters had been an accepted not-quite-dissident faction in the Kenmiri Empire, a group of aliens who'd left their homeworlds and lived on a collection of borrowed, bought and stolen skip-drive-capable freighters. Nomads, they'd made their way in the Kenmiri Empire by moving from system to system and trading goods as they traveled.

Even while remaining officially uninvolved, the Drifter Convoys had been one of the key sources of munitions and supplies for many Vesheron. They'd also hosted several covert Vesheron R&D programs along with their own research.

If an anti-grav-shield weapon had been developed by someone other than the Kenmiri, it would have either been the El-Vesheron or hidden among the Drifters.

"Were you specifically told that the missiles were meant for use against the UPA?" Henry asked.

"No," Attallis insisted. "Outside the moment of conflict, we may have been able to oppose Deearan if they had told us that. They did not tell us why we were in this particular system or even that we were hunting a particular vessel, if we were seeking your ship."

"Would anyone left know?" Todorovich demanded. "Any of the survivors?"

"Deearan did not share their thoughts outside their chosen Captains," Attallis admitted. "We junior captains were not trusted enough to know their plans, and no one below Captain was worthy to."

Henry liked this First Warlord less and less the more he heard about them.

"Do you know which Drifter Convoy?" he asked. He wouldn't be able to do anything about it on this trip, but he could put the information in UPA hands.

"Red Stripe Blue Stripe Black Stripe," the Drex officer told him. She put her hands together in what would have been a praying gesture for a Terran.

"If you release me and my people, I will provide you with everything we have in our files. You already have my recorded testimony for the Gathering. My ships and people...we must find a patron. A home, out here...not a hunting ground."

I think she's telling the truth, Todorovich sent Henry over their networks. *Her files and her testimony will be a useful tool at the Gathering, especially if someone is moving against us.*

Of course someone is moving against us, he replied. *The only question is who. She seems straightforward enough, but she could also be playing us.*

We don't lose if she is, the Ambassador argued. *I'd prefer not to leave pirates behind us, but I'm not willing to order mass executions. Are you?*

Not unless I must, he conceded. *What are you thinking?*

Trintar has managed to pull themselves together quite well near here, Todorovich told him. *Two Vesheron factions turned a relatively even balance of power into a combined military force and what's shaping up to be a functional civilian government. They'll be at the Gathering. If we send her to them, we'll know if she actually comes in from the cold and buy ourselves some goodwill with a potential ally.*

You're the Ambassador, Henry said. *That is* definitely *a diplomatic decision.*

"Are you aware of the system Trintar?" Todorovich asked.

Unaware of their network conversation, Attallis looked confused again.

"I think so," she said slowly. "The Kenmiri had a logistics base there that we raided before I became a Captain."

"The leaders there have combined two groups of Vesheron into a new system military under a civilian government," the Ambassador told her. "The UPA is in contact with them. If you go to Trintar from here with the three ships you can retrieve and place yourselves under their command, we will not pass on your confessions of piracy. We *will* still use your testimony about the First Warlord and the attempt to intercept *us*, but we will allow you a fresh start."

"The Ambassador wishes for you to become warriors again instead of pirates," Henry said firmly. "We will know if you betray us, Captain Attallis, and will provide Trintar and the other local governments with everything we have learned about your ships if you do.

"Do you understand?"

"I understand," she confirmed. "I will convince my people to do as you ask. It seems...a better option than continuing the First Warlord's plan." She grimaced. "The First Warlord would never have accepted being a subordinate. I see no problem with it."

"Good." Henry pinged the guards to let them know that Attallis would be leaving the room unrestrained after all. "Our troops will remain on your ships for a while longer, though.

"You understand that we must avoid unnecessary risks, after all."

CHAPTER SEVENTEEN

"Ser...I can't get ahold of the XO, and we need a senior officer in the officers' mess ASAP."

The noncom speaking in Henry's internal network sounded about as apologetic as a human could physically be. Given that the speaker was a second-class Petty Officer assigned to the mess, the likelihood that they'd started their calls as high as the XO was pretty low.

If they'd managed to bounce their way up to the Captain, the noncom was having a *bad* day—and with just about everyone of importance already racked out after the battle, Henry wasn't entirely surprised.

"I'll be right there," he promised.

He understood, intellectually, that the adrenaline surge of battle left most people feeling wrung out and needing to rest. That was part of why Ihejirika was holding down the watch while most of the senior officers were unconscious, after all.

Henry, on the other hand, took a *lot* longer to come down from that high than most people he'd known. It was useful in combat, but it also meant that he spent several hours pacing his quarters after a battle, waiting for his body and mind to relax enough to either sleep or do work that *didn't* need adrenaline.

His quarters weren't as close to the officer's mess as they were to the bridge, but he made it there within two minutes of getting the call. It turned out that a good chunk of the other officers who couldn't sleep after a fight had decided to deal with it with booze or food.

There were a dozen officers in the mess and two stewards under the supervision of PO Tasia Guarneri. The two stewards were giving the center of the bar a wide berth as Guarneri braved the storm radius of drunken pilots.

Three of them—including, Henry realized with a mental sigh, Commander Samira O'Flannagain. An inevitable Brownian motion had seen the other nine officers in the room move their chairs and tables away from O'Flannagain and her people.

"Another!" O'Flannagain bellowed, slamming a glass down on the table. "Hell, a round for everyone!"

"Ser, I'm sorry, but I have to cut you off," Guarneri said. Her gaze was focused on Henry as she spoke though, and he could read the silent pleading in her eyes.

"What, is my account not paid up?" O'Flannagain demanded aggressively. "I put good money in the damn system so that you can feed me booze *without asking questions*, Petty Officer! Now get me a damn bottle."

"Don't get her the bottle," Henry told Guarneri calmly. "The Commander's liquor privileges are revoked until further notice. *Completely.*"

It was amazing, he noticed, how fast even drunk pilots disappeared when the Captain showed up. Suddenly, he and O'Flannagain were alone in the center of the mess and she was slowly turning around.

"What, I kill a gunship for the man and I can't even get a drink?" she slurred at him. "What kind of bullshit is this?"

"The type where you're drunk beyond even bad stereotypes of

starfighter pilots and the Irish alike," Henry snapped. "Stand down, soldier."

"What's your game, Wong?" she replied. "Or is it wang? What's the wang on the Wong go for?"

"Commander O'Flannagain!" he barked. "You have two choices: go to your quarters and dry out, or go to the *brig* and dry out."

"Fuck that. Drink with me!"

She waved the bottle at him and he yanked it out of her hand. Absently, he noted that it wasn't even *good* Irish whiskey. Guarneri had clearly stopped serving the Commander good alcohol a while back already.

Taking the bottle was apparently the worst idea he'd had since entering the mess. O'Flannagain stared blankly at her empty hand for a moment...and then took a swing at him.

Unfortunately for *her*, she was drunk enough to telegraph the swing a mile away and he was still hopped up on adrenaline. Wong sidestepped the punch and sucker-punched his confused officer in the gut.

O'Flannagain went down, spewing vomit all over the floor before she hit the ground and stopped moving.

Sighing, Henry knelt and checked her pulse and airway. She was fine. She'd just passed out.

"Shame the Commander can't handle her liquor," he said loudly. "Got drunk, fell over. No one saw anything else, understood?"

He looked around the room, checking that the rest of the officers were now very determinedly focused on their meals or drinks.

"Apologies for the mess, PO," he told Guarneri. "Commander Turrigan, Commander Gaunt."

The two FighterDiv Lieutenant Commanders rematerialized as quickly as they'd vanished. They were drunk, but they were sober enough to recognize when they were in trouble.

"Get Commander O'Flannagain over to the medbay," he said flatly. "Now."

"Yes, ser."

Each pilot took one of their boss's shoulders and staggered her out.

Shaking his head, he turned back to Guarneri.

"Commander O'Flannagain is banned from liquor for the duration of this cruise," he told the Petty Officer. "Log it in the system."

"Yes, ser. Thank you, ser."

"You're supposed to have backup for just this kind of mess," Henry said quietly. None of the officers in the room were senior to O'Flannagain. With the pilots gone, the most senior officer in the room was an Engineering Lieutenant Commander.

"I'll check the rotations and make damn sure it's in place next time," he continued.

For now, though, he needed to touch base with his ship's doctor. If O'Flannagain had enough of a drinking problem to take a swing at the *Captain*, it was a medical problem...and one that should have been addressed before now.

RETURNING TO HIS QUARTERS, Henry dropped onto his bed with a sigh of mixed relief and exasperation. The not-quite-fight in the mess had sent his adrenaline surging again, which meant it would still be hours before he slept.

If O'Flannagain was going to turn into a problem, though, he'd rather it came up early. She'd get one chance to shape up, with help from the ship's doctor if the problem was addiction or another actual health problem.

The problem might well turn out to be that she was just an ornery troublemaker, though, and in that, Colonel Henry Wong knew his job. Her service record was such that he'd beach her rather than court-martial her, though.

He'd been a starfighter pilot once, after all. They were a breed unto themselves—and as O'Flannagain had drunkenly noted, *Raven*'s starfighters had killed a gunship for him. It was more than he'd expected from an eight-ship short squadron.

Sighing again, he realized he wasn't going to sleep and got back up. The main room of his quarters could do double duty as a social space or an office, depending on what he wanted it to be at any given time.

A gesture told the couches to retreat against the walls. He considered bringing his desk out for a moment, but then just brought up a massive hologram of the battlecruiser in the middle of the suddenly open space.

"Show me crew positions and system readiness reports," he said aloud. He gave the system a time stamp starting right when they had detected the bandit ships. Another gesture brought up a miniature display of the battle, but his focus was on his own ship.

Icons now cluttered the three-dimensional display. Just over two and a half meters long, the hologram filled the room from end to end, but at a 120:1 scale, he could pick out individual crewmen and systems.

"Begin playback, ten times speed," he ordered. The icons started moving. The ship only tracked crew who were on duty as a rule. Most spacers assumed that the Captain could pull tracking for any crew he chose, regardless of whether they were on duty.

They weren't *wrong*—but it wasn't easy, either. *Raven's* computers would require proper authorization from a minimum of two senior officers, logged for the record, before it would tell the Captain where someone who wasn't on duty was on the ship.

Readiness one, though, put two-thirds of the crew on duty. The battle-stations call shortly afterward put everyone on duty.

Plus, Henry didn't *care* if his crew were fraternizing or building a still in the underbelly of Engineering or anything like that. Without even *looking* for it, he presumed there were at least two stills on the ship and could pick the four most likely locations for them.

He'd have to make sure the word was quietly put out that

Commander O'Flannagain was cut off from *that* booze, too. The people running the stills understood that there was a tradition of genteel obliviousness on the part of the senior officers so long as no one was drunk on duty and the liquor bans that *did* get ordered got enforced.

It wasn't like the UPSF ran dry ships. The moonshine from the stills was just cheaper than the beer and liquor available in the messes and less bound by regulation.

Years of practice meant that he was able to track the playback of his crew's actions while making mental notes for future action. His crew had taken too long to get to readiness one and too long to get to battle stations.

Today, the battle had started at a long-enough range that it hadn't mattered. It might not next time. It probably wouldn't *ever* matter, he had to admit, but he wanted his crew ready for anything.

That meant getting the scramble time down to *less* than standard. He'd got *Panther*'s crew down to a minute from readiness one, and two minutes and twenty seconds on a full scramble from bunks to battle stations. It had taken six months on the front line to get to that point, though.

He'd settle for ninety seconds and three minutes. *Panther* had arrived in the Set Province with that standard, which was already three-quarters of the UPSF requirement.

A requirement that *Raven*'s crew had failed to meet in the face of the enemy. He doubted any of his chiefs or officers were going to let *that* stand, but he also needed to understand the reason.

Some of it was obvious as he watched the playback. A good third of his crew was clearly either utterly unused to their new ship or going into autopilot when the battle stations alarm went off—the autopilot for their *last* ship.

A lot of spacers went the wrong way for ten, twenty, even thirty seconds. Others had to pause and consider at intersections.

That he could drill out of them. He clearly needed to be running a more intensive set of drills than he had been—which made sense, really. The drills had been running at about twenty percent above the usual rate, but they were a scratch crew assembled from teams sent over from a dozen other vessels.

There was still over a week left of their trip, and he was going to have to drill his people until they *dropped*. There was no way he could risk having *Raven* look bad in front of the Gathering. The UPA's intentions and plans for the future were *not* going to be popular in a group that was almost certainly expecting the Terrans to help carry future campaigns to contain the Kenmiri.

With a shake of his head, he gestured for his desk to emerge from the wall.

He couldn't sleep and he had a handle on the problem. He'd want to go over everything he did now after he'd slept, to make sure he hadn't made any tired mistakes, but there was no reason not to start drawing up plans now.

CHAPTER EIGHTEEN

"A HUNDRED AND FIFTY–SECOND SCRAMBLE, SER?" IYOTAKE asked the next morning as the senior officers gathered for the meeting Henry had called. "That's a hell of a target to hold our crew to."

"I mean, we missed the Force standard and my chiefs are already chewing bulkhead and spitting nails," Song added. "But that's *half* the time the standard allows."

"And it's the standard over a third of the front-line battlecruisers were reaching at the end of the war," Henry said calmly. "Do I expect us to meet it *without* the pressure of repeated active combat and the accompanying drill?" He smiled.

"No. That scramble time requires not merely drilled veterans but *heavily* drilled veterans who have faced the fire together time and time again," he told his officers. "I'm not planning on holding our people to that target...but it's the target we're going to give them. I have every confidence that this crew can match everything *Panther's* people did for me in the long run, but we need to hold them to that standard and let them know what standard we want them to meet."

"I see the Captain's point," Ihejirika said. "As Colonel Song noted, my chiefs and junior officers are well aware we didn't even meet the UPSF standard for a readiness one scramble yesterday. They're working on my people already."

"My plan is for a minimum of one randomly scheduled battle station scramble per twenty-four hour period until we reach Resta," Henry told them. "We did acceptably yesterday, against First Warlord Deearan. I want that to be clear to everyone as well: we took on and defeated six Kenmiri light warships in rogue Vesheron hands and we took *zero* damage.

"Some of that was luck. Some of that was O'Flannagain's people nailing the first gunship right off the bat." O'Flannagain was the notably absent member of his staff this morning. Tactical, Communications, Engineering, Navigation and GroundDiv were all present.

The FighterDiv Commander was still in medbay. Which meant that *no one* was acknowledging that she was missing or would ever call her out for missing the meeting. UPSF had a laundry list of flaws, but they grasped the idea that healthy spacers were effective spacers.

"So, give your people a 'well done' before we start tearing into them for where we, as a ship, came up short," Henry ordered. "We're going to work them to the bone for a week, because we *should* have been working them halfway to the bone since we left Procyon.

"Anyone bitches, point them at me," he continued. "This one *is* my fault; I should have upped the drill schedule earlier. They want to burn me in effigy to make themselves feel better, well, the life-support team in Engineering will get to them *long* before I do!"

His team chuckled—though Song looked near-murderous at the thought of someone starting fires on *her* ship.

Captains, after all, only got to borrow Engineering's starships.

"What about our problem here?" Iyotake asked. "We still have GroundDiv troops on the intact warships."

"We've completed the search-and-rescue, right, Commander Thompson?" Henry said.

"We have," the GroundDiv Commander confirmed. "We dropped them all off on the two intact ships. I still have teams holding the bridge and Engineering of both ships."

"Colonel Song, how long for them to restart their reactors from cold?" the Captain asked with a momentarily mischievous grin.

"Minimum of an hour from when we initiate the full shutdown process, ser," Song replied. "Systems will automatically drain weapon capacitors and so forth to keep gravity and life support running, so no one will be in any danger..."

"But they won't be able to chase us or shoot at us. Are all of them back aboard?"

"Yes, ser," Thompson confirmed. "I can pass that order and have everyone back aboard in thirty minutes. Reactor shutdown will take ten of those."

"That gives us forty to get back on course at combat acceleration," Henry concluded. "Sound workable, Commander Bazzoli?"

"We'll still be in range if they decide to make trouble," Bazzoli pointed out.

"I don't really expect them to," Henry said. "I just want to buy us some safety margin and make a point. We cut a deal with Captain Attallis—that doesn't mean I *trust* her. And it definitely doesn't mean I trust her people."

"Then why did we cut a deal?" Iyotake asked. "Seems like we're just leaving pirates behind, ser."

"Because by the time we make it to the Gathering, she should have reported in at Trintar," Henry said. "If she *hasn't*, then we'll give her a couple more days at most and then dump everything we know about her and her people to every Vesheron Faction in Apophis Province.

"Either she turns a new leaf and they become protectors of the people working with the new fleet out of Trintar, or that same fleet hunts her down," he finished. "Either way, the situation is dealt with. *Without* us executing seven hundred and eighty-six people in cold blood."

Seven hundred and eighty-six Ashall, at that. Not all of Attallis's people were Drex, but all of them were from the Seeded Races. They all looked human enough to make mass executions a morale problem as well as a moral one.

"Especially since my people just spent twelve hours pulling two hundred of those people from wrecked ships," Thompson added. "I'd rather not rescue people just to shoot them. Nuking the wreckage is faster and cleaner."

"Fair enough," Iyotake conceded. "Either way, you're the Captain, Captain Wong. From the sounds of it, I think we're done here."

"We are," Henry confirmed. Neither of them was really talking about the meeting. "Commander Bazzoli, get your course loaded back in. Commander Thompson, pass the order to shut down our 'friend's' reactors and get your people back aboard *Raven*.

"This diversion has been fun, but we need to get back to our actual mission."

And if the mission was a glorified taxi trip, well...it was still the mission.

CHAPTER NINETEEN

HENRY GRUNTED AS THE SKIP DRIVE DECIDED TO TAKE THIS particular opportunity to knee him in the groin with a piece of his own reality. Exhaling against the unexpected impact, he glanced around the bridge to see if anyone *else* was looking unusually pained from this particular impact.

They were halfway through the ten-hour skip out of Apophis-Four, once again on their way. No pursuit, no trouble. One thorny problem dealt with and left behind to see if the situation resolved on its own.

Five skips after this one. He considered that with scant favor as he looked up how long it would be before the next bounce in this jump. It was more uncomfortable than most, but it would be two more hours until the next bounce.

He'd make sure to be in his office for that one. The crew didn't need to see the Captain looking like he'd just been kicked in the balls.

Shaking off the last of the pain, he checked the status reports. Mid-skip was generally pretty safe, though there was always *someone* who ended up in medbay.

The skip drive wasn't the best way to travel faster than light, just the only way. It was unusual for the injuries and adverse reactions to be serious, but it was a rare jump that saw only one person in the medbay.

On the topic of medbay, though, a new ping hit his network as he was checking the status. A meeting request from Commander O'Flannagain.

"Oh, this will be interesting," he murmured. And it would get him off the bridge if their icosaspatial momentum decided to groin-shot him again. He sent a response ordering her to meet him in his office in fifteen minutes.

"Commander Ihejirika, you have the con," he told his tactical officer. "I'll be in my office."

"The siren call of paperwork is making itself heard, ser?" the broad-shouldered Commander asked with a chuckle.

"Is that what we're calling it?" Henry asked. "I mostly go for the *crushing inevitability of paperwork,* myself."

"All of those things and more, Captain. Paperwork is a many-faceted beast that demands our worship."

Henry shook his head at his tactical officer.

"Behave, Commander, or I'll make you start an open-mic comedy night in the officers' mess."

That got an exaggerated shiver from Ihejirika as he acknowledged receipt of active command in the ship network.

In *theory,* Henry's internal network could overlay a pretty decent simulacrum of the bridge onto his eyes and allow him to run the ship from anywhere aboard. In practice, enough efficiency was lost not having everyone physically in the same room that the virtual bridge was used only when they were in the acceleration tanks.

After all, once you were submerged in specially designed gel and breathing via a mask, it was rather hard to have a regular conversation.

O'FLANNAGAIN ENTERED his office *exactly* on time, advanced to stand behind the chair across the desk from Henry and saluted with perfect precision.

He waited for her to sit down for several seconds, then sighed.

"Cut the mickey mouse," he ordered. "Sit your ass down, Commander, and tell me what you wanted to talk to me about."

She obeyed.

"It's not that I mind my regular check-ins with the ship's doctor," she finally said. "Always fun, those. I think I owe you an apology, ser. Rumor has it I took a swing at you."

O'Flannagain flushed, very clear on her pale skin.

"I don't actually remember."

"Neither do I," Henry said with a calm innocence. "*If* such a thing happened, it could potentially be ignored as a symptom of a mental health problem that you're addressing with the doctor. Am I clear?"

"Ser," she said flatly. "I also appear to have been cut off from all alcohol aboard the ship."

"Official and unofficial," the Captain confirmed. "Unless the chiefs *want* to have to deal with the stills...and they never do."

O'Flannagain swallowed.

"I'm not an alcoholic, ser," she noted. "You're not the first Captain to send me to a ship's doctor over that concern. After a fight, all I want is a long drink and a hard fuck, and the latter is hard to find when you're the damn CAG."

"Is that why you're trying so damn hard to lose a bar, Commander?" he asked, letting his own profanity match hers. "The degree to which demotion records are sealed is rather fascinating, but it's pretty clear to me you've lost that second steel bar at least once."

The flush darkened.

"Three times, ser," she admitted. "And that wasn't...*exactly* the plan."

"And frankly, Commander, I don't care what the damn plan

was," Henry replied. "You're not the best pilot I've seen in the last twenty years, not by a long shot, but you're probably in the top twenty.

"But I've seen better officers pull dumber stunts," he told her. "At war, you got docked a bar and everything got brushed under the rug. Reading between the lines, you missed out on more than a few medals and promotions due to getting drunk and starting fights.

"If there's a *problem*, Commander, we have doctors and counselors and a hundred solutions," he continued. "But if the answer is just that you want to be a whiny little bitch, there's a beach waiting for you.

"A peacetime Space Force isn't going to put up with this bullshit from even a top-tier pilot. You got drunk off your ass in public and ended up vomiting your guts out on the floor of the officers' mess. That's bad enough.

"You *also* managed to get a noncom with twelve years' experience of running the bar in a ship's mess concerned enough that she pinged the *Captain* for backup when she couldn't find anyone else," he concluded. "So, ask yourself, Commander O'Flannagain, was that *really* conduct becoming an officer?"

The room was silent.

"You're going to beach me, aren't you?" she said softly.

"Not yet," Henry told her flatly. "Because as you so pithily noted while drunk off your ass, you and your people killed a damn gunship for me and I wasn't expecting that.

"I don't usually play three strikes, but you've blown two strikes already. Fuck up one more time, Commander, and you're done. Your record already bleeds 'problem child.' I ask for a new CAG when this mission is over and you won't get a new post."

"I'm not even sure how I got this one," O'Flannagain snapped. "I doubt it's in my record anywhere, but I'm not *supposed* to end up as CAG. 'Personality unsuited for independent squadron command' was what Commodore Breslau said."

"Well, Breslau is *dead*," Henry pointed out. "She died in Golden Lancelot leading the combined fighter strike at Horus-One."

That had been one of the last big starfighter strikes of the war. Two of the UPSF's fleet carriers, backed up by the last of the old escort carriers and three battlecruisers. They'd launched almost four hundred starfighters in a long-range bombardment mission of the Kenmiri homeworld, under command of the only Red Wing still in FighterDiv...Commodore Sara Breslau.

Less than half of the birds had survived long enough to launch missiles, but they'd wiped out the largest concentration of Kenmorad breeding sects in the galaxy.

Seventeen starfighters had crawled back to the carriers. The escort carriers and two of the battlecruisers had been lost covering the retreat as well. Horus-One had been the single most expensive operation of the war, let alone of Golden Lancelot.

"But you're here, Commander O'Flannagain, because Commodore *Barrie* sent you over," he told his CAG. "Now I'm uninclined to speculate on your previous CO's motivations, but I should probably note that Commodore Peter Barrie is my ex-husband.

"So, the question, I think, is whether my ex-husband sent you to me because he figured I could make you rise above your bullshit or because he expected you to drag me down with you."

He smiled.

"Right now, I'm not thinking kind thoughts about my ex," he noted. "But in general, Peter and I parted amicably. So, *I* think you can be what this ship needs. Whether you do it to keep flying, do it to spite Commodore Barrie, or do it because *I asked you to*...I don't care.

"But there are seven pilots downstairs who are bound by law to follow you into hell if we order it. I think you owe it to them, if nothing else, to at least try. Am I clear?"

She was silent for at least twenty seconds, staring down at her hands.

"Commander O'Flannagain, I asked you a question."

"I don't know," she admitted. "I've screwed it up before and people died."

"And *that*, Commander, is what we're supposed to see counselors for," he told her gently. "Your strike against First Warlord Deearan's gunship? That was *perfect*. That was exactly what was needed, maximizing impact and minimizing the risk to your people.

"I need the officer who plotted that attack. I need her with her head on her shoulders and her heart in the game. Am I clear?"

"Yes, ser."

Henry shook his head.

"And for that matter, how the *hell* did you make it this long without all of this coming out with a damn counselor?"

"They're not pilots, ser," she said slowly. "They don't always ask the right questions."

"Well, take what you told *me*, Commander, and go tell it to the doctor. I will *not* let you self-sabotage yourself out of the cockpit; am I clear?"

"Yes, ser," she conceded.

IYOTAKE WAS silent as he watched the recording, then sighed and shook his head.

"*Rocket-jocks*," he swore with feeling. "Think she'll get it sorted with Dr. Pham?"

"I hope so," Henry replied. "I think *she* is a bit more aware of where she's at than she was before, but I'm no counselor. I'm a starship Captain."

"I'll keep an eye on her," Iyotake promised. "I'm guessing the liquor ban stays, though."

"Until she proves herself to me, yes," Henry agreed. "I'm half-convinced Peter sent her to me to knock her head on straight, and half-convinced Peter sent her to me to get me killed."

"I haven't served with Commodore Barrie," his XO said carefully. "I can't speculate."

"I can't speculate and I was married to the man for six years," Henry noted. "What else is going on aboard this ship that I need to know about?"

"We'll be launching the first battle-stations drill thirty minutes before we complete the skip," Iyotake told him. "You and I are the only ones who know the timeline, though Ihejirika and Song helped me set up the parameters."

"This is a straight report-to-stations drill, right?" Henry asked, the thirty minutes before skip timeline bringing a thought to mind.

"Yes, ser."

"Let's hold them at stations once they're there," the Captain ordered. "In fact, add that to our *announced* schedule for the next skip. From now on, we complete our skips at battle stations. It won't hurt anything, and it may just save our ass some day."

"Apophis Province is effectively unclaimed space at this point. So's Geb," Iyotake said. "No Kenmiri. Not even much in terms of Vesheron running around."

Henry nodded.

"That's part of why I'm worried," he told his subordinate. "Each province was five hundred star systems, Iyotake. We barely managed to name all twenty of the provinces, and we certainly haven't visited every Kenmiri star over the course of the war. I don't think we're over forty visited and labeled systems in any of the Kenmiri provinces.

"Even the Vesheron are barely aware of what's in the stars around them. The Kenmiri were the only ones to really know their space, and they've written it all off. It's going to be a chaotic hell for the next few decades as all of that gets sorted out."

"Feels like we should be doing more to hold that together," Iyotake said softly. "Never going to say the Kenmiri didn't need to get their asses handed to them, but it can't be a good thing that a state of ten thousand stars just shrank down to, what, four thousand?"

"Less," Henry replied. "They've pulled back to eight provinces of twenty, but they've abandoned peripheral stars in those provinces. And even what they're holding right now, they can't sustain.

"Worker drones only have a fifteen-year average life expectancy. In twenty years, there won't be any of them left." He shivered at the thought, letting the inevitable mental claim of responsibility flash through his mind without engaging with it.

"There'll still be billions of Warriors and Artisans, but they won't need four thousand stars and they won't be able to hold *on* to four thousand stars."

"It's going to be chaos," Iyotake said. "How the hell is anyone going to keep order?"

"It's not our problem, Lieutenant Colonel," Henry pointed out. "That's the General Assembly's decision. We deal with our worlds; that's it. Everything else is up to the Vesheron."

"At least they have subspace coms," Iyotake concluded. "Instant communication will help, like with us keeping an eye on Attallis and what she does."

"Exactly. There's enough Vesheron out there that if they work together, they can keep the peace, at least."

Iyotake looked past Henry for several seconds and the Captain followed his gaze. He was focusing on the blue UPA flag on the wall behind Henry, with its eight golden stars in a flattened V.

Like most federal unions before it, the United Planets Alliance had been born out of a bloody conflict to prevent future wars. Henry's guess was that the General Assembly was hoping for something similar to emerge from the Vesheron Gathering.

"What happens if the Gathering fails, ser?" Iyotake asked. "If it all falls apart and the Vesheron turn on each other now that they don't share an enemy? The only thing that defines us all is that we were fighting the Kenmiri."

"I don't know," Henry admitted. "I suspect the Londu want to leave the Gathering with a lot more territory than they're starting with—and I have no idea what the Terzan are going to want! The core Vesheron factions, though?

"I'm not sure most of them even know what they want. Until six months ago, I think they all expected to be fighting the Kenmiri for eternity. What happens next..." Henry shivered.

"I don't think anyone knows, XO. Part of our job is to help the Ambassador make sure the Gathering *doesn't* fail."

"Right. Good." The Lieutenant Colonel paused thoughtfully.

"How are we going to do that, again?"

CHAPTER TWENTY

PEOPLE DIDN'T HAVE SIT-DOWN MEALS DURING SKIPS. THE ODDS of losing any given meal were between thirty and seventy percent, depending on the individual and the skip, so UPSF crews stuck to ration bars during those periods.

With the timing of the next two skips, that meant it was almost four days after engaging the First Warlord before Henry once again joined Ambassador Todorovich and her people for dinner.

He wouldn't have needed Todorovich's warning that Leitz was upset with him. The chief of staff was quite good at hiding his expressions...except that Henry had learned to read emotions on Ashall faces, faces that weren't *quite* human.

He'd had to stop playing poker against anyone who hadn't had the same experience. One memorable casino night in the middle of the war had got him banned from every poker game in Tau Ceti—and made sure that his eventual retirement was going to be quite comfortable.

He hadn't been the first, but he'd been among the last before casinos starting checking who'd served on the front. Less than one percent of UPSF personnel had regularly interacted with the other

Vesheron, in his experience. Less than a tenth of those had learned Kem, and *maybe* half of those had learned to read Ashall expressions.

That was still a solid cadre of officers who the casinos were rightly somewhat terrified of.

It probably didn't help Henry's case, he reflected as he took his seat, that several of the Ambassador's staff had the telltale sheen in their hair of antiacceleration gel from the latest stint in the tanks.

"Welcome, Captain," Todorovich greeted him. "My understanding from my chef is that he is starting to run out of fresh ingredients. He wants me to apologize for the dinner."

"Em Todorovich, I was on a six-month deployment in Set Province only a few months ago," Henry reminded her. "If I can *recognize* what he's feeding me, we are definitely in the realm of my being perfectly happy."

"Fair enough." The appetizers started coming out and, regardless of the chef's complaints, they smelled fantastic.

"I'm assuming there's a reason the drill frequency went up after Apophis-Four?" Todorovich asked after they were most of the way through the flaky pastry shells filled with a mix of spiced meat and—presumably prepared-from-frozen now—vegetables.

"It didn't seem like things were that strenuous there," Leitz added. The chief of staff didn't have the sheen of tank gel in his hair, but his hair *was* damp. He'd clearly showered it out in the hour since the skip finished.

"We got lucky," Henry told the chief of staff. "Our scramble time was longer than UPSF standard, let alone what I'd find acceptable. The senior staff and I hadn't made sufficient allowance for how thrown together this crew is. We saw that their core competencies were present and forgot they hadn't worked as a team before.

"We should have been pressing the drills harder before. We're making up for lost time now, though I'll ease up on the crew once we reach Resta."

"I look forward to it," Leitz replied. "The acceleration tanks are...unpleasant."

"Try the one in a starfighter sometime," Henry replied. "At least the ones on *Raven* are *lit*. In a starfighter, it's all dark. Even with your internal net projecting an interface, it's claustrophobic."

"I believe you," Leitz said with feeling. "These ones are bad enough. I...will admit it seems odd we're going into them and then *not* seeing acceleration."

There was no bite to the man's tone, which was actually impressive. The chief was doing a good job of *not* projecting his frustration at the situation.

"My crew is trained to operate up to three pseudogravities," Henry pointed out. "Command consoles and so forth are designed to reorient under thrust gravity, and every part of the ship is rigged for movement and work under those conditions.

"Your people are *not* so trained. At three gravities, you're already at risk, Em Leitz. And at three pseudogravities, we're only at about point six KPS squared for acceleration. If I only need a twenty percent edge, I can push my crew to that without requiring them in the tanks—but I would be risking my passengers."

He shrugged.

"It's safer for everyone if you go in the tanks as soon as we call battle stations," Henry told Leitz. "We got lucky in Apophis-Four, but it wouldn't have taken a very different situation for me to push the ship to sixty percent acceleration." He snorted. "Had I decided to avoid engagement, we would have needed every scrap of power *Raven*'s engines could produce. Everyone aboard would have been in tanks...and given the scramble times I saw for everything else, that could have been a problem."

"I'm guessing you're drilling tank stations as well?" Todorovich asked.

"Not for the pre-emergence battle-stations call, but yes," Henry confirmed. "The pre-emergence call is only partially a drill. It is entirely possible we may emerge from skip into an unexpected combat situation. I don't want to add that extra layer of drill on top of the need to be ready for action.

"On the other hand, if we *do* enter a combat situation, knowing I can maneuver without risking the passengers this entire mission is about is useful," he finished with a grin. "I prefer not to break my diplomats, Ambassador Todorovich, Em Leitz. You're a nonexplosive payload, but no less effective for that in my experience."

Leitz nodded slowly, relaxing a couple of tense muscles he probably hadn't even realized were locked up.

"I appreciate the explanation, Captain," he said. "Thank you."

"Another question, if you don't mind," one of the junior members of Todorovich's staff said, barely loud enough to be heard. The younger woman was clearly being somewhat intimidated but curious.

"Well, the soup appears to be arriving," Henry pointed out. "But please, Em Morris, hold that thought."

HE REMEMBERED Sibyl Morris's *name* on his own, but the soup course gave him a chance to bring up the young diplomat's file, and he suspected he knew her question. Morris was a twenty-five-year-old Spanish brunette who seemed about as inelegant as a ten-week-old puppy and had spent the two years of her time with the UPA's diplomatic corps working entirely on trade deals between the member systems.

"Em Morris," he addressed her as the soup bowls were cleared away. "You had a question."

He didn't necessarily want to *answer* the inevitable question an unblooded diplomat was going to ask, but she was going to need to be educated sooner or later. That was Todorovich's job, really, but since he was *here* and she was asking...

"Yes, Captain Wong." She swallowed nervously, her eyes ticking ever so slightly around her.

Ah. She wasn't the only one among the junior diplomats and analysts supporting the Ambassador who wanted to ask the question. She was just the one who'd been put up to it.

He wondered if they'd drawn straws or played poker for it or what.

"Go on, Em Morris," he instructed. "I don't bite."

"Why *did* we engage?" she asked in a rush. "As you said, we could have evaded contact. We didn't know who they were, and we fired first. I thought this was a diplomatic mission!"

Henry held up a hand to Todorovich as the Ambassador leaned forward.

"It's an honest question, Em Todorovich," he said softly. "And not an unreasonable one. We are now at peace, everyone says. The war is over, everyone says. The Gathering is to shape the post-war world.

"*But no one told the Kenmiri that,*" he reminded his audience fiercely. "The Kenmiri have withdrawn from twelve of their provinces, yes, but there's been no formal peace negotiations. No surrender. No armistice.

"Any Kenmiri warship we encounter will still see us as the enemy and will still engage," he continued. "Which makes Kenmiri ships we encounter out here and can't validate as Vesheron units an active threat not only to ourselves but to anyone else in the region."

He raised a finger as Morris opened her mouth to try and extract herself.

"That said, I figured the odds they were Kenmiri at under forty percent," he told the young diplomat. "The other possibility was that they were exactly what they were: ex-Kenmiri units in Vesheron hands, turned to piracy.

"Their refusal to respond to our repeated hails and aggressive maneuvering may not qualify as 'firing first,' Em Morris, but they were a definite threat presented to *Raven*. More, their actions suggested that the ships in question presented a clear and present threat to neutral shipping in the area.

"Our long-term objectives may call for us to avoid entanglements in the former Empire, but we are *here*, right now. Pirates or rogue Kenmiri units alike, there was no way that engaging those ships wasn't going to leave this region better off than if we let them go.

"By acting, we cleared the local spaceways for civilian travel and may have provided a significant reinforcement to an at-least theoretically allied local power. I call that a win, Em Morris, and it's the win I expected when I ordered Commander O'Flannagain to engage the enemy."

He smiled.

"Does that answer the question your compatriots put you up to asking?"

From the flush on Sybil Morris's face and the uncomfortable shuffling of chairs and cutlery around her, he'd nailed *exactly* what had happened.

"It does, Captain Wong," she said. "I...appreciate your patience."

"You are far from the first diplomat to question whether violence was the appropriate answer to a situation," he told her. "You aren't even the first person on this ship to." He smiled. "The first person on this ship to question whether that was the right call, after all, was *me*."

DINNER WAS CLEARED AWAY, and Todorovich gestured for him to join her in her office. He followed readily enough, checking in with his internal network for messages as he did so.

Nothing had threatened to burn the ship down in the seventy minutes of the extended meal. They were ticking toward their next skip—their third and last within Apophis Province—in about seventeen hours.

"I apologize for Em Morris," Todorovich said when the door closed behind them. "I didn't realize my back office was going to be that troublesome."

"That wasn't troublesome, Ambassador," Henry replied. "*Troublesome* is when they ask that question and *argue* with me afterward rather than being willing to listen and learn. Morris, at least, seems bright enough to have picked up my point."

He grinned.

"I can't speak for the *rest* of your *back office*, but she had the forti-tude to ask a UPSF Colonel if shooting at the enemy was the right call. I like her."

Todorovich snorted and shook her head.

"Trust *you* to like the troublemaker that makes you think," she said. "I'm barely starting to get a feel for you, Captain Wong, but I'm starting to wonder if you're happy without someone trying to contra-dict you."

"On the contrary, Ambassador, I quite enjoy it when everyone agrees with me," he replied. "Of course, it also makes me worry I've done something *wrong*. A Captain who surrounds themselves with yes-officers sooner or later ends up a *dead* Captain, Ambassador...and their crew with them."

She shook her head.

"We're alone, Captain," she noted. "You may as well call me Sylvia."

"Only if you call me Henry," he said. He tilted his head to get a better view of Todorovich's face to read her...but *she* had learned to conceal her expressions from everyone. It was more impressive, to his mind, than his ability to read people across cultural and racial lines.

"Fair enough, Henry," Todorovich conceded. She opened a cupboard and produced a bottle. "Wine?"

"I won't argue, Sylvia," he agreed, letting her name roll off his tongue carefully. A glass of the dark red liquid almost magically materialized in front of him, the dint of long practice on the Ambas-sador's part.

"I'll warn you, I'm not a wine drinker," he told her. "If this is any good, you're probably wasting it on me."

"I'm afraid I don't keep cheap wine on hand for people with no taste," she replied with a grin. "You'll have to suffer the waste, I'm afraid."

He snorted and saluted her with the glass.

"To the United Planets Alliance," he toasted.

"The UPA," she replied. "The UPA and absent friends."

"God knows we all have enough of them," Henry agreed, and drank. The wine was good, smooth and dry on the palate. There were probably a billion layers to it he was missing, but it was acceptable to him.

"Even us diplomats," she agreed. "Let alone officers like you, Henry. Not many still in uniform who were here at the beginning."

"More than you'd think," he said. "All of the Admirals were around then. I think the most junior Rear Admiral now was a Commander when the shooting started." He shrugged. "There aren't many Colonels or Commodores who weren't in uniform seventeen years ago, either. A few, yeah, but I think you'll find most of the senior ranks were in UPSF service from the beginning."

Of course, even with the dramatic expansion of the UPSF over the war, there were a lot fewer command- and flag-rank officers now than there had been Ensigns and Lieutenants twenty years before. Attrition had taken its toll, and for every officer promoted, there'd been half a dozen flag-draped coffins brought home or fired into a star.

"Fair," she conceded. "It was a smaller war in many ways than ones we've fought in the past. We didn't feed an entire generation into the meat grinder."

"We're better off this way," Henry agreed. "Though I wonder sometimes if the General Assembly might feel more committed to the stars we just spent ten years fighting through if it really *had* been total war on our side."

The gravity shield hadn't made the UPA's ships invulnerable, but it had made them tough beyond any rational amount of firepower. They'd taken far fewer losses than their allies, which had allowed the UPA to maintain the war with only a moderate commitment from the member systems.

"It's intentional that the UPSF is far weaker than the old colonial fleets," Todorovich noted. "The Novaya Imperiya and the USCA are better left in the ashbin of history."

"I'd take *Raven* against the massed fleets of the USCA *or* the Novaya Imperiya, thanks," Henry said with a chuckle. "A hundred years of technological advancement will give you that."

He shook his head. The UPA had banned its member systems and their lower tiers of government—like, for example, Russia or the USA—from owning skip-capable warships. Those were the sole province of the United Planets Space Force.

It was hard to wage war between star systems without skip-capable ships, after all, and the UPSF was less likely to be drawn into politics between member systems.

"I'm not sure a bloodier war would have made the General Assembly more concerned about what happened afterward," she told him. "I think the war-weariness factor might have been even *worse*. We were only just starting to see new colonies get to the point of asking for entry-level Assembly membership when the war started.

"There's a dozen systems begging for more attention and money to grow new colonies—attention and money that's gone to the UPSF of late. The Assembly has focuses closer to home that they'd like to deal with.

"They don't want commitments outside our borders."

"I know," he allowed. "But I know these people out here, too. If we hadn't tangled with the First Warlord, it would have been years before Trintar or the other local powers could have dealt with six escorts without exposing their home systems.

"We happened to be passing through, and we probably saved dozens of ships and thousands of lives. What happens without us?"

"I don't know," she conceded. "But I *do* know that you and I? We don't make those decisions. Even diplomats get their marching orders, Henry. And we follow them. Whether we like them or not."

"So do soldiers," he said, looking at the wine. "I guess we have at least that in common."

CHAPTER TWENTY-ONE

With one last kick—relatively gentle, all things considered—*Raven's* skip drive delivered her to the Resta System. Once the homeworld of four minor colonies, all settled with sublight ships that had taken twenty to forty years to reach their destination, it had become almost a provincial sub-capital under the Kenmiri occupation.

And according to the updated briefing Henry had just received by subspace, the Restan had done the impossible when they'd been conquered and occupied: they'd *hidden* the fourth colony.

Not only that, they'd *kept* it hidden. A good chunk of that, Henry had to admit, had been by not telling even their Vesheron allies about it. The Vesheron factions had been enthusiastic and determined but not...good at spycraft.

The Restan clearly were. That, unlike the news of the fourth world of the reborn Restan state, was not a surprise. They'd been one of the handful of factions fully briefed on and involved in Operation Golden Lancelot. The fleet that had covered the carriers while Commodore Breslau and her fighters made their bombing run on the Kenmiri homeworld had been almost entirely Resta.

Henry had served with dozens of Restan ships and hundreds of Restan officers, but he'd never set foot in the Resta System itself. He took in the scans with a smile as *Raven's* sensors trawled the theoretically friendly system.

"Well, that is...a *lot* of floating metal," Iyotake noted from CIC. "And I'm *not* talking about the infrastructure."

"I'm more impressed by the infrastructure," Henry replied. "The Kenmiri took over most of the Restan infrastructure intact and then added to it. They're not going to be hurting for industry going forward."

Ost was a densely populated world of ten billion souls, once home to a garrison of a hundred million Kenmiri. Most of those drones had even managed to evacuate before being murdered.

The three Kenmorad sects that had split the rule of the system hadn't died in space battle like most of the targets of Golden Lancelot. The Restan had smuggled tactical nukes into the three supposedly super-secure palaces and set them off.

Much less destructive than full-scale space battles, and part of why the industrial infrastructure the Kenmiri had built was intact... and working.

"The infrastructure is going to make a huge difference for whatever they want to do going forward, yeah," Iyotake confirmed. "But can we pay *some* attention to the hundred-odd *warships?*"

"That's the Gathering, XO," Henry pointed out. Swift gestures highlighted the key points.

"We won't be going anywhere near Ost," he continued as he highlighted the Resta homeworld. "Right now, they're guarding that like the holy grail. I make it twelve capital ships, fifteen escorts. They're what, half-and-half Kenmiri and homebuilt?"

"*Fifteen* capital ships, Captain," Iyotake corrected. Three icons blinked inside the Lagrange point station clusters. "I don't know if the last three are intentionally hiding or just there to support the forts they took from the Kenmiri, but that's three ex-Kenmiri dreadnoughts in close to the shipyards."

"Okay, so the Restan have thirty ships defending their home planet," Henry agreed. "That's...mostly irrelevant today. No one is going after Ost unless they're insane.

"The coordinates we have put the Gathering here." He pinged a location on the scan of the system for Iyotake. "Looks like a big space station, which was what I expected. It's on the edge of the asteroid belt, so it was probably a mining station or a mining ship base originally."

The Resta System had one of the biggest asteroid belts he'd ever seen. Ost was the fourth planet of a hot-burning F-sequence star. It shared a similar orbit to Mars in Sol but was even warmer than Earth.

The fifth planet was a small gas giant. The sixth planet was a larger gas giant, and the two were close enough to each other that their gravity wells had formed a giant catcher's net over the untold millennia.

Both gas giants had smaller-than-normal rings. The system's outer ice cloud was sparser than usual. There were even fewer *comets* than most systems.

All of that debris was bound up in an asteroid belt that had a radius twenty percent larger than Sol's, half again the width, and almost twice the density. Even under the Kenmiri, that belt had to have been swarming with mining ships—and faced with building a new fleet to defend themselves against a potential Kenmiri return, the belt now practically glowed with the energy signatures of Restan mining ships.

"And the Gathering is around that station," Iyotake agreed. "All eighty fucking starships of it."

"I leave it to Todorovich to guess who's late, who's early and who we needed to beat here," Henry said dryly. "We can figure out who's here, at least."

He wasn't the only one doing so. The combat information center analysts around Iyotake were already at work.

"Hardest part is splitting up the ex-Kenmiri ships," Iyotake told him. "The rest are easy enough. There's another three capital ships and three escorts from the Resta. That's a Terzan...whatever they call it."

Henry chuckled. The Terzan were the strangest of the Vesheron. Like the UPA and the Londu, they were El-Vesheron—outsiders rather than rebels, despite what the word *Vesheron* meant—but unlike the UPA and the Londu, they were not Ashall. They were, in fact, insectoid sentients with ten legs and some kind of low-grade organic radio communication with each other.

The UPA had *no* idea how the Londu had brought them into the alliance against the Kenmiri, but the other El-Vesheron power was credited with making contact. And even with translation equipment, the Terzan were hard enough to communicate with that they couldn't really dispute that assessment.

"Starfang," he told his XO. "The mind-concept they use for their lighter warships translates as *starfang*. Just the one of them?"

"Isn't that enough?" Iyotake replied. "I don't suppose *you* know why I've got an intel warning here classifying the starfang as the biggest threat here?"

"You're not cleared for that," Henry admitted. "If you need to know, I'll brief you. Otherwise, let's just not pick a fight with the ten-legged spiders, okay?"

He *had* been briefed. One Terzan ship during Golden Lancelot had demonstrated a form of gravity shield when under pressure. The sensor data was unclear, but it had suggested that the Terzan not only shared the system the UPA had regarded as their main advantage over the rest of the galaxy...but that their version was *significantly* more sophisticated.

And if they had a grav-shield, they almost certainly had grav-shield *penetrators*.

"Right." Henry could hear Iyotake's lack of enthusiasm. "As for the rest, well, I see a Londu battleship with four escorts, a Drifter Convoy's Guardian that I *think* two of the ex-Kenmiri escorts are attached to, a pair of homebuilt corvettes from Trintar...ten other midsized homebuilt ships from factions the UPA doesn't care about, six ex-Kenmiri dreadnoughts that could belong to *anybody* and fifty or so ex-Kenmiri escorts and gunships of the same stripe."

"Start digging into the IFFs and intel files and see if you can at least flag who the dreadnoughts belong to," Henry ordered. "With the Restan ships, that gets us to ten dreadnoughts in the system, and the last I'd heard, the entirety of the Vesheron factions had only captured fourteen!"

"We should be able to ID them," Iyotake promised. "What about the rest?"

"Moon?" Henry turned to his communications officers. "Do we have an orbit from local control?"

"Just arrived, ser."

"We set our course for the Gathering, then," he told his officers. "I'll touch base with the Ambassador and with Command to see if we have any last-minute adjustments.

"For us, however, it looks like the hardest part of the job is done. Well done, everyone. We made it in one piece."

THE CALL WITH UPSF COMMAND, Henry and Ambassador Todorovich had been scheduled since before they even left Procyon. It had been rescheduled after the delay in Apophis, but now they had reached their destination and it was time for the final updates.

It was just the two of them in the secured conference room, and as Todorovich fussed with a carafe of coffee, Henry input the codes that locked everyone else aboard *Raven* out of the subspace communicator.

Usually, they were running multiple parallel channels to allow for a dozen different necessary communications to take place. For a secure call like this, everything else would have to wait.

"We're locked in," he told Todorovich. "Ready?"

"For the biggest and messiest challenge of my life? Of course," she replied with a smile. She slid a coffee cup across the table to him and took a seat herself. The fussy nervousness of a moment before was gone, vanished behind a mask that would have fooled even Henry if he hadn't seen her a second before.

"I learned to read microexpressions to deal with Ashall," he noted. "You *scare* me, Em Ambassador."

"Good," she said calmly. "That means the Ashall can't read me, either."

He shook his head at her, put on his own professional mask—far less controlled than Todorovich's, if still enough to conceal his emotions from his crew in the middle of a battle—and opened the subspace communicator link.

"This is *Raven* reporting in," he said aloud. "Authentication code is Michael Gabriel Raziel Aziraphale One Six Niner Four One. Captain Henry Wong on the call."

"This is Ambassador Sylvia Todorovich reporting in," the Ambassador added a moment later. "Authentication is Raven Raven Wolverine Seven Niner Badger Duck."

A green light flashed in the middle of the table, replaced a moment later by a rotating image of the eight-star seal of the United Planets Alliance.

The seal lasted through one twelve-second rotation and vanished. The empty chairs around the conference table were suddenly full, each of them mirroring a chair somewhere in the UPA.

Given the collection of stars and titles around the table, Henry would have been *very* surprised to learn that the rest of the call was in one room.

"Em Secretary, we now have Captain Wong and Ambassador Todorovich on the call," the clear organizer of the meeting reported. Even Henry recognized Senna Dirksen, the extraordinarily pale and androgynous Senior Undersecretary of the United Planets Alliance.

"While I'm certain Ambassador Todorovich knows half the people on the call and Captain Wong knows the other half, perhaps some introductions would be in order, Undersecretary?" the woman Dirksen had addressed replied.

Vasudha Patil was so dark-skinned as to nearly blend in with the tailored leather chair she was sitting in but wore a traditional Indian sari and had the red-dot bindi tattoo of a married Hindi woman on her forehead.

She was also the Secretary-President of the United Planets Alliance. Her power inside the actual member star systems of the UPA might be limited, but there was still no question that she was the single most powerful human being alive.

"Of course, Em Secretary," Dirksen replied lightly. They gestured at the other six people at the table, neatly divided into military on one side of the table and civilian on the other side.

"Captain Wong will be familiar with Admirals Saren, Kosigan, and Bailey," they said, indicating each of the officers in turn. "Lee Saren is the head of SpaceDiv, Miles Kosigan heads IntelDiv and Jean Bailey heads GroundDiv."

Lee Saren was a shaven-headed Asian individual almost as androgynous as Dirksen. A Tau Ceti native, she'd come up through FighterDiv and switched to SpaceDiv much like Henry. And like him, she wore the Red Wings of someone who'd been a combat pilot in that first bloody campaign.

She, however, had been the third-most senior pilot in that desperately thrown-together fleet and had been in *charge* of feeding the massed starfighter wings of the UPSF into that meat grinder again and again. And again. And again.

Miles Kosigan, on the other hand, was a tall and dark-haired Slavic man from Russia's Epsilon Eridani colony. In Henry's experience, he combined an exceptional personal attractiveness with a dizzying intellect and a degree of hyperactivity normally seen in small terriers. It had apparently been a dangerous combination in a spy and was a deadlier one in a *leader* of spies.

Henry didn't know Jean Bailey as well as the other two, but the broad-shouldered woman from Altair had a nasty scar along one side of her face. That could easily have been healed, so the simple fact that Bailey still *had* that scar said volumes about the GroundDiv Admiral.

Dirksen gestured to the other side of the table. "Ambassador Todorovich, on the other hand, knows Trade Undersecretary Shahira Saqqaf, UPA Intelligence Director Njal Vang, and Undersecretary of State Sukhon Wattana."

Saqqaf was a petite woman in a niqab marked with a constellation pattern in what Henry suspected was actual gold and gems. Only her eyes were visible through the embroidered veil, but they were bright green and sparkling with interest in the discussion around her.

Vang was a study in contrasts with his military counterpart. Where Kosigan was tall, dark and Slavic, Vang was short, blond and Scandinavian, with a neatly braided beard that reached down to the collar of his perfectly tailored business suit.

Wattana was one of the three Earth natives on the call with Dirksen and Henry, a heavyset broad-shouldered Thai woman with piercing black eyes.

"We currently have most of the civilian and military administration of the United Planets Alliance on this call," Secretary-President Patil noted. "This conference was not entirely about the Gathering, but it does behoove us all to move with alacrity."

"And to make sure we cover things completely," Dirksen added, earning themselves a vaguely accepting wave from Patil.

"Kosigan, Vang. Have there been any major changes in our situation with regards to our allies since *Raven* departed Procyon?" Patil asked.

"Our agents on the ground are suggesting that we're seeing even more of a pullback on the part of the Kenmiri military than we are seeing of their population," Kosigan told them. "We're seeing every sign that the Kenmiri are on the edge of dissolving into civil war over how to proceed without the Kenmorad."

"Our contacts with the Vesheron closer to the Horus Province agree," Vang added. "At least one of those factions, I must note, is suggesting a campaign of mass genocide into the former Empire. The logic, I suppose, being that if they can't rule, no one will."

"If they launch such a campaign, can the Vesheron stop it without us?" Patil asked.

"It won't matter either way," Kosigan said. "Without prepositioning Admiral Saren's ships throughout the former Empire, there's no way we could get forces into position in time to stop the Kenmiri remnants if they launch a suicide campaign.

"To make sure we secured our allies against that kind of attack would require the forward deployment of almost the entire UPSF."

"And the cost of that kind of deployment would be extravagant," Wattana pointed out. "Saqqaf? Do we have numbers on that?"

"Every battlecruiser deployed outside UPA space costs us approximately one point two million dollars per day more than a battlecruiser on deployment inside UPA space," the Trade Undersecretary said instantly, though she seemed oddly unenthused with giving the numbers to Henry. "That is in additional wear, the need to supply precious metals for trade goods for acquisition of fuel from allied sources, hazard pay and similar costs."

"The UPA can't *afford* to continue prosecuting this war," Wattana concluded.

That, Henry noted, had *not* been what Saqqaf had said. Someone was playing games here...and he didn't think he liked the one being played.

"We know that," Patil said calmly. "Even if that wasn't the case, the General Assembly and the member systems have made it clear that they have no interest in continuing a war far beyond our borders now the threat to us has been neutralized.

"This does, obviously, impact your potential options, Ambassador Todorovich," she continued. "While I have categorically refused to forbid you from offering deployments of our ships to secure trade routes, the General Assembly has made the limits of what can be offered in that case very clear."

She gestured to Saqqaf. Henry only had the Undersecretary's

eyes to go on, but he would *not* have wanted to be the target of the anger he saw in them.

"The General Assembly has officially authorized you to offer deployment of up to two battlecruisers or an equivalent mass of lighter units," Saqqaf said flatly. "I don't personally see how that could possibly be sufficient to secure trade lines even through the Ra Province, let alone all the way to, say, Resta."

"We answer to the Assembly, not the other way around," Patil said, the only concession Henry was seeing to the fact that Saqqaf kept getting pulled into the conversation.

"We might be better off with a half-dozen destroyers than two battlecruisers," Admiral Saren noted. "How heavy are pirate forces likely to *be* in the wake of the Empire's fall?"

"Heavy," Henry injected calmly. "I presume only summaries of our reports from Apophis-Four made it all the way up the chain, ser? We faced a six-ship flotilla of ex-Kenmiri ships, including two gunships, that had been acting as pirates."

"That had to be an isolated incident, though," Saren argued. "They were Vesheron gone rogue. We can't be expecting to see much of that..."

From the way she trailed off, she could see the expressions on the intelligence officers' and diplomats' faces.

"The likely situation is that *most* of the smaller Vesheron are going to turn to banditry," Todorovich said quietly. "Unless there are specific groups trying to sweep them up to form new nations in their area, they're going to go home. And they're not going to find anything waiting for them there. Certainly, few of the Vesheron were in position to step back in as a government in exile like the Restan were.

"Piracy, warlordism, violence and chaos...this is going to be the Kenmiri Empire for the next hundred years," the Ambassador noted. "That is why this Gathering is taking place—because many of the larger Vesheron *realize* that and want to head it off."

The table, with its mix of holographic and physical people, was silent.

"We know," Patil finally said. "The truth of the matter, Ambassador, is that it is always about money. The United Planets Alliance is limited under the constitution to a one percent flat income tax on all individuals. Systems under our direct administration see us receive the full revenue of a more standard income tax structure, but we only control minor colonies at best.

"To fund the expansion and operation of the UPSF required special funding agreements with the member systems. Those agreements are up for renewal in less than six months. With the Kenmiri no longer an active threat, they will *not* be renewed."

"And without those agreements, every battlecruiser we send beyond our borders is a battlecruiser back home we need to decommission," Saqqaf said flatly. "Expanding our external trade options will increase the funding available to the UPA, and in the long run, we see that eventually being self-funding with regards to the force necessary to secure those routes.

"In the short term, however, we need to limit what we can deploy to what we can afford."

"Which is why Ambassador Todorovich has the instructions she has," Wattana concluded. "We cannot get involved in the future—or even the *current* problems—of the Vesheron. We want a series of stable successor states.

"Unfortunately, in at least some cases, those successor states will be born out of the warlordism that Em Todorovich mentioned. Stability is going to be more important than palatability for a long time, people."

That chilled the conversation again. As the American in the room, Henry could reflect on *exactly* how well policies like that had worked in the past.

"That brings us back to the intelligence briefing," Kosigan noted. "Our sources in the Londu military have been...quite open about their desires at the Gathering."

"This is new information, I take it?" Patil asked.

"Our agent on the scene wanted to confirm the details as best they could before risking a subspace transmission out of Londu space," the Admiral replied. "But there's no question now: the Londu are preparing a new battle fleet, at least a dozen battleships, with attendant escorts...and invasion forces.

"If the Gathering does not provide the territorial gains they want in the Isis Province, they have every intention of taking them by force," Kosigan noted. "The Londu Scion wants to double his territory as his price for their aid in the war. They're aiming for a hundred stars and at least a dozen inhabited worlds."

"The Vesheron are not going to give that up," Henry said softly. "The worlds closest to the Londu like them well enough that voluntary annexation is entirely possible, but that's a fifth of the Province. They're not going to sign over a dozen inhabited worlds, of which maybe three will have a voice at the table."

"If they don't, they're going to be looking at another war. A war *we* can't fight," Kosigan replied.

"I hate to say it, but we may need to back the Londu up," Wattana said. "Their presence would secure an entire former province. They will not tolerate chaos near their borders. Our influence may well swing the decision on conceding to their ambitions."

She smiled coldly.

"Of course, *they* don't need to know our objectives. Ambassador Todorovich should be able to extract quite a price for our assistance."

Henry felt a little sick, but he understood the point. If the alternative to letting the Londu gobble up a dozen inhabited worlds and a hundred star systems' worth of resources was to see *five hundred* systems with fifty inhabited worlds degrade into chaos and bloodshed, then let the Londu gobble away.

And since the UPA's objectives lined up neatly with what the Londu wanted—they wanted stable trading partners in Kenmiri successor states, after all—they could support that. But since what the Londu wanted was against the desires of most of the Gathering, Todorovich could extort quite a price for her help.

"That's not a bad basic plan to apply overall," Patil noted. "Kosigan, Vang, I want you and your people to sit down and flag who are the most likely stabilizing influences in each province. If we can subtly direct the weight of authority in their regions to them, then we increase their ability to stabilize entire sections of space.

"The Gathering isn't going to create some grand Vesheron federation to replace the Kenmiri Empire. The Vesheron simply don't have enough in common with each other to manage that.

"Our focus has to be on the Ra Province, with Apophis and Hathor second and the rest a distant third at best," the Secretary-President admitted. "The General Assembly has tasked us to see to our own matters first, so that is your guiding light, Ambassador Todorovich.

"We can't save six thousand stars from chaos, even if the Assembly handed us an infinite budget. So, let's use this Gathering to help create islands of stability among those stars, islands that we can trade and negotiate with to mutual benefit."

"Those are my instructions, then?" Todorovich asked stonily.

"They are," Wattana confirmed. "They're not much different than what you already had, but I'll make sure it's all codified in writing for you, Em Todorovich."

"And as for you, Captain Wong," Admiral Saren said, locking her gaze on Henry, "your task remains as it always has been: no matter what happens, Ambassador Todorovich is to be kept safe. If the Gathering comes under threat, your first priority is the Ambassador. You *are* authorized to attempt to protect the Gathering from any external threat you believe you can safely engage, but if you do not see a way to victory, you are to extract Todorovich and her staff and get the hell out of Resta.

"Am I clear?"

Any situation where the massed fleet at the Gathering couldn't, combined with the Restan defense fleet, stand off an incoming threat...well, Henry wasn't sure he'd be *able* to get the Ambassador out in that situation.

"I understand, ser," he replied. Saren knew the limits and knew exactly what kind of scenario she was postulating. Her orders covered his working with the Vesheron against any threat short of a doomsday scenario.

Which was good...because that was probably what he'd have done anyway.

The Medal of Valor came from the Red Wings Campaign. He'd probably done at least two or three other things that would have earned him that since, but they'd been a bit busy to be submitting awards to the General Assembly for people who already had them.

"Soldiers," she said dryly, but it wasn't really a curse. "How many times do you have to nearly die to get that level of signage?"

Henry grimaced. At least Todorovich understood how the things were usually earned.

"I've lost count," he admitted. He tapped a particular decoration in the row of miniatures. "That one is memorable, though."

"Oh?" she asked, her tone careful.

"Turquoise Star. It's for going Dutchman in a crippled starfighter and living," he told her. "The Idiot-Who-Lived badge."

THE STATION HAD DEFINITELY BEEN BUILT as a mining base. Like many Kenmiri large space installations, it had started life as an asteroid that had been partially melted with Kenmiri plasma guns and spun up to create a neatly cylindrical shape of mostly pure metal.

Artificial gravity turned those former asteroids into multi-kilometer-tall skyscrapers in space. This one was just over three kilometers high, with docking collars evenly spaced every three hundred meters to allow for ten sets of ships to be docked.

The docks were designed to make sure they could handle escort-sized starships, even if their main purpose was to host smaller sublight ships. Studying the collars as their shuttle decelerated toward the station, Henry was comfortable in his initial assessment: he could have docked *Raven* with the station.

There was no chance in *hell* he or any other Captain here was going to do that. The Restan hadn't even bothered to tell anyone they couldn't. They'd just assigned everyone orbits without asking if they wanted to dock.

A single Restan battleship orbited fifteen thousand kilometers away from the station, and everyone *else* was at least one light-second away.

Very few of the weapons available to the Vesheron factions had a range of over a light-second, and none of the ones that did were light-speed weapons. The distance the Restan had put everyone at meant that no one could shoot the station without that battleship having a chance to intervene.

"Ser, we're handing you off to Gathering Station Control," Lieutenant Commander Turrigan reported. He was the commander of the two starfighters escorting the shuttle in. "You're in the perimeter of their defensive lasers now, and they're taking over responsibility for your security."

Turrigan paused.

"It's not been *explicit*," he noted, "but they implied pretty strongly that while we were fine escorting you in, we're not welcome this close to the station otherwise."

"Understood, Lieutenant Commander," Henry replied. "We'll be fine. Safe trails back to the hangar."

"Good luck with the diplomacy, Captain," Turrigan said before dropping the channel, drawing another sigh from Henry.

"Why am I here, again?" he asked Todorovich.

"Because we need to show off," she told him. "Everyone is showing up with escorts and staff. Plus the commanders of our starship escort, because we all brought very decorated people that everyone here knows the name of.

"So, yes, Captain Wong, you're the UPA's prize stallion today, and we get to show you off."

She smiled at him as she gave him a calmly assessing gaze.

"I think it will definitely have the intended impact."

"I hope so," he muttered. "I *hate* this uniform. I feel like the dictator from some bad three-D serial."

"Perhaps," she conceded. "But remember that neither that actor nor that dictator *earned* their decorations. I've seen your record, Henry. You earned every damn thing we hung on you. Deal."

Regardless of Henry's opinion, this was definitely Todorovich's part of the mission. He had his orders...and he would soldier on.

Even if he hated his dress uniform. And had to wear a sword.

TODOROVICH HAD BROUGHT thirteen people with her, including a chef, analysts and junior diplomats. Henry had added sixteen GroundDiv troopers to the party going aboard Gathering Station, bringing them to an even thirty.

He was the odd man out, but he didn't expect to be on the station for long. His place was aboard the battlecruiser with the rest of the escorts, not taking part in the stream of meetings, parties, dinners and politics that he knew was going to consume this station for the next few months.

"Clear," the Chief Petty Officer in charge of the half-platoon GroundDiv team announced. "Locals waiting for you, sers. Looks all decorative and friendly, though."

"Play nice, Chief," Henry murmured.

"Never nicer, ser," the other man replied.

The Captain carefully levered himself out of his chair, taking a few tentative steps to rebalance his weapons and get a feel for the local artificial gravity.

"I see the Restan got into the gravity controls as soon as they took over," Todorovich noted, clearly doing the same. "Always good to see."

He chuckled and nodded. The Kenmiri set gravity on any facility they used at around 1.15 gee. It was light enough that other races could adapt to it, but it still sucked for anyone who hadn't grown up on a high-gravity world—GroundDiv trained in 1.5 gee for just that reason.

Ost, on the other hand, had a gravity of 0.97 gee, comparable to

Sandoval in Procyon. The Restan had turned Gathering Station's artificial gravity from where its Kenmiri builders would have set it to where the new management found comfortable.

"I believe it's us first," he told the Ambassador. "Shall we, Ambassador?"

"Let's get this game started," she confirmed, gesturing for him to fall in beside her.

They stepped out of the spacecraft together, walking down the short ramp to where the locals were waiting for them.

As the Chief had said, they were definitely decorative. There was a line of ten Restan soldiers on either side of the pathway forward. Unlike many Ashall, the Restan didn't need a hood and distance to pass for human. Most of their ethnotypes had equivalents on Earth and most Terran ethnotypes had equivalents on Ost.

Clad in silvered body armor and carrying homebuilt energy weapons, they could have passed for GroundDiv troopers with ease. As Henry and Todorovich approached, each pair of soldiers saluted crisply with their fist to their chest.

Henry returned each salute with a firm nod as they made their way through the paired soldiers, his own soldiers following behind with the rest of the staff.

Civilian clothing, at least, was different on Ost. The diplomat waiting for them could pass for human, but she was clearly not a UPA citizen. Her formal wear consisted of long purple leggings, a knee-length red kilt, and a sleeveless vest in a matching purple to the leggings.

A gold torc around her neck declared her a senior official, if the fact that she was waiting for them with her two companions one step behind her wasn't enough of a clue.

"Ambassador Sylvia Todorovich, Colonel Henry Wong," she greeted them, the two English titles slightly distorted on the tongue of someone who didn't speak that language. After that, she switched to the Kem trade language they shared.

"Welcome to Gathering Station. I am Under-Speaker Sho Lavah

and I am the senior Restan diplomat for the Gathering." She smiled. "That also makes me your host, and it is a pleasure to meet you both. Your reputations are known to us."

"Greetings, Under-Speaker," Todorovich responded with a small bow. "I look forward to our conversations. We have much work to achieve in the days ahead of us."

"That we do." Sho Lavah glanced past the two of them to the party waiting by the shuttle. "Quarters have been prepared for yourselves and your staff. Before we send everyone on their way, however, I promised to allow one more greeting."

Henry's focus had been on the Under-Speaker and her eye-catching outfit. He'd registered the two officers in their kilted uniforms behind her, but he hadn't really looked at them beyond classifying them as "not threat."

Now the taller of the two Restan officers stepped forward and bowed to Henry. She represented one of the ethnotypes that *didn't* have a Terran equivalent, a dark-haired woman with dark blue eyes and pale green skin.

"Colonel Henry Wong, it has been a while," she said as she offered her arm to him.

He'd spent enough time with Restan to recognize the gesture— and the green-skinned woman had been one of the Restan he'd spent that time with! He grasped her arm, forearm to forearm, and grinned at the other soldier.

"Ship-Voice Ta Callah," he greeted her. "It has been too long. You are well?"

"I am well," the woman replied. She'd been the flag captain of the Restan force sent into Set Province along with *Panther*. Their ships had reinforced the disorganized Vesheron factions on the far side of Kenmiri space from the UPA and helped turn them into an actual fighting force.

A fighting force that had struck the killing blow against the Kenmorad.

"It is Squadron-Voice now," Ta Callah continued. "I was honored and promoted for our victory over the Kenmorad."

"I received a new command, our newest and most advanced warship," Henry told her. It wasn't quite for the same reasons that Ta Callah had been promoted, but that wasn't worth explaining to the alien...and definitely couldn't be explained on the reception deck of the space station.

"So, the UPA also recognizes the Destroyer," Ta Callah said. "That is good."

The Destroyer.

Henry didn't even need to ask what she meant by that. *Panther* had killed the last Kenmorad. His hands had struck the last blow of the genocide of the Kenmiri. It would take decades for his actions to actually *end* their enemy, but he was the one who'd destroyed them.

"Many here will want to meet the Destroyer," Sho Lavah added. "There will be time later, but Squadron-Voice Ta Callah commands the station's defenses. She wanted to meet with you before you were swept up by the diplomats, and her duties demand much of her time."

"All soldiers understand that," Henry said with a small bow to the Under-Speaker. "I, too, will need to return to my ship, but I am at Ambassador Todorovich's disposal for now."

"So I understand," the Under-Speaker confirmed, her glance at Todorovich more amused than Henry was probably supposed to pick up. "We shall have to see what her schedule for you allows, Colonel."

CHAPTER TWENTY-THREE

THE FIRST PARTY WAS THAT EVENING, A PRIVATE GATHERING FOR the ambassadors and one invited guest apiece. The list was that restrictive, Henry knew, because there were already a lot of ambassadors on the station.

Every faction that had fielded ships against the Kenmiri was recognized as deserving a seat at the table there. He had *no* idea how Todorovich and the diplomatic staff were going to be identifying who actually mattered and who had three starships and no home base.

"Everyone here will speak Kem," she told him as they crossed the main promenade of the area the Gathering had taken over. It was an open space, twelve decks tall, with balconies and elevators all around it.

"I can't see the factions sending anyone who doesn't," he replied. They were speaking English, though there would be enough computer translators around that it wouldn't protect their privacy alone.

"They have to *have* someone to send," Todorovich said. "Not all of the factions are worth our time...or anyone's, really. The first week of this mess is going to be sorting out which groups are even worth talking to."

Mixed in with that, Henry realized, would be the assessment of which factions the UPA would back to create those "islands of stability" the Secretary-President wanted. Resta was obviously one, and it looked like Trintar in Apophis Province would be another. He doubted they'd be lucky enough to find easily picked-out candidates in the rest of the provinces.

"So, tonight is what, mingle and make friends?" he asked.

"Tonight is to show you off," she told him bluntly. "If we'd brought *any* of the Captains from Golden Lancelot, we'd have had rep to spend. Bringing *you*, though…

"They're going to fall over themselves to meet the man who struck the final blow." She held up a hand before he could say anything. "I've got a pretty good idea of how you feel about that, Henry, but it's another weapon in my arsenal and I'm *not* giving it up, understand? So, soldier on. I'll make it up to you later, I promise."

Henry had no idea how she planned on doing that, but he knew how to *soldier on*.

"Understood," he said. "Just…keep an eye on my back, Sylvia. I'm not a diplomat and I may accidentally encourage some knives to get pointed in that direction."

"No one's expecting you to be a diplomat," she told him as they crossed the last balcony to the space their networks told them held the party. "You won't be the only soldier here, either. I suspect that since this party is in *our* honor and they know I'm bringing you, most of the ambassadors will bring their escort commanders.

"You should know at least some of them."

"That's not exactly a selling point," Henry murmured, but he shook himself and nodded firmly. "But it's the game and I'm under your orders for this part. Let's go scout out enemy territory, shall we?"

The chuckle he surprised out of the Ambassador got them the rest of the way into the hall.

THE FIRST PERSON TO greet them as they came through the door was their host on the station as well as for the party. Sho Lavah wore the same formal style of outfit she'd greeted them at the dock in, though tonight the kilt was longer and a dark green to go with black leggings and vest.

"Welcome to the Gathering once again, Colonel, Ambassador," she greeted them in Kem. The titles were in English, but that was normal. Kem was acquiring a lot of loan words from the various Vesheron languages, mostly ranks and titles.

That the language of their enemy remained the only tongue they had in common wasn't lost on Henry. He suspected it made a great metaphor for the overall problem the Gathering was going to face.

"We are grateful to be welcomed," Todorovich said for them both. Henry spoke fluent Kem, but the Ambassador's smooth mastery of the language was a step above his own. "We are eager to get to work, as well."

"We all are," Sho Lavah said softly. "But these affairs are a necessary beginning. They help us divide the..." She paused, probably trying to parse a Restan idiom into something Kem could handle.

"They help us divide the grand-wielding from the grand-speaking," she concluded.

The wheat from the chaff was the equivalent metaphor from Henry's own farm upbringing.

"How many ambassadors are here tonight?" Todorovich asked.

"One hundred and sixty-two," Sho Lavah told her. "There are only seven on the station who were unable to attend. Few can be seen to miss a party to honor the UPA and to honor the Destroyer. Fewer still would desire to."

Henry was surveying the crowd. A hundred and sixty-two ambassadors and their plus-ones meant there were over three hundred people in the room, and it definitely looked like it. Over seventy percent of the people he could see were Ashall, too.

That still left over eighty truly alien aliens in the mix, but there was one he was *looking* for who was missing.

"Either we are early or the Terzan Ambassador declined to attend," he murmured. The Terzan, after all, would be neither early nor late. They would have arrived *exactly* when they were asked to.

"Takik declined to attend," Sho Lavah confirmed. "Do not be offended, Ambassador Todorovich. They have yet to attend *any* social event. It is not their way."

"We know the Terzan, Under-Speaker," Todorovich said. "We understand."

"Come, my friends. There are people here you *must* meet," the Under-Speaker told them.

Henry concealed a smile as they fell into the wake of the woman who was basically *running* the Gathering.

People she felt the Terrans "*must* meet" were almost certainly people the Resta, at least, had decided were actually going to be worth negotiating with.

HENRY WAS COMPLETELY unsurprised to see Sho Lavah cut through the entire crowd to guide them unerringly to a pair of Ashall men in familiar garb. Both were eerily skinny and extremely tall, with almost translucent blue-white skin. Their particular variety of Ashall only grew hair in a mane that stretched from the back of the skull to the base of the neck, and both of their manes were pitch-black.

The taller man, reaching at least ten centimeters over two meters, wore a pitch-black robe under a corset-style chest piece. The robe had a hood, but it had clearly been embroidered to be left down rather than put up.

The corset was worked with filigree in gold and some kind of bone or ivory, and the hood was embroidered in gold and red. Otherwise, there was no decoration on the distinctive black robe of a Londu government official.

The shorter of the two Londu was only shorter relatively, still edging over two meters and overtopping Henry by easily fifteen centimeters. Instead of a corset, he wore a matte-black fitted chest piece over a white robe that was fitted closely around the torso and loosely around the legs.

There was no hood on the dress uniform of an officer of the Blades of the Scion, the Londu space force. A black iron collar, its hand-hammered crudity completely intentional, hung around the officer's neck and bore the vertical gold bands of the man's rank.

Three bands marked him as a Lord of Ten Thousand Miles, roughly a UPSF Commodore, and almost certainly the Captain of the battleship outside...but likely *not* the commander of the entire escort.

"Ambassador Todorovich and Colonel Wong of the United Planets Alliance, it is my pleasure to introduce Ambassador Saunt and Lord of Ten Thousand Miles Kahlmor," Sho Lavah told them, gesturing from one pair to the other. "They are, of course, of the Londu, servants of the Great Scion."

"It is a pleasure," Saunt said, bending his incredible height into a deep, swooping bow. "Ambassador Todorovich and I have met, though I doubt she remembers me. I was much less tall then."

"I remember you, Ambassador Saunt," Todorovich replied with a smile. "Your father was memorable enough for both of you."

A silent ping on Henry's internal network popped up with a picture of a group of Londu, very clearly being led by a man who was *unquestionably* a close relative of Saunt. The younger Londu at the leader's left hand—the place of honor in Londu culture—was a good seventy centimeters shorter than Saunt was now, but he could tell it was the same man.

Eleven years ago, when we first arrived in Londu space, Todorovich's silent message told him. *Saunt's father was the regional governor. Kelant is also the Scion's younger brother.*

"We are honored to see that the Scion places enough value on this gathering to send his finest," she continued, as if she'd never sent the silent message. "I look forward to working closely with you, Ambassador Saunt."

"It is good to be remembered," the Ambassador replied.

Now, of course, Henry was wondering if Saunt was here because of his *ability* or because of his *blood*. The Londu couldn't be more than twenty-five years old.

If the Ambassador was potentially a callow youth, his companion was most definitely not. Henry wasn't familiar with this particular Lord of Ten Thousand Miles, but he knew what to look for on that matte-black breastplate.

Where Henry had miniature ribbons laced together on a plaque on his chest for most of his awards, the Londu had inscriptions on the breastplate. They were only visible in perfect lighting unless you were looking for them, but Henry knew what to look for—and his network was more than up to picking the lines inscribed on the armor out in poor light.

The Lord of Ten Thousand Miles had seen a *lot* of elephants in his time, and had spent enough time with Terrans along the way to know to offer his hand in a proper handshake.

"It is an honor to meet the Destroyer," he told Henry as they shook hands. "I led a cruiser force in support of the Golden Lancelot operations in Isis Province. It did not fall to us to strike the final blow, and I envy you that privilege."

"Duty," Henry corrected the other man. "It was a duty, perhaps, but not a privilege. It is never a privilege to take lives, regardless of the need."

Kahlmor's smile tightened as he clearly failed to understand Henry's point. That was fine, though. Just because the Ashall *looked* human enough didn't mean they shared anything resembling Terran culture.

And there'd been enough *Terran* cultures that wouldn't agree with a twenty-fourth-century Asian-American's opinion on violence, after all.

"I see," was all he said, though. "You have a fine ship, Colonel Wong. Would it be possible for me to tour her?"

"I will have to consult with my superiors," Henry replied. "*Raven* is our most advanced warship, and even among close friends, we must keep some secrets."

"I understand," Kahlmor said brightly. "Regardless of whether your superiors will permit me to tour *Raven*, I would be delighted to invite you aboard *Rigid Candor* for a tour and supper."

That was not an offer Henry had expected. He hadn't looked at the Londu battleship closely, but he doubted the Great Scion had sent less than his best to the Gathering.

Like the UPA, the Scion knew there was a component of a dick-measuring contest to the forces escorting the ambassadors...and unlike the UPA, the Scion couldn't send one ship with the implicit message of *yes, this one ship can take all of yours.*

The Blades of the Scion didn't have gravity shields, after all.

"I am honored by the trust and respect your offer shows," Henry said slowly. "I gladly accept."

He glanced over at Todorovich and Sho Lavah. They'd continued to speak with the Londu Ambassador as he and Kahlmor had their own conversation. They looked done now, though.

"In any case, it appears that I am being called to meet others," he told Kahlmor.

"We must speak again," the Londu officer replied. "But I understand the demands upon the Destroyer tonight. Until we do speak."

He bowed his farewell and Henry allowed Todorovich and Sho Lavah to pull him back into the fray of ambassadors and escorts, hoping that his poker face was good enough to have concealed his confusion.

CHAPTER TWENTY-FOUR

"I DO BELIEVE OUR LONDU COMMODORE FRIEND IS HITTING ON you, Colonel," Todorovich told Henry as they moved away from the conversation. Most of their meetings were quite short, barely more than an exchange of greetings. Over the course of the evening, after all, Todorovich had to meet all one hundred and sixty-two ambassadors.

"That would make some sense," Henry admitted, going back over the conversation in his head. "I *think* it's mostly professional courtesy, but you may be right." He shrugged. "Not that it matters. Kahlmor isn't my type."

Todorovich started to say something, then swallowed her words as they approached the Trintar delegation.

"You're not dodging the question this time," she hissed under her breath. "But I'm not asking it here, either!"

He chuckled at her before dropping his mask back into place and smiling politely at the two pairs from their "most likely stabilizing faction" in Apophis Province.

"Ambassador Todorovich and Colonel Wong of the United Planets Alliance, it is my pleasure to introduce Ambassador Koss

Tamar and Strike Commander Osu Don of the Trintar Commonality," Sho Lovah told them.

Koss Tamar was Ashall; Henry assumed she was from Trintar though he couldn't be sure—the planet was home to another of the galaxy's seemingly infinite varieties of Ashall. She could have easily passed for Terran, a petite woman with neatly braided brunette hair and a button-nosed face that would have made her dangerously adorable on Earth. She wore a toga-like wrap in a deep russet orange.

Osu Don was *not* Ashall. They shared the same basic upright bipedal form most tool-using species ended up with, but their species had been *hexapods* at one point. Their third set of limbs was a pair of impressively feathered wings that emerged from the joint in their torso where their ribcages met their spine.

The way the wrap garment Osu Don shared with Koss Tamar wound its way easily around the wings suggested an explanation for why it was popular among the Commonality. Osu Don's people, the Kraital, were the natives of one of Trintar's two inhabitable planets.

"A pleasure to meet you both," Todorovich told them. "We have heard many things of the success of the Commonality in bringing together people in the wake of the Kenmiri withdrawal."

"And we have heard many things of your United Planets Alliance," Koss Tamar told them. "Most recently, I have a report of several new ships reporting in at Trintar and volunteering to join our fleet.

"Their leader, one Captain Attallis, said that you had liberated them from a rogue warlord and sent them our way. She asked for me to pass on her regards."

Henry was relieved to hear that. He'd worried that his mercy had enabled continued piracy in the Apophis Province.

"While I know the needs of the UPA are quite different, the gesture is not insignificant," Osu Don told them, their wings wrapping around their shoulders like a cloak of white feathers. "Three escort-type ships is unlikely to ever be an insignificant part of our forces. Not until we start building heavier warships of our own."

"Those are details for more specific discussions, Strike Commander," Koss Tamar pointed out. "Osu Don commands the strike wing that accompanied me here." She smiled. "They would, of course, prefer that said wing consisted of dreadnoughts instead of our new-build corvettes."

"Any commander would," Osu Don conceded. "But we have need for our heavier ships back home. This Gathering is less...immediate."

Henry could easily hear the words the officer had cut off. *Less important. Less relevant. Less likely to achieve anything of value.*

"And yet, this Gathering will decide how all of those immediate things are dealt with in the future," he noted to the other officer. "Less immediate, yes, but we all need to be here."

He gestured at the crowd around them.

"Regardless of whether the party is to our taste or not, we all need to be here," he repeated.

Don laughed softly.

"You are not wrong, Colonel Wong. But your people, at least, are not actively in combat while you eat small foods and drink small drinks and talk small talk."

Henry was going to have to do some research. He wasn't aware of active combat going on in the Apophis Province. On the other hand, most people likely weren't aware of Henry's battle against the First Warlord's little fleet. Minor actions didn't raise that much attention.

"Some must always stand behind the diplomats while others face the enemy," Henry told Osu Don. "If we are worthy of our commands, we hate every second of it. But it does not invalidate that the work still needs to be done."

The winged alien bowed their head.

"Of course. I apologize for my manner and thank you for your words," they said delicately. "It seems, sadly, that our limited time is up. I am sure we will encounter each other again, but today, you are the center of the party, and everyone must have their minute, must they not?"

"Even if we hate every second of it," Henry repeated with a grin —and was rewarded with a clear laugh from the other officer.

"Good luck with your battle, Colonel Wong," Osu Don told him.

WITH A HUNDRED AND sixty-two ambassadors to meet, the meetings grew shorter and shorter as the night went on. The names of the factions grew less and less recognizable, too. After the first sixty or so meetings, Henry stopped trying to even remember names.

His internal network could handle that if they ended up being important, but UPA Intelligence files suggested that fewer than sixty of the Vesheron factions could field more than six warships. He figured most of the people who'd managed to send a ship and an ambassador to the Gathering were at least connected to planets, but unless those planets had functioning governments and had enough ships to actually be able to project force outside their own system... they were the small fish in the game.

There were two noticeable gaps in the list, though, and they became more noticeable as the night drew on as well.

"Under-Speaker," he finally asked Sho Lavah. "Is there no one here from the Ra Province?"

Ra was the closest province to the UPA, the one they most needed to be stable and secure for easy trade. If there was no one there worth talking to from Ra, that suggested problems in the future.

"The Kozun sent an ambassador," she told him. "He declined to attend tonight. There are two others who are here, but they have made no effort to move themselves up my list."

Translation: they were small powers the Restan didn't regard as worth paying attention to *and* hadn't tried to make direct contact with their largest nearby neighbor. And the one *significant* power was intentionally ignoring them.

That was never a good sign.

"What about the Drifters?" he asked. "I saw a guardian out there without a convoy to watch, so I'm guessing there's an ambassador here?"

"Ambassador Sarkal pled illness," she told him. Sho Lavah paused, glancing at Todorovich. "The Kozun's Ambassador made no excuse; he simply declined attendance."

So, the biggest mobile power—one that Henry very much wanted to ask pointed questions about gravitic resonance warheads—and the biggest power close to the UPA had both declined to show up to the party held in honor of the UPA.

He nodded calmly in acceptance of Sho Lavah's words. The Restan official was being helpful tonight, but she was probably being helpful to *everyone*. Her job was to make the Gathering go smoothly and make sure Resta got what they wanted.

The UPA didn't need her to know that their commander on the scene was concerned.

CHAPTER TWENTY-FIVE

HENRY WASN'T SURE HE WANTED TO KNOW WHAT THE CLEARLY segregated and secured sections being used for the ambassadors' quarters had originally been built for. His guess was hostages when the Kenmiri had first taken the system—they had been known to do that, and the hostages had generally been kept in reasonable comfort.

Whatever their purpose, though, the Restan had renovated the spaces quite heavily to make them appropriate for the ambassadors and their retinues. He suspected the UPA had one of the more decorated sections along with having one of the larger ones, but that wasn't really his problem.

His point of concern was that there was only one way in or out of the apartments. A pair of Restan guards in entirely un-decorative battle armor stood outside the vestibule, matched by a pair of GroundDiv troopers in similar gear inside.

Once they were past those guards, at least, he was able to relax a little bit. They might be trapped inside this space, but no one *else* was getting in.

"Ser!" The GroundDiv Chief, Bilal Roi, in charge of security seemed to materialize out of nowhere, thankfully waiting a few seconds after announcing himself for Henry to readjust his mind back to English. "We've swept everywhere for bugs. I'm one hundred percent certain that the Restan are using the station systems to observe us, but I think we've found and disabled everyone *else's* microphones and cameras."

Henry snorted as he traded a glance with Todorovich.

"How many?" he asked.

"Average of fourteen per room," the Chief replied. "We've also got some portable jammers and white-noise generators set up in a couple of key rooms. You should be able to have the conversations in private that you need to, Ambassador."

"Good. Thank you, Chief," Todorovich told the man. "Your work is appreciated. I assume you have guard rotations and everything set up?"

The desperately-trying-not-to-look-bored pair that had escorted Henry and Todorovich to and from the party—without being allowed *into* the party—were already disappearing to their quarters.

"Yes, Em Ambassador," the Chief replied. "I have two guards on duty at all times, with two for backup or escort as required. We would prefer that no civilians leave the apartments without at least one trooper for escort."

"Your soldiers also don't leave on their own," Todorovich countered. "We move through the station in pairs at a minimum, Chief Roi. If you need more troopers, we'll bring them over, but I only trust about a third of the people on this station to have a weapon in front of me, let alone a weapon behind me."

"Understood, Em Ambassador," Roi confirmed. "I have fifteen troopers and myself. If necessary, I can have a trooper with every civilian and keep two here to guard home base."

"Good. That shouldn't be necessary, but some of the staffers will be in separate meetings on their own and they will definitely need escorts." She smiled. "Now, I may be exhausted, but the Colonel and I need to debrief. Where were those secure zones?"

"Follow me, sers."

CHIEF ROI HAD PICKED the most comfortable place he could find for his secure zones. The spot he left Henry and Todorovich in had a selection of excessively plush couches placed in a neat triangle, with small tables for food or computer tablets as needed.

The security generator looked like a decorative statue, wrapped in gold foil and with ivory inlays hiding its entirely functional interior.

"This is going to be exciting," he said dryly. "So, the Londu want to use us, the Drifters might be actively moving *against* us, and the Kozun are what, ignoring us?"

"And those are only the first three key points of the evening," Todorovich said with a chuckle. "It's the Drifters that worry me, to be honest. Everyone relied on them, everyone needed them, but no one ever really managed to ask what *their* agenda was.

"They did damn well out of the situation under the Empire, but they helped bring everything down. Somehow, I don't think that they did it all out of the goodness of their hearts."

Henry sighed.

"Our Set operations alone last year handed over eighty metric tons of gold and platinum to the Drifters for fuel and missiles," he noted. "We checked the weapons for bugs every time. They didn't rig them every time, but they did it often enough."

"Wait, seriously?" Todorovich asked. "They sold us *missiles* with bugs in them?"

"Everybody was using Kenmiri missiles," Henry pointed out. "Even the ones we're building are functionally identical to them. Even on extended logistics, our machine shops could build more, but it was easier to buy them from the Drifters when we could.

"But yeah. They bugged them. Fantastically complex little devices that worked in concert to make sure that whatever one of them knew, the rest did, and any that were left were supposed to transmit everything to any Drifter ship in the area."

He shook his head.

"I think our nomadic caravan merchants knew a hell of a lot more about what was going on throughout the entire rebellion than just about anyone else," Henry said. "I'm not sure the Vesheron would have *survived* without them, but I don't know their agenda and it makes me nervous."

"Especially when they start making deals to get people to test weapons that can actually threaten our ships?" Todorovich asked.

"Especially then," he agreed. "It's not like they need it, either. That guardian out there? It's got more turrets than a Kenmiri dreadnought, and its turrets are *bigger*, too. There's a reason the Kenmiri left the Drifters be, and it's those things."

A guardian wasn't a particularly *stable* ship in a lot of ways. The Drifters had no ability to build a contiguous hull as large as a dreadnought, so their guardians were a mix of unmatched parts and modules welded together and roughly armor-plated.

They had more powerful turrets than the Kenmiri, but that came at a much higher risk of failure. Henry had seen a guardian lose turrets in a straight fight with a Kenmiri dreadnought. The guardian had *won* that fight, but it hadn't been a clean win.

"And the Londu?" Todorovich said. "I find it interesting that the Lord of Ten Thousand Miles is coming on to you, Colonel. It suggests at least some research on your personal tastes. I doubt Kahlmor is inviting you aboard his battleship for dinner without encouragement, let alone permission, regardless of his actual interest in you."

"It doesn't take much research to know I was married to a man," Henry replied. "It would take more for them to work out they're completely off base. Kahlmor isn't my type."

"What *is* your type?" Todorovich asked, sounding almost relieved to get the question out there.

The Colonel laughed.

"Based on historical evidence? One girl I grew up with in

Montana who is now married with two kids and mayor of our hometown...and my ex-husband."

The Ambassador didn't quite seem to know how to take that for a moment.

"Wait, two people? Ever?"

"Ever," he confirmed. "Well, a couple of attempts at other relationships in the Academy, but those petered out fast enough to confirm what the counselor figured. Demisexual was the term they used." He shrugged. "Academy counselors pay a *lot* of attention to things the Academy administration can't officially know about."

"Not your type, indeed," Todorovich murmured. "Poor tall bastard. Try not to start a war when you break his heart?"

"We both know any attempt at flirtation with a UPA officer on the part of a Londu Lord of Ten Thousand Miles is carefully calculated and authorized at the highest levels," Henry pointed out. "I'm more concerned about the Scion's bloody *nephew*."

"They're monarchists," she pointed out. "Sending a close blood relation of the Scion is a sign of how serious they're taking this. Saunt was at his father's side for some pretty tense negotiations at age fifteen. I doubt that was the first time he'd sat at the negotiating table.

"Don't let his age fool you; that man has been an active diplomat for over a decade and speaks with his uncle's voice. There's almost certainly more experienced advisors in his staff, but he's not here because the Scion doesn't trust his judgment."

"He's the man the Scion sent to tell the Vesheron to bend over and spread," Henry noted. "That's going to be an interesting sell."

"That's understating it, Henry." She sighed. "If I can manage to conclude the Gathering without a war, that's a hell of a feather in my cap back home. That really is the extent of my orders: just make sure that we're not involved in any wars."

"Odds of that?" he asked.

"Decent. The Gathering doesn't officially start for two more days, and it's going to be a week just to get through everyone's opening remarks. There's a reason I'm not expecting some delegations until day five or six."

"And the Kozun?" Henry asked.

"They arrived a day before us," she told him. "I didn't recognize the name of the Ambassador, either. Something Rojan, apparently. I thought I at least knew *of* all of their diplomats."

"Kal Rojan?" Henry asked.

"Yeah," she confirmed after a moment's thought. "Why?"

"Kal Rojan isn't a diplomat," *Raven*'s Captain told her. "He's barely a damn soldier. Kal Rojan is an assassin and a terrorist, the personal bloody-handed knife of the First Voice of the Kozun. He's an enforcer, not an Ambassador."

"What the hell is he doing here?"

"I don't know," Henry admitted. "But I'm starting to think that I might be more valuable to you from the bridge of *Raven* than acting as the UPA's poster boy. And not just because I *hate* being lauded for Golden Lancelot."

"You may be right," she allowed. "I was planning on dragging you to at least one more round of parties and events, but I'm looking at Rojan's file right now and it agrees with you."

Todorovich shook her head.

"You *are* right. I need you on *Raven*, Captain Wong—and I need Thompson to send me more troops. My back has this itchy feeling, like someone's measuring it for a knife."

CHAPTER TWENTY-SIX

A PAIR OF HENRY'S STARFIGHTERS RENDEZVOUSED WITH THE shuttle less than twenty thousand kilometers clear of Gathering Station, the two Dragoons falling in neatly on either side of the transport.

"Ser, we have a laser com from Commander O'Flannagain," the pilot reported. With only Henry as a passenger, he'd joined the crew in the cockpit.

"Put it through to my network," he ordered, blinking a virtual screen up in his view and adjusting his mental state to talk through the network instead of aloud.

The image he received of Commander O'Flannagain was an avatar rather than the woman's current state. He *knew* what a pilot looked like in the heart of their starfighter, and O'Flannagain's feed was entirely lacking in viscous gel and oxygen masks.

"And just what is my CAG doing flying escort, Commander?" he asked dryly.

"I was on the rotation, ser," she replied. "I only have eight birds and eight pilots, counting myself. We're keeping two in space at all times, so I'm taking a rotation a day with everyone else. What did you expect, ser?"

"About that," he conceded. On a carrier, the CAG being in space on a day-to-day combat space patrol would arguably be a minor dereliction of duty. On a battlecruiser, with its single understrength squadron, it was almost necessary.

"What did you need, Commander?" he asked.

"I was hoping for some reassurance," she told him, her tone light. "My pilots are out and about in this mess more than anyone else, and it's making me twitchy. I swear at least a third of the ships out there are measuring us up for an alpha strike."

Henry concealed a shiver.

"I'd have expected a quarter at worst," he replied. "But then, I'd be expecting the rest to be watching each other. You're out there, Commander," he agreed. "Want to take a guess at who has *Raven* dialed in?"

There was a long silence.

"Yeah," she said quietly. "The Kozun flagship. One of the Restan dreadnoughts—though, to be fair, I think the Restan have at least a turret pointed at every capital ship in this mess. The Drifter guardian. A couple of others I'm not sure about, but those three are the ones we've flagged as highest-threat."

"Iyotake knows?" he asked.

"It's in our reports and I flagged him down in person," she confirmed. "Ser...I get the Resta, they're watching everybody, but the Drifters? The Kozun? I figured the Kozun were going to play nice with us."

"The Drifters are, if nothing else, experimenting with anti-grav-shield weaponry to sell to everybody else," he told her. "The Kozun sent an assassin to the Gathering, not a diplomat. I *think* that's because the First Voice trusts said assassin more than any of their diplomats, but still..."

"And the Restan are being justifiably paranoid, because if my people are reading the passive sensor array layouts right, half the ships that delivered the Gathering's ambassadors have the other half locked up," O'Flannagain said. "Hell of a peace conference, ser."

"The Vesheron share one language: the Kenmiri's," Henry reminded her. "They only shared one thing in common: a hatred of the Kenmiri.

"Without the Kenmiri, what do the Vesheron become?"

His pilot didn't have an answer.

"Exactly, Commander," he told her after ten seconds or so of silence. "Nobody else knows either, but the Vesheron weren't lacking in internal conflicts even *during* the war. The main purpose of the Gathering is to set up protocols to try and mediate those conflicts before they become their own wars."

IYOTAKE WAS WAITING for him when he disembarked the shuttle, his executive officer giving him a crisp salute with almost-concealed relief.

"Welcome back aboard, ser," the Lieutenant Colonel told him.

"I relieve you, Lieutenant Colonel Iyotake," Henry said with a gentle smile.

"I stand relieved," the XO confirmed. They were as alone as it was possible to be on the flight deck, with the pilots focused on their craft. "I'm guessing O'Flannagain took the chance to fill you in?"

"She did," Henry confirmed. "I'm guessing CIC and Tactical agree with her?"

He started walking toward his office, gesturing for Iyotake to fall in beside him.

"If anything, she's underestimating it," Iyotake told him. "I think she's missing part of the equation, too."

"Which is?"

"Not counting our birds, there are a grand total of twelve starfighters flying combat patrol around the Gathering," the XO said. "*Twelve.* Two are from Trintar—their corvettes carry four apiece, it looks like. Two are from the Londu. Two are from the Drifters. Four are Restan and two are from the Slant from the Bes Province."

"And ours are the only ones with a gravity shield," Henry said slowly. "The Dragoons are getting eyed for capture, aren't they?"

"Exactly," Iyotake confirmed. "I'm not sure who in this mess to even call allies, ser, but even the Restan wouldn't hesitate if they thought they could manage to snap up one of our starfighters. Even if they had to give it back in a day or two, having unrestricted access to one of our birds to dissect for even twenty-four hours..."

Henry nodded. They'd *never* based grav-shield starfighters off Vesheron ships, and while the occasional *pilot* had been picked up by the UPA's allies, they'd always ditched and destroyed their fighters.

It had taken a ruthless degree of paranoia to get through the war without the grav-shield technology ending up in Kenmiri hands. The price had been higher than Henry thought many of his superiors guessed. A *lot* of the Vesheron were bitter over it.

"The longer I'm here, the more I expect the Gathering to explode before it actually resolves anything," he admitted. "And the actual Gathering itself hasn't started yet."

"Tomorrow?" Iyotake asked.

"Day after," Henry said. "And it's going to take them a week just to get through opening remarks. I'm looking forward to hearing how the Londu Ambassador spins the Scion's position. I suspect that is going to throw as much of a wrench into this affair as our own desire to get the hell out and be left alone."

They reached his office, and his XO was shaking his head as they stepped inside.

"It doesn't feel right, ser," Iyotake told him. "We had a big hand in breaking the Kenmiri, but now we just walk away and leave everyone to their own devices?"

"Twenty-four battlecruisers. Six thousand stars. How much can we really *do*?" Henry asked. He shook his head.

"Getting the Vesheron aligned and focused on peace will make a far larger difference than sending us out into the wilds, XO."

"I get that, ser," Iyotake confirmed. He tugged on his braid. "It just feels...wrong, ser. Like we should do *something*."

"I agree with you, XO," Henry pointed out. "But unless you think you can get yourself in front of the General Assembly with a presentation to change their minds, there's not much we can do."

Iyotake chuckled.

"I can't do that," he agreed. "But I bet I know who could. *Ser*."

Henry shook his head.

"I think you overestimate how much my name can conjure," he pointed out. "I'm just one Colonel."

"We may not use the nickname the Vesheron have hung on you, ser, but believe me that 'the Destroyer' is not a meaningless distinction back home, either," Iyotake told him. "Not least since even our government is growing a guilty conscience, even if most of it is in denial."

"Let's focus on the problem in front of us, Colonel," Henry suggested. His XO probably wasn't wrong, but it wasn't something he'd ever thought about. He'd been too busy trying to hide from any public recognition or adulation for his role in "ending the war."

Could he *use* that? Possibly. It wasn't his skillset or his usual battlefield...but it *was* Sylvia Todorovich's. A conversation for another day, perhaps.

"Did Command get back to us about Lord of Ten Thousand Miles Kahlmor's request to tour *Raven*?" he asked.

"They did," Iyotake confirmed, a flash in his eyes suggesting that the conversation around the UPA's responsibilities in Kenmiri space wasn't over yet. "It's an entertainingly phrased response."

"Oh?" Henry asked.

"Admiral Hamilton managed to remind you that a tour of the ship is entirely at your discretion, recognize that you asked them for an opinion so they could say no, and give us a neat sound bite to provide to the Lord of Ten Thousand Miles," the XO replied. "The Admiral *suggests* that we not give any tours out here, in general."

"But it is my decision," Henry concluded. "By kicking it upstairs and letting Admiral Hamilton say no, however, we keep a potential channel with the Londu officer on the scene open."

"Like I said, she recognized that," Iyotake said with a chuckle. "Shall I have your staff talk to his staff, ser?"

"He offered me a tour of his ship even if I couldn't let him tour mine," *Raven*'s Captain replied. "Let's set that up. Todorovich thinks he's flirting with me *and* trying to establish a back channel." He snorted. "*I* think he's just trying to establish a back channel.

"Either way, we need to find out what the Lord of Ten Thousand Miles is about. And I'm not passing on a tour of one of the Londu's newest battleships!"

"Understood, ser. We'll get it set up. How soon?"

"First day of the talks, I think," Henry replied. "I suspect we'll both need the distraction."

CHAPTER TWENTY-SEVEN

THE COMMANDS TO THE HONOR GUARD WERE IN A LANGUAGE Henry Wong didn't understand, and the uniforms were vastly different from what he was used to...but the structure of the drill was entirely recognizable as a double file of Londu soldiers lined a pathway from his shuttle.

They wore a red version of the armored-robe dress uniform Lord of Ten Thousand Miles Kahlmor had worn to the party and held energy rifles in front of them, barrel tips resting on the floor in a formalized sign of nonaggression.

Henry gave the dozen soldiers a crisp salute and then made his way down the pathway to meet the Lord of Ten Thousand Miles himself. Like Henry, Kahlmor was wearing a slightly dressed-up version of his space duty uniform.

Where Henry's uniform was slacks and a turtleneck that could link together to act as a bodysuit, the Londu uniform was a perfectly fitted black bodysuit that linked into the iron collar of his rank. The soldiers were probably wearing a version of it under their robes, though Henry hoped it had climate-control functions, if that were the case.

In place of Henry's undress uniform jacket, Kahlmor wore a knee-length open white robe. It was held in place by a strip of metal on either side of the opening—and that metal bore the same inscriptions as Kahlmor's dress uniform breastplate.

"Lord of Ten Thousand Miles," Henry greeted his host with a salute. His Kem would serve today, a better choice than computer-translated Londu, he figured. "I appreciate your invitation aboard *Rigid Candor* and your flexibility."

"Your suggested time worked well for us both, I think, Colonel Wong," Kahlmor replied in the same language. "My Lord of Hundred Thousand Miles required my time yesterday. The number of ships here at the Gathering always raises concerns."

A Lord of Hundred Thousand Miles was more senior an officer than Henry would have expected to command the Londu escort, the equivalent of Vice Admiral Hamilton in the UPA. The Londu really had sent a detachment able to speak for the Scion and act on his behalf.

"It does," Henry agreed. "But we are all trusted allies here, are we not?"

"Allies, yes," Kahlmor confirmed. "But I imagine you are no more trusting of everyone here than I am. We shared an enemy once. Who we are now..."

"Is what the Gathering is meant to decide, isn't it?" Henry asked.

Kahlmor laughed.

"This is true," the Londu officer conceded. "Come, Colonel Wong. From your record, I presume beginning the tour with *Rigid Candor*'s starfighter bays is acceptable?"

"She is your ship, Lord of Ten Thousand Miles," Henry replied. "I will follow as you lead."

THE STARFIGHTER BAYS WERE IMPRESSIVE. If Henry had needed any reminder that *Rigid Candor* was almost twice the size of

Raven, the bays would have been enough. Where his ship had eight ships in individual cramped bays, *Rigid Candor* had twenty-five sharing ridiculously spacious working bays.

They only had five of those bays, though, with the starfighters themselves stored in a rotating magazine with an automatic system that delivered them into the bays for maintenance or rearming.

Henry made the appropriate appreciative noises at the system, a clever way to maximize the limited space any line warship could devote to its parasite missile platforms. Despite the lack of grav-shield, the Londu starfighters were otherwise extremely similar to the Dragoon. They had the same spherical shape to maximize the volume-to-armor ratio, similar divots for modular weapon systems, even similar-looking engines.

The Londu craft could accelerate at two KPS^2 to the Terran ships' one point five, though. They'd needed the extra maneuverability against the Kenmiri.

The former rulers of the region had never bothered with fighters, mostly because their lasers were *very* effective at shooting them down. Unfortunately for them, a living pilot at the controls added just enough randomness to make it worthwhile for many of the Vesheron powers.

And while the Kenmiri defenses could shoot down missiles and starfighters, they had serious problems trying to do both at the same time. Once the starfighters had launched, they were often allowed to escape—because a wing of a hundred starfighters put four hundred missiles into space. That would strain the missile defenses and energy screens of even Kenmiri dreadnoughts.

"Unfortunately, I have been advised that I am not allowed to show you our energy-screen projectors," Kahlmor told Henry. "Would you rather see our plasma cannon or the bridge?"

Henry chuckled. The UPA had enough samples of the Kenmiri version of the technology that they could readily duplicate it—if they ever found a way to make it compatible with the gravity shield. Since the UPA didn't deploy the system, though, he understood why the Londu might be protective of their version of it.

"I have seen a lot of Kenmiri plasma cannon. Are yours particularly different?" he asked.

"I would like to *think* so," Kahlmor replied. "We get the same power out of a somewhat smaller installation...but truthfully, I don't think they look that different, myself."

"The bridge, then, Lord of Ten Thousand Miles," Henry said. "It is always good to see the brain and beating heart of a warship, don't you agree?"

"Indeed," his host confirmed, gesturing for him to follow. "I always did love our starfighters, though I never flew one myself," Kahlmor continued as they left the bays. "They seemed a more... elegant system than yours. Requiring more skill to evade enemy fire than a ship that can just bull through on the strength of their gravity shield."

Kahlmor wasn't just talking about the starfighters, Henry knew. For all that *Rigid Candor* was twice *Raven*'s volume and three-quarters again her mass, *her* base safe acceleration was the same one KPS squared that Henry's ship could make only with every crew member and passenger in the acceleration tanks.

Of course, *Rigid Candor* didn't *have* any acceleration tanks, since her engines weren't capable of pushing her past about one point one KPS^2 and an attendant five pseudogravities of thrust.

"And it is not like you can even mount energy screens on a starfighter," Henry agreed with a smile. The defensive systems could significantly enhance a ship's survivability, shrugging off everything from lasers to the plasma blast of a conversion warhead...but they were massive installations, too big for anything smaller than a battleship to fit them aboard.

They had to pause the conversation to climb a ladder—Henry figured the Lord was taking him on the shortest route, which always led to visiting some entertaining portions of the ship, in his experience.

"Even energy screens do not allow the same cavalier behavior I've seen in your ships and fighters," Kahlmor told him as they approached a set of heavy security doors. The six-layer-deep armored bulkheads were open right now, but a pair of Londu soldiers in decidedly non-ceremonial armor stood outside them.

"I have watched your battlecruisers charge right through entire Kenmiri dreadnought groups, convinced of their own immortality," the Lord of Ten Thousand Miles continued. "Your shield is a powerful tool, but in everything I have seen of your people, they have used it as a replacement for actual skill in battle."

Stepping through the security door, Henry stopped at the top of the bridge and stared. He was confident he was concealing most of his outright awe, but he still had to just *look* at the massive space that controlled a Londu ship of the line.

From the entrance Henry stood at, a peninsular platform extended out into the middle of the bridge, hanging above the working spaces. The floor of the peninsula was transparent, allowing the Captain and his senior officers to look down and see what everyone was doing.

Stairs swept down to the left and right, allowing access to the neatly subdivided sections of the floor. There were at least a hundred individual stations on the floor beneath him—and the entire space in front of the command peninsula was taken up by an immense hologram.

He took a slightly deeper-than-normal breath and looked around again, trying to find the mundanity and weaknesses in the design. It was awe-inspiring, yes, but it could easily hurt crew morale—and *necks*—to have to literally look up at the command staff. It wouldn't help that the lower level resembled nothing so much as an array of office cubicles, where the data-entry drones happened to be doing data entry on missiles and starships instead of transactions and assets.

Plus, there was a reason the UPA didn't use holographic projectors on their ships. They were inherently fragile things. It didn't matter how much better Londu tech was, a few solid hits to the warship would knock out the big display.

And a Londu battleship was supposed to be able to *take* those solid hits and keep fighting.

"Impressive, is it not?" Kahlmor asked. "Come, Colonel. Follow me."

Henry obeyed, following his host out onto the clear peninsula. Now that he was standing on it he could see the support struts linking it to the roof, the floor and the surrounding walls. It was still a structural vulnerability, even as it required the bridge to take up precious volume that could have been used for magazine space for easily forty or fifty missiles.

He had to admit, though, that it gave Kahlmor as thorough a view of what everyone on the bridge was up to as his own double-sided screens. And the holodisplay allowed for a spectacular view of the star system around him.

"Were you suggesting, Lord of Ten Thousand Miles, that your crews are inherently more skilled than UPA crews?" he asked, delicately picking up the challenge that Kahlmor had laid down.

The Londu officer grinned brilliantly.

"It follows logically, does it not?" he asked. "Your officers rely on the security provided by the gravity shield. It allows them to take their maneuvers more slowly, to miss shots because they know they will get a second one. Those of us without such systems, well, we must become better if we are to survive."

Henry could tell when he was being set up, but he could also see the value in what he was being set up *for*.

"That sounds, Lord Kahlmor, like something we should put to the test," he noted softly. "A test of maneuvering and gunnery, perhaps? Skills that would atrophy aboard my ship, according to your logic.

"We would need to arrange an environment where your ship's acceleration advantage would be irrelevant as well," he continued.

"Since it may well be that *your* crew relies on speed to escape what we must face."

Kahlmor grinned and stepped up to the main command seat on *Rigid Candor*'s bridge. It was practically a throne, but the arms were inlaid with the same kinds of controls Henry had on his own ship.

The Lord of Ten Thousand Miles tapped one of those commands, and the hologram of the star system in front of them zoomed in...on Resta's massive asteroid belt.

"The belt would provide much of that environment, would it not?" he asked. "If we have our hosts lay out an obstacle course and arrange the deployment of gunnery targets, neither of us would have an unfair advantage. I think we could both trust them to arrange a fair contest?"

Henry wasn't certain his ship was ready to be put up against the best of the Londu Blades of the Scion. He had good people, he knew that, but he'd had mere weeks to pull them together. *Rigid Candor*'s crew hummed around him with the calm confidence of a crew that had worked together for months or even years.

"We can certainly trust the Restan for that," he said aloud. "Surely, though, there must be *some* kind of wager for a contest like this."

They couldn't *officially* wager "biggest dick in the dick-measuring contest that is the Gathering escorts," after all.

"I have a flat of covilla liqueur in my mess deck stocks," Kahlmor replied. "I think two hundred bottles should suffice for your entire crew to sample my Scion's preferred drink?"

"It should," Henry agreed. "I think we can manage to counter that with a thousand bottles of Earth wine. Ambassador Todorovich adores it."

That was easily half the stock of wine aboard *Raven*, but he hadn't thought to come prepared for this kind of challenge. The crew would just have to win.

"Done," Kahlmor agreed. "We will have the Restan set it up, and in a few days, we shall see just who truly has the better crews!"

"So we shall," Henry murmured.

"And just so you know what we are offering, I have arranged for covilla liqueur to be served with dinner," the Lord of Ten Thousand Miles told him. "Which should be ready by the time we reach my dining room."

"Lead on, Lord Kahlmor," the UPA officer replied. "I look forward to it."

CHAPTER TWENTY-EIGHT

HENRY DRANK SPARINGLY AT THE BEST OF TIMES, AND A PRIVATE dinner with an untrusted ally captain was *not* that. Covilla liqueur was extremely pleasant, with the fire he associated with spiced drinks but far smoother than any Terran-made drink he'd had with that heat.

Nonetheless, he was still stone-cold sober when he returned aboard *Raven* and promptly downloaded the entire recording of his trip aboard *Rigid Candor* for review. Most likely, only Intelligence would go through it unless there was reason to think he'd acted inappropriately, but just having it on file was a shield against accusations of colluding with the enemy.

And would make Admiral Kosigan's Intelligence wonks happy, a good thing on its own.

"Iyotake, meet me in my office," he ordered as he left the shuttle bay. He'd been gone for less than four hours this time, so no one was officially greeting him aboard. "Get a secured subspace link to the Ambassador as well.

"I need to brief you both on what I just agreed to—risks and benefits alike."

The channel was silent for several seconds.

"I'll make sure of it, sure," Iyotake replied. "Just...just what did you do?"

"I committed us to a gunnery and maneuvering contest against *Rigid Candor*," Henry explained. "We're betting wine against liqueur, quantities sufficient for the entire crew of each ship."

"Do we *have* that much wine?" his XO asked.

"I'll have to check, but I'm pretty sure I put up half of our mess stock," the Captain answered calmly. "So, let's make sure we don't lose. Set up that call, XO. I'll see you in five."

He was in his office by that point and poured a pair of coffees. He'd just finished adding the XO's preferred mix to the other man's cup when Iyotake arrived.

"Coffee?" he asked.

"Please." Iyotake took the cup. "I know you know how much of a headache you just dropped on me. How much alcohol is in this?"

"None right now. How much would you like?"

"He doesn't get any," Ambassador Todorovich's voice cut in, and both men looked up as her holographic image settled in in the corner of the room. "He's going to need his head clear for dealing with this."

"A bet, Captain? Why does this sound like a terrible idea?"

"Because it is one," Henry confirmed. "It's also a brilliant idea. Which it ends up being depends on whether we win, lose or draw. Putting all context aside, the contest itself lets us assess our skills against the Londu's best.

"That has value, both in motivating the crew and in helping the UPSF assess where we stand against one of the other major powers of the Vesheron."

"Context, Captain Wong, is often everything," Todorovich pointed out. "I'm not seeing the context for this as particularly good."

"It isn't," he agreed. "But it also is. We all know the main reason everyone brought the biggest and baddest warships they could spare here is because the escorts are a dick-measuring contest." He shook his head. "There's a hundred ambassadors on that station that either came on unarmed ships or hitched a ride on somebody else's warship.

They know damn well they're getting automatically dumped to the bottom of the list.

"Everyone is looking to the ambassadors who showed up with the biggest guns. Right now, ignoring the Restan, who have the advantage of being the hosts, that's the Londu, who showed up with a battle group; the Drifters, because everyone is terrified of guardians; and us...because everyone knows that *Raven* could take the massed firepower of every other ship here and have a decent chance of not even *noticing*.

"So, if we and the Londu throw down in a formal contest intended to judge not who has the better *ship* but the better *crew*, that changes the balance. Whichever one of us wins that contest has more weight to throw behind their words."

He smiled thinly.

"Am I wrong, Ambassador?"

"No," she confirmed. "Do you know how much influence we'll lose if you lose?"

"Enough to put us solidly behind the Drifters in the diplomatic weight game," he guessed. "But given that all we really need is to walk out of here without committing warships..."

"I'd rather have the weight to smother some of the likely conflicts before it's over," Todorovich told him. "My hopes for any kind of long-term balancing organization out of this meeting are shrinking by the minute."

"I don't plan on losing," Henry said. "I'm not expecting to win, either, if I'm being honest, but I figure we can at least bring Kahlmor to a draw with even honors."

"That'll help us more than it hurts, I suppose," she conceded. "But I can tell you now, Henry, it's going to be hard enough to get anything done here as it is. Losing influence because of some military game..."

"I think Kahlmor is playing on more than one level, too," Henry pointed out. "He suggested going into the asteroid belt. Once we have a location, I'm going to take a closer look at it. The nature of the exercise will require a relatively dense chunk of the belt...probably chock full of radioactives."

"He just had you aboard his ship," Todorovich reminded him. "If he wanted to have a private conversation, he could have done it then."

"We're on an encrypted subspace call with two of us in the same room and you in a white-noise field," he replied. "Even so, what do you think the odds are that no one in this system is listening in?"

The silence he got *was* his answer.

"I don't know if that's the game Kahlmor is playing. Even just aiming to beat us in the contest could be played multiple ways, depending on Saunt's plans," he noted. "Either way, I think we had to take the bet. We need the Londu to respect us, and subtle as the challenge was, I think we'd have lost some critical points with them if I'd dodged it."

"Probably," Todorovich conceded. "And you've done it, anyway. I'll talk to the Under-Speaker and get things rolling."

"Then I need to go warn the crew," Iyotake said. "They'd be rather upset to discover they lost their wine stock because they weren't fast enough or sharp enough, so I figure it'll be a handy motivational tool."

He smiled wickedly.

"*They* don't need to know we're only aiming for a draw, after all!"

AFTER THE XO WITHDREW, Henry turned his attention back to Todorovich. With only the two of them on the call now, her hologram was showing more of her fatigue than it had before.

"You all right, Sylvia?" he asked. "I hope this contest isn't adding that much to your workload."

"God, no, not really," she admitted. "Ten hours, Henry. I just sat through ten hours of the official Gathering, and my hopes of getting anything actually done here are disintegrating.

"Everybody is getting to speak. Opening remarks of twenty to *seventy* minutes apiece. We're up to a hundred and seventy-five ambassadors, with nineteen more expected in the next three days."

That was a week of ten-hour days, even with the shorter speeches.

"Better you than me, Sylvia," he concluded. "I might have shot someone already today."

She shook her head and sighed.

"We'll get through it, and it's not like no business gets discussed around the opening remarks," she said. "I mean, we got something resolved today!"

Her tone was a warning, but he picked up the trap anyway. He figured she needed him to spring it.

"It didn't sound like the day was that productive," he noted. "What did you get resolved?"

"That we won't call the Kenmiri provinces that anymore," Todorovich said bitterly. "*That* took an hour of debate. In Kem. Since the Kenmiri no longer rule them, we can no longer call them provinces.

"Of course, since those five hundred star divisions have been in play for between sixty and *three hundred* years, we're still going to *use* them. We're just going to call them sectors instead of provinces now."

She snorted.

"So, now Resta is in the Geb *Sector* instead of the Geb Province. This was very important, you see, for people to get sorted out."

"I see," he acknowledged, while making a note to have the not-quite-useless change included in the morning briefing for his Kem speakers and the translator programmers. "It's not meaningless, I suppose."

"No, but it wasn't worth an hour's debate with the core diplomats of two hundred Vesheron and El-Vesheron factions present," she told him. "Though, let's be fair, getting something through a hundred and seventy-five diplomats in an hour is a miracle. *Eto piz'dets.*

"I met Kal Rojan, at least," she continued. "Man has dead eyes, even for a Kozun. I'm pretty sure he was seriously planning on killing the four-eyed *mu'dak* nattering on about the Kem etymology of the word *province*."

Henry had *never* heard Sylvia Todorovich degrade into Russian profanity. It was probably a good sign that she was relaxed enough to do that around him, but still...

"Is it that bad, Sylvia?"

"Probably worse," she told him. "I'm blowing off steam because I *can*, Henry, but unless we start semi-officially dismissing half of the ambassadors as meaningless or breaking out into committees, this Gathering is going nowhere quickly."

"How would you run it?" he asked.

She snorted.

"Honestly? *Short* opening remarks, then split into committees," she admitted. "I'd *maybe* put some restriction over who was a big-enough deal to get opening remarks in the first place, but the Restan aren't too far off what I'd do yet.

"We'll see how it goes," she concluded. "Thanks for letting me rant, Henry."

"I'm here to support your mission any way I can," he told her.

"I appreciate it," she replied. "But, Colonel Wong?"

"Yes, Em Ambassador?" he answered, matching the formality of her tone.

"Kick Kahlmor's ass in this contest of yours. It would make *my* life a lot easier."

CHAPTER TWENTY-NINE

HENRY'S SENIOR OFFICERS LOOKED AT THE HOLOGRAPHIC IMAGE hanging in the middle of the room in a shared uncomfortable silence.

"Let's run down the numbers, shall we?" Ihejirika said, his voice surprisingly calm as the tactical officer looked around the room at his compatriots. "*Rigid Candor* is roughly four hundred and eighty meters long and two hundred wide, massing approximately four megatons when fully fueled and armed."

The width was somewhat deceptive as it was from the widest point, and the ship was a rough, flattened teardrop shape. It was much like *Raven* in that sense, though the battlecruiser's wings were narrower than the battleship's flared-out engineering section.

"She has an acceleration capacity of up to one point one KPS squared but can easily maintain a full KPS squared with full inertial dampening," Ihejirika continued, his voice edging toward dry from its base of calm. "Her primary armament is six heavy plasma turrets of a version notably superior to that of the Kenmiri, backed by missile launchers, heavy lasers and twenty-five starfighters.

"She is one of the most advanced ships of the Londu Blades of the Scion. And we're supposed to beat her in a competition. What are we competing on? Taking a hit?"

"With her armor and energy screens, she's not much worse at that than we are," Henry replied. "For the first few hits, at least. It's probably relevant that while *Rigid Candor* is one of their more advanced ships, she's only middling in size for a battleship."

He smiled coldly.

"I have every confidence that this ship could destroy *Rigid Candor* in a straight fight," he continued. "The question is whether we can *perform* better than her in a contest. A contest, I remind everyone, that is supposed to be structured to even out our various advantages."

The conference room was silent again.

"How exactly are they going to *even out* the fact that *Candor* has twice our acceleration?" Bazzoli finally asked, the navigator staring blankly into space at a set of data only she could see. "There aren't that many clusters dense enough to even that out in the galaxy, let alone in the system."

"My understanding is that the Restan will be placing a series of navigation beacons through the cluster we'll be exercising in," Henry told her. "We will need to approach each beacon at a specific vector, ping it with a tightbeam from within one thousand kilometers and proceed to the next beacon.

"Without hitting any of the beacons."

She grunted.

"Tight quarters and specific maneuvers make up some of the difference," she conceded. "But they're still going to have the advantage unless we send the crew to the tanks."

"So we send the crew to the tanks," Iyotake suggested. "We can match her gee for gee if we seal ourselves in the tanks and juice up."

Henry grimaced.

"I hesitate to ask the crew to take acceleration drugs for a contest," he replied. "Plus, we'll lose a small but critical edge on the *gunnery* part of the contest if the crew is in acceleration tanks or coming down off the drugs.

"Bazzoli, *can* you do it without the crew in the tanks?" he asked the navigator.

"You're asking the impossible, ser," she complained.

"I know. If it was merely very difficult, I wouldn't be asking," Henry told her.

"They have twice our acceleration," she repeated. "That's twice our velocity change. Twice our maneuverability. Easily twice our speed averaged over any open stretch. We're a bit more agile, we can change our thrust vector about thirty percent faster than they can, but that's it."

Henry studied the battleship in the hologram again.

"I suppose we could ask them to limit their acceleration to keep it a fair contest between crews instead of between the ships' engines," he murmured.

Bazzoli sighed.

"I'll do what I can, ser, and I know I can fly rings around *any* Londu helmswoman," she told him. "But the odds are against us."

"We'll deal with what comes," Henry said. "So long as everyone is okay with having to drink beer on the way back home, anyway."

"I'm less worried about the gunnery portion," Ihejirika told them. "That's a straight accuracy test for the main weapons. From what the Restan sent me, there's a time *limit* but not a time score. Which makes sense, given that they have *six* main guns and we have one."

"And our main gun would gut *Rigid Candor* where her main guns would tickle us," Henry replied. "You can outshoot them?"

"I can bull's-eye a mosquito buzzing around your ranch on Earth from Mars orbit," Ihejirika boasted. "I think we can manage a few dead-center hits to even up the contest."

Henry had to swallow a wince at the mental image from the boast.

"Let's not bull's-eye mosquitos with cee-fractional weapons, shall we?" he suggested. "Perfect shots on the target drones, though, those I'll take. Some will be immobile; some will be moving and evading."

"We can handle that," the tactical officer promised. "Plasma guns aren't precision weapons. A good crew can achieve incredible things with them...but I *know* my crew can do better with the grav-driver."

"Good," Iyotake replied. "Because I don't know about the rest of the crew, but I *hate* beer and I don't want to have to give these bastards our wine!"

THE OTHER OFFICERS dispersed to try to motivate and corral their teams for the mission ahead of them, leaving Henry and Iyotake sitting in the room, staring at the hologram of the Londu battleship.

"I don't think there's a question that we could take her in a straight fight," Henry said quietly. He drew a line in space with his hand. Two of the six heavy plasma turrets were on the tip of the teardrop, both opening up arcs of fire and protecting the ship from potential blowback from the powerful weapons.

A single grav-driver strike with a kinetic armor-penetrating round would shatter the spine of the battleship and send a third of her heavy firepower spinning off into space. Missiles with conversion warheads would keep the lasers engaged while they used further AP rounds from the grav-driver to disable the energy screens.

Once the energy screens were done, conversion rounds from the grav-driver would finish the job. It wouldn't be quick or clean, but *Rigid Candor* was a battleship. It was designed to survive.

The tactics would be familiar to Lord of Ten Thousand Miles Kahlmor, too. They were the same ones he would have seen *Jaguar*-class battlecruisers use against Kenmiri dreadnoughts.

The UPSF had a lot of practice at killing other people's capital ships.

"Killing the people we want to work with is generally frowned upon," Iyotake replied. "So, we play a game and see who wins. I think one of the most interesting parts of this is going to be how the Restan set up the contest."

"Oh?"

"They have a pretty good idea of the limits and advantages of each of our ships," the XO noted. "Energy screens are at their worst at stopping physical objects, where the grav-shield is at its best against them. We can fly through a meteor shower or debris cluster without blinking.

"Kahlmor can't. On the other hand, as Commander Bazzoli pointed out, he's far better off at a straight sprint than we are. It's a similar story with the gunnery contest. They have more lightspeed or near-lightspeed weapons than we do. Depending on how they set up that time limit Ihejirika mentioned, they could leave us in a position where we can't use the grav-driver on every target."

"That wouldn't be that much of a disadvantage," Henry argued. "Ihejirika and his people are *good* with the lasers."

In simulations, at least...

"The lasers are new, though," his XO replied. "The Restan don't know how good we are with them, but they know we're going to be deadly with the grav-driver.

"As the hosts, they're setting the terms of engagement, which means they can very easily tilt the entire contest toward one of us." Iyotake studied the battleship's hologram and tugged on his braid.

"I think that whether they do so—and *who* they tilt it toward if they do—is going to be fascinating."

"I won't be feeling quite so fascinated if we actually *lose* this, XO," Henry noted. "Winning opens doors for our Ambassador. Losing may close them. I'd rather *not* have Todorovich more pissed at me than she already is."

"Now, that, ser, I understand completely!"

CHAPTER THIRTY

THE TWO SHIPS ACCELERATED AWAY FROM THE GATHERING IN close company. Closer, really, than Henry was comfortable with. He appreciated Kahlmor keeping his ship's acceleration down to *Raven*'s standard 0.3 KPS^2 for the trip, but it made his neck itch to have another capital ship within thirty thousand kilometers.

Of course, given the setup of the ships around Gathering Station, his neck had a lot of practice at itching of late.

"Turnover in an hour," Bazzoli reported. "Arrival at our destination two hours after that. There's a pair of Restan destroyers hanging out by the cluster we're heading for. I'm guessing they're our adjudicators?"

"Either that or the Restan are going to take advantage of this opportunity to stab us in the back with a dramatically insufficient force," Henry replied. The Restan ships were rough equivalents to the Kenmiri escorts, with missiles and heavy lasers, and while they could probably damage *Rigid Candor* or *Raven*, they'd need complete surprise to seriously threaten either ship.

"We're receiving a transmission from them," Moon reported. "Looks like an entry point and a timeline. They're suggesting that

Rigid Candor push their turnover and deceleration slightly and arrive ten minutes before us."

"Let them go first?" Henry asked. "Makes as much sense as anything. They can get there faster."

"Plus, if we go first and bull our way through a debris field, we clear a path for them to follow," Iyotake noted. "Commander Ihejirika, can you double-check this? CIC is picking up some heat trails inside the cluster that don't link up to the destroyers."

"Looks like civilian shipping," the tactical officer replied. "Mining ships that were ordered to clear out to safe the area."

"I'll run that by CIC, but it makes sense," the XO agreed. "That's about what I figured, but I wanted a second check in case they looked like warship signatures to you."

"Not even close," Ihejirika replied.

Henry was pulling up the data and double-checking to assuage his own paranoia, and he had to agree. The signatures were at least a day and a half old and too weak to have been warships. They were too old to have been helping the Restan set up the contest, but the timeline was about right for them to have been ordered to clear the area after it had been picked.

"Kahlmor has agreed to go first," Moon reported. "He wants a channel to you, ser."

"Link him to my network," Henry agreed.

The channel clicked into his head, and an image of the Lord of Ten Thousand Miles appeared in front of him.

"We are going to leave you behind here, Colonel Wong," he said in Kem. "*Rigid Candor* will be first to the challenge, but I'm sure you will do more than merely follow in our trail. Good luck, Colonel.

"May the best crew win."

"And good luck to your people as well, Lord of Ten Thousand Miles," Henry replied. "May the best crew win."

RAVEN HIT TURNOVER, flipping in space to shed velocity as they headed toward the entrance point. *Rigid Candor* kept going for several more minutes before mirroring the motion, decelerating slightly harder to make sure she reached the designated spot ten minutes early.

The Restan destroyers were the markers of the beginning of the course, but *Raven's* sensors were starting to pick up hints of the beacons hidden inside the cluster.

"That is a *mess* for sensors," Ihejirika exclaimed. "I should be able to see the entire cluster, but the radioactivity is so bad, I can only see the outskirts."

"Is there a chance this is an ambush?" Henry asked. No wonder the cluster had shed mining ships after the order had been given. There were enough radioactives in those asteroids to fuel Resta's munitions industry for at least a century.

"There's *always* a chance," the tactical officer replied. "I'm sure I'd be picking up any actual ships inside the cluster, though, plus we'd see heat trails from their drives if they'd entered anytime in the last week or two."

"How *sure* is 'sure'?" Henry asked. "This is what I was expecting, but I didn't expect it to be *quite* that jammed."

"Seventy percent," Ihejirika admitted. "Maybe seventy-five. Our hypothetical ambush would have to have known we were going to be having this contest in this particular location weeks ago, though."

"That would only require that the Londu and the Restan be working together," Henry replied. "I've heard much worse conspiracy theories."

Ahead of them, *Rigid Candor's* velocity dropped to zero at the entrance point. The battleship hung immobile in space, a half-kilometer-long lump of iron and technology.

In another time and another place, the Londu would have been the UPA's enemies. An expansionist semi-totalitarian monarchy, they made for unlikely allies at best. In the face of an expansionist polity that controlled ten thousand stars and enslaved entire races to fuel their industry, the Londu had been the lesser evil.

Suddenly, Henry found himself questioning if he *trusted* them. If they were working with the Resta, luring him into close range of *Rigid Candor* inside an area no one in the star system could see would be a perfect trap.

He chuckled at his own paranoia.

"Of course, ambushing us when everyone *knows* that we're in a contest with the Londu that we had the Restan organize would make both of them look bad at what's supposed to be a diplomatic conference," he said aloud. "I don't think it would serve either of their goals, so we're just borrowing trouble, aren't we?"

"Probably, ser," his tactical officer conceded. There was a silent pause. "*Rigid Candor* has commenced the course. They are entering the cluster at point seven KPS squared at vector thirty-six by seventy-nine."

"All right. Track her as long as you can see her," Henry ordered. "Feed everything you see to Bazzoli. If we have to outfly the big bastard, let's see just what they got up to."

THEY LOST track of *Rigid Candor* well before they reached the entry point themselves, a disturbing reminder of how radioactive the region they were going to be maneuvering in was.

Bazzoli stopped *Raven* in the exact same spot that the Londu battleship had been stopped, and the bridge crew eyed the designated path with wary eyes.

"I'm picking up beacons marking themselves as one, two, and three," Ihejirik noted. "No debris fields or anything that *Candor* couldn't have flown through. Tight turns and tight spaces, but clear flying."

About as even between the two ships as possible, then. It seemed fair enough so far.

"XO, is the ship prepped for thrust?" he asked.

"We are prepped," Iyotake confirmed. "All loose objects are secure and crew are strapped in."

It wasn't the same as putting everyone in the tanks, but it would buy them four pseudogravities of thrust. That would give Bazzoli another tenth of a KPS squared to work with.

"Transmission from the Restan destroyer," Moon reported.

"On the main screen," Henry ordered.

"*Raven*, this is Lesser-Ship-Voice Nad Ahlane," a dark-skinned Restan officer introduced herself in slightly choppy Kem. "Are you picking up the first course beacon?"

"We are, Lesser-Ship-Voice," Henry responded. "And at least one past that."

"That is positive," she confirmed. "There are thirty-six beacons positioned in the cluster, following a course that will bring you to the gunnery area at the center, where a dozen drones await you. Points will be assessed for speed of your journey through the cluster and closeness of approach to the beacons. Points will be removed for the destruction of any beacon.

"Once you reach the center, you have six minutes to destroy all twelve drones. Points will be assessed for accuracy in terms of both missed shots and proximity to center of mass on the drones.

"Good luck, Colonel Wong."

He inclined his hands.

"Thank you, Lesser-Ship-Voice. Are we clear to begin?" he asked.

"The timer will begin on the activation of your engines. Carry on, *Raven*."

The channel closed and Henry smiled beatifically at his crew.

"Ladies and gentlemen, the flag has dropped. Make it happen."

Bazzoli had been waiting for the order. Thrust pressed Henry back into his seat as she took the battlecruiser's massive engines from zero to sixty percent in under three seconds. Four large men settled onto his chest, but *Raven* flung herself forward.

"First beacon contact in forty-two seconds," Ihejirika reported, his voice not audibly impacted by the acceleration.

"We'll change vector seven seconds before that," Bazzoli said aloud. "Inertia will take us within ten kilometers of the first beacon as we burn for the second."

Henry didn't even nod in response. This was Bazzoli's chance to shine, and the navigator had control of the ship. They were going to win this or lose this on her skill...and on whether or not the Restan had left any places in the course where a willingness to plow through debris would save them time.

"Beacon one tagged," the report came half a minute later. "Closest approach, seven point one kilometers."

Beacon two's closest approach was at eleven kilometers seventy seconds later, as *Raven* contorted in space toward beacon three.

"I've got four and five on the scopes," Ihejirika reported. "Feeding them to the nav console."

Henry was already watching everything Bazzoli did on the two-sided screen. The new icons popped up, and he suppressed a moment of frustration as he saw them. So far, all of this was clear space. The tight turns required to keep the sequence going were slightly to *Raven*'s advantage, but he wasn't seeing anything that wouldn't let *Rigid Candor*'s greater acceleration carry them forward faster.

Beacons six and seven popped onto the screen as Bazzoli whipped them around beacon three at barely *two* kilometers. They were separated by a lengthy stretch of open space, exactly the kind of stretch that would give the Londu an advantage.

He had to admit, though, that Bazzoli was *terrifying*. The sheer skill with which she danced a two-million-ton battlecruiser through the obstacles on the course was mind-boggling. Each beacon after two was tagged from less than ten kilometers away as she tried to score points for proximity.

More beacons appeared on the screens and *Raven* wove her way through the course. It was, he had to admit, mostly a fair course.

There was the stretch between six and seven that took *Raven* four minutes and had probably taken *Rigid Candor* half that, but the rest was the kind of tight turns and maneuvers where helm skill made all the difference.

By the time they spotted the eye of the storm, though, he knew how things had shaken out. *Rigid Candor* was waiting in the clearing at the center of the cluster...and the only drones on the scanners were tagged for *Raven*.

They had at least five minutes left of the course, which meant that the Londu ship had probably cleared the course at least twelve minutes or more before.

Despite Bazzoli's skill, *Raven* had clearly lost the maneuvering portion of the contest.

"Ihejirika," Henry said softly.

"Yes, ser?"

"The contest screwed us on the maneuvering, but they *can't* do that on the gunnery." He smiled coldly. "Bazzoli did a fantastic job. Match *her* and we'll remind the Londu why they should be damn happy they can outrun us."

⁂

RAVEN DECELERATED all of the way into the clearing from the final beacon, reducing her velocity to less than a tenth of a kilometer per second by the time the drones registered her as being in the zone and sent their active signals.

Henry mentally cataloged the drones as they came online. Four were immobile targets, sitting ducks for whatever Ihejirika chose to hit them with. Six were maneuvering at various rates, ranging from 0.1 KPS^2 all the way up to one accelerating at the 10 KPS^2 of a missile.

The last two were maneuvering *and* were running some of the nastiest electronic countermeasures he'd seen in recent years. In his mental list of targets, those were the last ones he'd have fired at—better to remove the easy targets first, after all.

So, of course, Ihejirika shot them first. *Raven's* heavy lasers spoke before her main gun, the power-capacitor icons on the screens losing a third of their contents as the beams flashed out.

Maneuvering or not, ECM or not, those drones died instantly to direct hits—and then Ihejirika truly set to work.

The first grav-driver shot was a conversion round that managed to take out two of the immobile targets. The second finished the other unmoving drones off, while the lasers took out four of the dodging drones in the same time period.

There was a moment after the second conversion round, then the lasers fired one last time.

Twelve drones had taken two grav-driver rounds and eight laser shots...in under ninety seconds.

"Course complete," Ihejirika purred. "I show the clearing as complete. Just us and *Rigid Candor*."

"We are receiving an encrypted tightbeam from *Candor*," Moon reported. "Really?" she asked in credulousness at what she'd just said. "We're a thousand klicks from them and behind a nearly solid wall of uranium asteroids. *Encrypted tightbeam?*"

"Link encryption protocols and send it to my network," Henry ordered. "Let's not critique our allies' paranoia, people. I was expecting something like this."

"Colonel Wong," the image of Kahlmor greeted him as it appeared. "Your gunners are...impressive."

"I believe *terrifying* might be the word you are looking for, Lord of Ten Thousand Miles," the UPA Captain suggested.

The Londu chuckled.

"Perhaps," he conceded. "I will leave it to the umpires to decide when we deliver the data to them, but I believe this contest has been a draw. We took the maneuvering, but you have handily outshot us."

"And that is not why you are talking to me on an encrypted

implant-to-implant channel," Henry pointed out. "This far out, I don't believe we could get more secure."

"We can," Kahlmor said calmly. "And we must. I ask that you meet me on a shuttle between our ships, Colonel Wong. There are... discussions between us that should be private. And even here, I do not trust computers or radio to be safe."

"Very well," Henry agreed.

The Londu seemed almost taken aback.

"I expected more argument," he admitted.

"I expected this," Henry told him. "We each bring a shuttle to the exact midpoint. But we meet on *my* shuttle, understood?"

"A fair request," Kahlmor conceded. "It shall be done."

The channel cut and Henry shook his head.

"XO? Get a shuttle prepped for me. I'm meeting our friend in person in the middle of nowhere."

"Why?" Iyotake asked. "That's *insane*."

"No. It's the Scion wanting to talk to the UPA without anyone else knowing the details," Henry said grimly. "He's sent a man he trusts, but the Scion hesitates to trust even his own crew."

He shook his head.

"We pulled a draw, so we get to keep the wine," he noted. "I would bet *all* of it that Ambassador Saunt is aboard that shuttle."

"Like I said, ser, I *like* wine," his XO replied. "I'm not losing it on a sucker bet!"

CHAPTER THIRTY-ONE

LIEUTENANT COLONEL IYOTAKE'S WINE SUPPLY WOULD HAVE been safe, it turned out. Henry had agreed with his XO that it was a sucker bet, but when the two shuttles linked airlocks in the middle of the eye of the asteroid cluster, only Lord of Ten Thousand Miles Kahlmor crossed over.

Without maneuvering, Henry was wearing mag-boots to remain locked to the shuttle deck. The Londu shuttle had artificial gravity, but the UPA's version of the tech was too finicky to easily install in that small of a ship.

The systems aboard the shuttle could compensate thrust to allow the craft to accelerate at half a kilometer per second squared, but they couldn't provide gravity while the shuttle wasn't accelerating.

The lack clearly surprised Kahlmor, and he nearly overbalanced and fell into the ship before Henry grabbed his arm.

"Here." He passed the other man a pair of mag-boots.

"You are the masters of gravity technology among the Vesheron, yet your shuttle lacks artificial gravity?" the Lord of Ten Thousand Miles replied in Kem. He put on the boots regardless, and based on the ease with which he locked himself to the floor, the tall Londu man wasn't unfamiliar with the concept.

"Creating a basic gravity field with a device that can fit in the free space in a shuttle that has to match her mothership's acceleration is a very different project than projecting a gravity shear with enough tidal force to deflect a laser," Henry said. "Our gravity technology is rather...focused."

It also wasn't true that the UPSF *couldn't* put artificial gravity in their shuttles. They'd chosen to spend that mass and cubage else-where. Most of the time, after all, a shuttle was either in motion or in someone else's gravity field.

"And that focus has made you among the most powerful of the Vesheron," Kahlmor replied. "Which is why I am here."

"I will admit, I expected Ambassador Saunt," Henry said as he led the way into the shuttle's main space. The crew were sealed in the cockpit and they were alone. His network was recording every-thing he saw and heard, as were the shuttle systems, but those were the only recordings of what was happening.

And even the shuttle crew didn't have access to those cameras right now. The shuttle's passenger space was probably the most secure meeting space Henry had ever been in.

"This is not a matter for ambassadors and diplomats," Kahlmor told him. "This is to be between soldiers, between commanders who have fought the same enemy and know the limits of each other's ships and crews."

"That sounds intimidating, Lord of Ten Thousand Miles," Henry said calmly.

"This is a time for clear honesty," the Londu officer replied. "We have arranged this moment of complete security so that you and I can discuss what is to come now that the Kenmiri are no longer a factor."

"We keep assuming that," *Raven's* Captain noted. "Has anyone asked the Kenmiri what they think of no longer being a factor?"

"They have abandoned almost seven thousand stars to their fates. The remnants of their empire have a lifetime measured in decades at most, but even those remnants have retreated entirely from twelve sectors.

"The Kenmiri remnant will cause problems in the future, but we must establish the fate of those abandoned stars now."

"That is what the Gathering is about, is it not?" Henry asked. "That's what those diplomats and ambassadors are discussing."

"My Scion has committed vast resources to this war," Kahlmor replied softly. "He will demand his price now, and I must know whether the UPA will fight us."

And there it was. The flat question of whether the United Planets Alliance would fight the Londu for the other Vesheron. Henry *knew* that answer. He didn't like it, but he knew it—and he knew it wasn't his place to give it.

"That is a question for ambassadors, I think," he said, slowly and carefully to make sure his intent transferred across languages. Fluent as everyone sent to the Gathering was in Kem, it was still a barrier that everyone was negotiating in a second language.

"And the answer will depend on what price the Scion desires," he admitted.

"The sector you call Isis," Kahlmor said. "All of it."

Henry stared in silence for several seconds, even his control of his emotions and expressions broken by that shock.

"That is *five hundred star systems*," he replied. "At least sixty inhabited worlds. There are over a dozen ambassadors here at the Gathering from those systems. You lack the ships and the soldiers to secure five hundred stars."

"Not all at once, no," Kahlmor agreed. "Some of those worlds have already agreed to join us voluntarily. Others will kneel if the rest of the Vesheron will not support their stand. And if Terra stands aside, the rest of the Vesheron will not fight us without you."

Henry knew the UPA was prepared to surrender the hundred star systems they'd expected the Scion to chase. To...well, to betray their allies in those systems, if he was going to be honest with himself.

But to freely yield five hundred star systems and somewhere in the region of eighty *billion* sapient beings to an expansionist empire...

"I cannot answer that question, Lord of Ten Thousand Miles," he told the Londu.

"You hesitate, Colonel Wong," Kahlmor suggested. "We both know that the Isis Sector will fall to the Blades of the Scion. The Vesheron here, the non-Vesheron scraps in Isis, they lack the ships and the will to stand against us.

"And if we do not secure the sector, those five hundred stars and sixty worlds will descend into chaos and anarchy. If those worlds yield without a fight, they will only benefit from our rule," the soldier continued. "You have already seen this on your journey here. Without the Kenmiri to stand against, the Vesheron will shatter. This Gathering will fail. The strong must maintain order or the weak will suffer.

"The diplomats can phrase it how they wish, but you and I? We are soldiers. We understand that there must be ships and warriors to guard the innocent from the evil. Scattered and disunified, a few honorable Vesheron squadrons cannot turn back the night. Only *governments* and *fleets* can replace the Kenmiri Empire in providing peace.

"Here, the Restan will do it. In Apophis, Trintar. Ra? You, I presume. But Isis has no home for the Vesheron, no government already risen from the ashes to command their loyalty and shape their power to the betterment of all people."

Henry shook himself.

"You would replace one foreign ruler and enslaver with another," he pointed out. "There is providing security for a region, and there is *conquering* it...and your Scion clearly plans the latter."

"It is the price we must demand," Kahlmor said softly. "And I must know, Colonel Wong, if I should expect that you and I will meet across the field of battle. Here? Now? This is not a question of price. We both know that the UPA's support would turn the tide of what my Scion wants.

"Your aid would bring a dozen worlds to bend the knee without bloodshed. Save tens of thousands of lives. My Scion's orders are clear: your Ambassador may name her price. But we must know your answer."

"If it were up to me, we would defy you," Henry finally said. "Were it *my* will, you would face our fleets at every star. At every front, our carriers and battlecruisers would hammer you back. We would teach you that tyrants *always* fail and empires *always* fall."

The shuttle was silent, Kahlmor clearly as taken aback by Henry's words as Henry had been by his.

"But it is not up to me," Colonel Henry Wong of the United Planets Space Force said, his voice suddenly tired and small. "And all the will in the universe will not conjure warships or fuel from nothing.

"Is that the answer you seek, Lord of Ten Thousand Miles Kahlmor? The United Planets will not oppose you. Saunt and Todorovich can establish what our price looks like, but we will not fight you."

He shook his head.

"We *cannot* fight you."

"And that is why we have to act," Kahlmor said, his voice gentle. "Because you are not alone in your limits, and my Scion will not stand by and watch chaos consume the Kenmiri Empire. We can act to control the Isis Sector and protect the people there. We seek citizens and brothers, not slaves."

"You say that now," Henry replied. "But my people have known tyrants and empires in the past. They always fail. It's only a question of how many people they kill on their way down."

THE SHUTTLES SEPARATED, Kahlmor's whisking the Londu back to *Rigid Candor* like he hadn't just broken Henry's illusions with a hammer. Henry's own shuttle made its own way back to

Raven while he sat in the cargo bay and studied a holographic map of the stars.

UPA Intelligence's best guess was that the Great Scion of the Londu commanded eighty battleships and two hundred or so escorts. They had a surprisingly solid idea of the industrial capacity and population of the hundred stars the Londu already claimed and their fourteen inhabited worlds.

Without imposing conscription or any drastic demands, UPA Intelligence estimated the Londu could field somewhere in the region of fifty to a hundred million ground soldiers. It would strain their economy for them to do so, but the Scion was a near-absolute monarch.

If he wanted to invade and conquer the Isis Sector, he could bankrupt his nation trying. He might even pull it off...but he could also end up making the situation in the Isis Sector *worse* and feeding the whole disaster back into Londu space.

But there was nothing Henry could do. Without writing new temporary funding agreements that dramatically expanded upon what had been provided for the last decade of the war, the UPA couldn't afford to field a fleet that could match the Londu's.

Their best option was to support them at the Gathering, hoping to reduce bloodshed and score major concessions in terms of future trade with the soon-to-be-dramatically-larger Londu Imperium.

"We'll be back aboard in a few minutes, ser," the pilot informed him. "Anything you need us to do?"

"Lock down the recordings from the cargo bay," he ordered. "They're to be double-encrypted and transferred to *Raven*'s systems under my personal seal. Once they're transferred, wipe them from the shuttle's memory."

There was a pause.

"Yes, ser. As you order."

The whole meeting was a ticking bomb, and he was going to lob it to Ambassador Todorovich before he even told *his* superiors.

CHAPTER THIRTY-TWO

Back on *Raven*'s bridge, Henry began to feel slightly more in control of the situation.

"Do we have a course out?" he asked Bazzoli. "Or are we following the same path we came in on?"

"There is a second set of beacons to guide us out," his navigator replied. "It's a much straighter route."

"*Rigid Candor* is getting underway now," Ihejirika reported. "A nice gentle point four KPS squared."

"That's practically an invitation," Henry said with an only partially forced chuckle. "Let's take the Lord of Ten Thousand Miles up on it. Position us ten thousand klicks behind her, watching her back."

"On it, ser."

He settled back in his seat and studied the Londu battleship. Eighty of those versus twenty-four UPA battlecruisers...he wasn't entirely convinced it was an unwinnable fight. Being able to beat the massed Londu fleet in open combat, though, didn't enable the UPA to magically *get* that fleet to the Isis Sector or force that fleet engagement.

It wasn't his call. It had never been his call, but Henry still felt dirty for having been the one to admit to the Londu that the UPA wouldn't stop their conquest of sixty new worlds.

Mostly to distract himself, he started to go over their course out of the asteroid cluster. From inside the swarm of radioactive rocks, they couldn't see much outside of it. Few of the rocks were big enough or close enough together to really stop *Raven* bringing up the grav-shield and taking the shortest route out. On the other hand, these particular radioactive rocks were probably rather valuable to the Restan, and shattering asteroids your hosts wanted to mine was rude.

The route they'd been given took them off the shortest course back toward Gathering Station by enough to dodge around a denser zone of the cluster that was hard to scan into even from this close.

It would keep them safe, which was important for *Rigid Candor*, but they were still passing close to the cluster, and something about it was making him nervous.

"Commander Ihejirika, can you give that cluster a focused radar pulse?" he ordered, tossing the location he was studying over to the tactical console. "And get me a radiation breakdown. Ten thousand kilometers *should* be plenty of distance, but let's be sure."

It would take a star to be dangerous at ten thousand klicks, not an asteroid of heavy metals, but the jamming effect was making him nervous—

"Threat alert!" Ihejirika barked. "*Fuck.* Those are anti-radiation targeting systems! I have multiple missile signatures inbound from the cluster!"

"Get the shield up," Henry snapped. "Lasers out. Spin up all the reactors—but *drain* those capacitors. Battle stations!"

They were farther away than whoever had laid the trap had been hoping, he noted absently. Even at the missiles' ten KPS^2, fifty thousand kilometers was over ninety seconds' flight time.

It *should* only take ninety seconds to get the grav-shield up, but unprepared response times on *Raven* still weren't where he thought they should be.

Defensive lasers under bridge control were their first line of defenses, and *those* were online in forty seconds. With the active radar quiet now, the missiles had to use their own sensors to aim, which helped target *them*.

There were still at least thirty of them targeting his ship, and he didn't have a grav-shield yet.

"*Rigid Candor* is maneuvering to light up the cluster, but they're out of position to shoot at the missiles coming at us," Iyotake noted. "They are charging their main guns, targeting the cluster. They'll fire about as the missiles reach us."

"They won't reach us," Ihejirika said grimly as the first half-dozen red icons vanished from the display. "It's the fighter missile problem. Short range means low terminal velocity, and *we* weren't moving fast enough to make up the difference."

More missiles died. As the weapons flashed toward *Raven*, they started disappearing faster and faster...and then the shield came up.

"Grav-shield online," Lieutenant Henriksson reported, the engineering relay officer relaxing as she spoke.

"Six missiles converted," Ihejirika reported. "No shield failure. We're clear, ser."

"From *that* round," Henry replied. "What did the radar sweep get us, Okafor?"

They'd been so focused on the missiles that had lit up in response to their radar, they'd missed the *rest* of the trap. Fortunately, they weren't alone in this mess, and *Rigid Candor* had also picked up the reflections from their radar pulse.

Unfortunately, *Rigid Candor*'s main heavy plasma cannon paid for their lighter profiles and greater flexibility with longer initial warmup times. A Kenmiri dreadnought might have been able to fire before the mines realized the ARAD missiles had fired, woke up their own sensors, located their targets and detonated.

The Londu battleship fired before *most* of them detonated. Dozens of laser mines were vaporized, but at least ten triggered.

Nuclear warheads flared in the dark of the void, feeding X-ray lasers that stabbed deep into *Rigid Candor*'s hull.

"Report, is *Candor* still with us?" Henry asked as new scarlet details flashed across the icon of the other capital ship.

"Her energy screen took the worst of it, but it's offline now," Ihejirika reported. "She's bleeding atmosphere and fuel, and at least half her turrets went offline with the energy screen. Energy signatures suggest she just emergency-scrammed multiple reactors."

"Please tell me that was everything," *Raven*'s Captain snapped.

"It looks like *Rigid Candor* swept the cluster clean, but...I wouldn't have set this up with only one round of weapons," his tactical officer replied.

"Right. Keep the shield up, keep us at battle stations," Henry ordered. "Bazzoli, swing us out in front of *Rigid Candor*. Ihejirika, once we're out in front of them, start hitting every cluster between us and empty space with the hardest radar pulses we have. I want to be able to tell the damn Restan which asteroids out here are the best places to start mining, am I clear?"

"Understood, ser."

The battlecruiser dashed forward as Henry studied the situation. There was at least one more cluster that their route had been intended to take them around. It wasn't as dense as the first, which limited how much weaponry could be concealed in it.

It was still suspicious to him. He was going to have some *long* conversations with the Resta. Speaking of which...

"Where are the Restan destroyers?" he demanded.

"They just brought their engines online," Ihejirika reported. "They were headed back to Gathering Station. They appear to have flipped and are heading back to us at maximum acceleration. I'd *like* to think they're coming to help."

"They probably are," Henry conceded. "Are we seeing anything in that last cluster on our path? Bazzoli, can we detour around it?"

"We could," the navigator confirmed. "We wouldn't get a lot of distance, but we could probably put at least a hundred thousand kilometers between it and us. *Rigid Candor*, on the other hand, is currently ballistic.

"They're going to cut within fifteen thousand kilometers, and there's nothing we can do until they get their engines back online."

Henry swallowed a curse.

"All right," he said calmly. "Hold the shield and take us right at that cluster with full evasive maneuvering. If sensors aren't picking up anything, let's give whatever is hiding there something to see."

If there was one more jaw to this trap, he was going to let it close on his ship. The odds that whatever it was could punch through his grav-shield were low. He could be *wrong* on that assessment—and he'd pay for it if he was—but he had to act.

"And now is when we find out how many of those grav-shield disruptors the Drifters sold," Iyotake's voice murmured over his internal network. "And if they've improved the design."

"You think this was the Drifters?" Henry asked. Their conversation was functionally silent, a network-to-network connection linked through the ship's systems.

"My guess? Kenmiri-built weapons someone bought from the Drifters," his XO replied. "The Drifters don't pick sides; I doubt we're somehow on their hit list."

"*Someone* with a Drifter Convoy made a deal with First Warlord Deearan," Henry reminded Iyotake as they closed with the second cluster.

"Someone *aboard* a Drifter Convoy made a deal," the younger man replied. "Didn't have to be one of them. A lot of people rent space on those convoys, everything from passage to entire covert research facilities."

"Hell, we did the latter," Henry admitted. "Let us tear apart Kenmiri weapons without risking our own ships or worlds—and they rented us people with the expertise to help us do it without risking theirs, either."

The UPSF had paid the Drifters a vast quantity of platinum, gold, uranium and plutonium over the years of the war. They'd bought everything from fuel to missiles to medical care for injured crewmen.

Henry had always known the Drifters would take anyone's money, but that hadn't really been a problem when everyone they *would* work with was fighting the same enemy.

"There is *something* in that cluster," Ihejirika reported. "I'm not sure... *Missile launch*. Multiple missile launches. Ser—they had military-grade launchers in there. *UPSF* launchers!"

Everyone might be using the same missiles, but only a few of the Vesheron were able to build fully functional missile launchers. Kenmiri launchers, and their homebuilt equivalents, added a thousand kilometers per second to the initial velocity of the missile.

There was enough variety in the energy signatures and final velocity for Henry to completely trust Ihejirika's assessment. And if they were UPSF missile *launchers*...

"Double those evasi—"

They were only twenty thousand kilometers away. The missiles' acceleration was basically irrelevant—and the sparkle of warning lights on his screen told him his worst-case scenario was true.

Ten missiles made it through the defenses to the gravity shield... and vanished. Fractions of a second later, their icosaspatial skip ended and they reappeared.

Inside *Raven*'s defenses.

Bazzoli had already *been* evading. For all that they'd been accelerating at ten KPS^2 the whole way, the missiles had essentially been fired dumb.

Seven missed. Two, despite all odds, were shot down in the final fractions of a second before impact.

The last missile hit at an angle, failing to penetrate into the inner hull but dragging a long gouge along the top of the battlecruiser before finally stopping near the engines.

"That's it, ser," Ihejirika said, his voice small. "I've confirmed fourteen launchers. All were destroyed by nuclear scuttling charges after firing."

"Colonel Song," Henry called his engineer, his own voice surprisingly calm. "That was a kinetic warhead, not a nuke. There must be something you can retrieve from the wreckage. I want a team to retrieve it *now*.

"Commander O'Flannagain? I want your birds in the air now," he continued as he flipped channels. "The missiles that made it through the shield are gone, but there's four wrecked missiles out there. It doesn't look like whoever fired them managed to access their guidance controls, so I'm hoping the safeguards are inoperable as well.

"I need you to catch me a dead missile, Commander," he told her. "I need answers, and those missiles are the best source we're going to have."

No one was supposed to have icosaspatial grav-shield penetrator warheads except the UPSF. What he'd seen suggested that someone had retrieved the launchers and missiles from one of their destroyed ships...which wasn't supposed to be possible.

And suggested all *sorts* of ugly scenarios down the line.

CHAPTER THIRTY-THREE

"SER?" MOON ASKED SOFTLY AS THE RESTAN DESTROYERS BEGAN to slow down to assist *Rigid Candor*. "*Candor*'s coms are back online and Kahlmor is ordering the Restan to stand off."

"I would too, in his place," Henry admitted. "But I'm not dropping the gravity shield. We can't tow him, so..."

"They are arguing the same thing and insisting they had nothing to do with this," Moon confirmed. "They say they're approaching with weapons offline."

"Ihejirika?" Henry turned to tactical.

"Sensors confirm," he said. "Should we send that to *Candor*?"

"Do it," *Raven*'s Captain ordered. "Sanitize the data to as low a resolution as you can confirm the lack of weapons cha—"

"*Candor* *is firing!*"

It was a warning shot, Henry realized inside a second. For that second, he thought he was about to see the entire Vesheron disintegrate into open warfare right then.

The blast of plasma missed the two Restan ships by at least ten thousand kilometers, but they both adjusted their vectors away from the Londu battleship immediately.

"Get me a channel to Kahlmor," Henry said. "And get that sanitized data packet for me."

"On it," his officers replied in chorus.

A moment later, a new icon popped up in the corner of his vision, and he mentally clicked on it to link into the channel.

"Lord of Ten Thousand Miles, we can confirm the Restan are approaching with weapons cold," he said without preamble. "Beyond that, what is your status?"

The only visual on the channel was an avatar, a computer-generated image of the tall Londu officer as he chose to appear. He guessed that *Rigid Candor*'s bridge was visibly damaged. The Blades of the Scion would refuse to show weakness to anyone.

"Our status is less than optimal," Kahlmor said slowly. "I have contacted Lord of Hundred Thousand Miles Intahlrahn via subspace, and she is on her way to retrieve us with the rest of the battle group.

"Let the rest of these so-called warriors think my engines are offline," he continued. "If my weakness allows Saunt to draw our enemies out of the shadows, they will be sorely disappointed."

Henry had a summary of *Rigid Candor*'s status as best as CIC could assess it running on his network. Only half her turrets were online, and the energy-screen projector was simply *gone*. His analysts figured she could get about a quarter of her engines back online, but they were raising questions around her inertial dampeners.

And her artificial gravity, which might also explain the avatar in the call. *Candor* was less damaged than her ballistic course toward Gathering Station implied, but far more damaged than Kahlmor was pretending to Henry.

"I will confirm with my Ambassador, but I should be able to maintain position on you until your battle group arrives," he told Kahlmor. "I need to remain to retrieve my fighters anyway."

"Your vessel is also damaged," the Lord of Ten Thousand noted, his tone surprised. He probably hadn't had time to look at anything outside his own hull since the first bomb went off. "What happened?"

There was no point in dissembling, not when Kahlmor's ship had been right there. Sooner or later, he'd look at the sensor data and see what had happened.

"Whoever triggered this was in possession of several UPSF weapons," Henry admitted. "My people are attempting to trace those. It may give us more clues than the collection of Kenmiri missiles and mines used for the rest of the attack."

Kahlmor grunted.

"Any of us could have acquired Kenmiri missiles," he agreed. "The mines...those are different."

"We have encountered them before," Henry said. "We just usually knew where they were. Mines are pretty useless in space, after all."

"If you learn anything, the Blades of the Scion will be in your debt," Kahlmor promised. "For now, Colonel Wong, I must attend to my ship."

The channel cut and Henry leaned back in his chair.

"Did O'Flannagain catch anything?" he asked.

"It looks like one of the missiles might be intact enough to be worth retrieving," Ihejirika reported. "She is vectoring in on it now."

Of course the CAG was trying to do the damn fool stunt he'd ordered herself. Henry realized he needed to remember how rocket-jocks thought more often.

"Understood," was all he said, though. "And our status? Colonel Song?"

"We got lucky," his engineer told him bluntly. "Even a slightly steeper impact angle and that round would have punched right through the armor and *ricocheted* down the length of the ship's interior."

That was a mental image Henry probably could have lived without.

"As it is, we basically don't have armor on the top of the ship's core hull anymore," Song continued. "I've got drones out looking, but you're not going to find much of a weapon that impacted at over a thousand kilometers a second, ser. That kinetic energy became heat, and even if most of that heat got dispersed into our armor, the original projectile is in pieces at best."

"I know," Henry conceded. "Priority is the ship, but we *need* to know where they got those missiles."

"We'll see what we and the fighters get, and I'll go over everything when we have the parts," Song promised. "I can tell you one thing, though."

"What's that?" Henry asked.

"Ihejirika, your data shows that they all were off course after they emerged from their penetration skip, right?"

The tactical officer was silent for a few seconds.

"Yes," he finally confirmed. "That's why most of them missed... they were pointed *directly* at us, but once they'd skipped the shield, they were off course."

"If they'd had the guidance systems online, the software was designed to compensate for that," Song told them. "That means they were Gen Two or Gen Three missiles. I'd say Gen One, but Gen One was never deployed forward.

"It took three generations of design and analysis before we finally sorted out compensating for the gravity shear's icosadimensional effect," the engineer continued. "Gen Four missiles were the first that would emerge from their skip in a straight line from where they entered. Everything before that adjusted their impact angle to account for the divergence and was programmed for final adjustments in the terminal approach."

"We started seeing Gen Four missiles eight years ago," Henry said slowly. "I don't think they were fully deployed through the Force until five years ago, though. We weren't using penetrators, after all."

His own magazines held sixth-generation grav-shield penetrators. In theory, the weapons would be almost as useful against energy screens and even heavy armor as they were against grav-shields, but the UPSF didn't want to give anyone ideas.

The one major advantage *his* missiles had over the ones he'd been shot with was that his weren't kinetic weapons. Gen Six penetrators were the first to carry a condensed two-hundred-megaton fusion warhead.

"So, if we're looking at Gen Three weapons, we could easily be seeing missiles stripped from any ship lost in the middle ten years of the war," Song told him. "You know was well as I do that the grav-shield never made us invulnerable."

"They also had the launchers, which means that a ship's self-destruct protocols failed," the Captain replied. "Fourteen launchers, too. That means at least two destroyers were taken somewhat intact by *somebody*."

His guess was Drifters. He wasn't going to go so far as to claim the Drifters were behind the attack, but he could definitely see them deciding that UPSF ship parts were worth enough to others to not even let the UPSF bid on them.

"What's the ETA on the Lord of Hundred Thousand Miles and her battle group?" he asked.

"Two hours, twenty minutes," Ihejirika replied. "Your orders?"

"We stand here like a friendly guard dog until Intahlrahn gets here, then we get back to Gathering Station," Henry said. "Keep me in the loop. I'm going to call the Ambassador."

✶⋆
V
✶⋆

"ARE YOU ALL RIGHT, HENRY?" Todorovich demanded the moment he had the subspace connection live. "Is your *crew* all right?"

"A few minor injuries, no severe casualties," he told her. "I've had skips that were worse in terms of crew injury. *Raven* took a heavy hit, but it didn't penetrate our armor." He shrugged. "Warships are built to take a beating, Sylvia. We're fine."

"That's good." The sharp-faced woman shook her head. "The rest of this has the potential to turn into a goddamned clusterfuck, so I'm glad your ship is okay."

"How bad?" Henry asked.

"The Restan are assigning everyone's escorts new orbits, and the ambassadors are promptly freaking out," she replied. "The ships are not only being set up at least a light-second from the station, they're being set up at least a light-second from *each other*. That makes perfect sense to *me*, but a lot of people think they're basically being accused of setting up the attack."

"My suspect list only has three groups of people on it," Henry said dryly. "The other however-many-hundred ambassadors present are in no danger from me."

"Let me guess: the Restan, the Drifters, the Kozun?" Todorovich asked. "I'd honestly swap the Restan out for the Londu. Kahlmor seems straightforward enough, but Intahlrahn is a twisty one."

"God." He shook his head as he remembered the conversation with Kahlmor. "I don't know about *straightforward*. The whole contest was apparently a setup to get me somewhere where Kahlmor could talk to me face to face and be entirely certain that no one was listening in."

"So, of course you're going to brief me over subspace," the Ambassador said with a chuckle. "Because we don't care about Londu paranoia."

"They want the Isis Sector, Sylvia," Henry said quietly. "All of it. Kahlmor wanted me to say, one way or another, whether we'd fight them."

The call was silent.

"What did you tell him?" she finally asked.

"He told me that you could name your price for our support at the Gathering for that," he said. "So, I told him the truth: we can't fight them. Most of our soldiers would *prefer* to, but we cannot wage a war against the Londu."

Todorovich nodded.

"Probably better. You lie better than most Force officers, I suspect, but the truth serves our purposes. If they want an entire sector...I have a shopping list."

"They won't be able to hold it," Henry warned.

"Then I should make sure my shopping list is short-term, should I?" she asked. "I don't know if the Gathering is going to work out for anyone at this point. Right now, there are sixty warships out there whose captains—and the ambassadors they report to—are arguing with their hosts over where they should be orbiting.

"No one is shooting yet, but from what I'm overhearing, there's a lot of charged weapons systems out there...and not all the Vesheron like each other. Think you can get back here without igniting any new sparks of chaos?"

"I didn't think my contest was going to turn this into a tinderbox," he admitted.

"Oh, don't give yourself so much credit," Todorovich replied with a smile. "This was a jug of gasoline before that. Now people are just realizing what the jug they were hauling around was full of.

"Ambassador Saunt, Under-Speaker Sho Lavah and I are playing elder diplomat. I think we'll have everyone calmed down in a day or two and ready to get back to the table...assuming nothing *else* goes wrong."

"Well, I have one more spark that we'll want to keep quiet as long as we can," Henry admitted. "We didn't have a shield blowthrough, Sylvia. They hit us with penetrator missiles. Fourteen of them."

Todorovich's response was silence and a gesture for him to continue.

"From what my engineers are telling me so far, they were definitely ours. Our missiles fired from our launchers. No ship, just launchers and an isolated power source. Best guess is early generation missiles stripped from a couple of the destroyers we've lost.

"Downside to that is that if a mythical someone got their hands on two destroyers, well...we can assume that seven launchers were lost to whatever damage took the destroyers out without triggering their self-destruct, but they should still have had thirty penetrator warheads in their magazines.

"Each."

"The nukes and the conversion warheads would be irrelevant,"

Todorovich said softly. "The computer cores should have slagged even if everything else failed, correct?"

"They didn't seem to have access to the proper codes for the missiles," he agreed. "They managed to bring them live and fire them with active penetrator systems, but the guidance systems were offline. I'd guess the ships were wrecked, but the overall self-destructs and the magazine security measures failed."

"But someone out there probably has at least another dozen penetrator warheads...and as many as forty-five of them?" she asked.

"My *hope* would be that they only got the magazines from one ship," Henry said. "But yeah. And I give you two guesses who I think at least *found* them, even if I figure they *sold* them rather than using them."

"You know," Todorovich said after a pause, "there was a time when having an available bunch of nomadic merchants with a grand total of one principle was *useful*."

"It's the same problem we're going to have with the rest of the Vesheron, Sylvia," Henry reminded her. "So long as we were all fighting the Kenmiri, it was fine."

He brought up a hologram of the ships' locations around Gathering Station above his desk.

"We've been moving you around to date on our standard shuttles," he noted. "I have two heavy-duty insertion ships. Weaponry is modular; if we replace it with fuel tanks, one of them can reach Gathering Station in three hours, well before *Raven* can get back.

"The shuttles have gravity shields," he told her. "I'm going to send it with a pair of fighters for escort. You'll need to convince the Restan to let O'Flannagain's birds dock."

"It's not going to happen, Henry," she told him. "And trying is going to burn some of the goodwill I've been building by trying to keep things calm.

"Send the shuttle," she agreed. "I'm not going to complain about having a near-invulnerable getaway vehicle on hand, but a pair of loose starfighters in the middle of this is just asking for trouble."

"Sylvia, we're four hours away," he pointed out. "We should be underway in two, but that's still six hours until *Raven* is back at the station. If things go to shit before we're there..."

"I'll deal. Even if everyone is arguing over moving orbits, they're still outside easy weapons range of Gathering Station. If this falls apart, the ambassadors will be the prize everyone is fighting over, not the target they're shooting at."

"I'm not sure I'd be so blasé," he admitted.

"You're the one with a warship. You should be the calm one," she replied. "Send the shuttle, Henry. I'll get the Restan to fuel it up, and I'll have my people settle into our equivalent of your readiness one.

"If things fall apart, we'll be on that shuttle in five minutes. We'll be fine."

"All right," he conceded. She was assuming an *external* threat, but he had to live with what she was willing to do. This was, after all, her mission.

Right up until "things fell apart," anyway.

CHAPTER THIRTY-FOUR

HENRY WATCHED THE ICONS OF THE RETURNING FIGHTERS ON his screen with a concealed sense of awe. The missiles hadn't been moving *that* fast in the grand scheme of things, having been accelerating for only a handful of seconds when they were disabled, but when they'd lost acceleration, they'd done so violently.

That meant that *Raven* didn't have a guarantee on exactly what moment the engines cut out—and even fractions of a second mattered at ten KPS^2—and the impact itself had added an unknown random vector.

Ihejirika had localized probability zones for three of the four missiles he'd shot down, but even those were simply identifying the haystack the needle was in.

O'Flannagain and her people had found two of the needles. The CAG herself had matched vectors with the more violently spinning one and caught it with tow cables.

"There's a reason we don't catch missiles, ser," Ihejirika noted. "That was damn impressive flying on our people's part."

"It was," Henry confirmed. "I'm not the pilot I once was, but I can still manage a fusion rocket better than some." He shook his head. "*I* couldn't have done that."

He watched the icons from the bridge for a moment more, then shook his head again.

"I'm going to go meet O'Flannagain on the deck," he told his bridge crew. "Iyotake has the con."

ONCE ON THE DECK, automated movement systems closed around the spherical starfighter. They whisked it into its bay as the craft's internal systems moved the "coffin" to the exterior and opened the accessway.

Commander Samira O'Flannagain emerged from the goop of her acceleration tank clad in a head-to-toe bodysuit and helmet. The helmet came off as soon as she was outside the tank, taken by a waiting FighterDiv support tech.

Henry was waiting as the helmet was removed and gave the woman a crisp salute.

"Ser!" she greeted him, returning the salute.

"Commander," he replied. "Well done. I saw the vector data on those missiles."

"Neither is in great shape, ser," she reminded him. "I figured we needed both if we were going to track *anything* useful from them."

"You're right," he agreed. "Two half-wrecked missiles are worth a hell of a lot more than one. The missile Gaunt brought home? Decently clean vector, for all that Ihejirika's people put a laser through its engines.

"But you forget that I can fly that ball of metal behind you," Henry continued. "I'd have gone after the missile Gaunt did, because that one was *possible*. The one you pulled in? That was impossible, Commander."

"Nothing is impossible, ser. Not to a pilot with something to prove." She smiled. "You know that, I'm pretty sure."

"I do," he confirmed. "You shouldn't have done it, Commander, and it's enough of a bad look on the CAG that I can't officially condone or commend what you did. Understood?"

"Yes, ser," she said crisply, the smile fading.

Henry *had*, however, stopped at the officers' mess on the way down. The bottle of brandy was the most expensive the ship had in stock, probably the single best liquor on the entire warship, and even his mess account had cringed at its acquisition.

He pulled it out from behind his back and offered it to her.

"*Raven*'s Captain cannot commend you for taking the risk or condone the CAG showing off like that," he repeated as she stared at the bottle. "But that missile may make sorting this whole mess out a hell of a lot easier. So, consider this a gift from *Colonel* Wong. Am I understood, Commander?"

"Ser, yes, ser!" she said crisply.

She paused after taking the bottle. She studied it for a few seconds, then chuckled and passed it to the same tech who'd taken her helmet.

"Get that in my locker, PO," she told the woman. "There'll be another time for it, I think." The tech obeyed and the two officers had a moment in private.

"I get the full lecture, ser," she conceded. "CAG shouldn't have done it, but I was the only pilot there who could. I owe it to my people not to take risks like that...but I owed it to *Raven* to make sure that missile came home."

The *full* lecture, indeed. It seemed that Commander O'Flannagain might be at a vastly reduced risk of being beached when this tour was over. If it took an ex-pilot as her Captain to show her how to be a better officer, well...

It wouldn't be the first time Henry Wong had hand-reared an officer worth the time.

"I'm going to see what Song makes of your prizes," he told her. "Go get cleaned up, Commander." He paused, considering the situation back at Gathering Station.

"We're holding the ship at readiness two, but I want your pilots at one," he told her. "This system is a time bomb in a tinderbox, and I'm not sure it's a question of *if* it's going to blow up...or *when*."

"Understood, ser. *Raven*'s starfighters will be ready for your orders!"

THE MISSILES HAD BEEN aboard for less than ten minutes by the time Henry located the workshop Song and her people were working in, but they'd already been dismantled and spread across the entire space.

It was easy to pick out the missile that had hit *Raven*. For one thing, there wasn't as much of it left, and what was left was in far smaller pieces.

"Anything useful yet?" he asked. "I know it's only been a few minutes, so I'm not expecting miracles."

Song removed her head from inside the chassis of one of the missiles.

"I saw what O'Flannagain pulled to get this one," she said, rapping the casing with her fist. Around her, a dozen senior chiefs continued tearing into components of the three-meter-long weapons.

"It was dumb, but we all figured it would be worth it," he told her.

"Yeah, well, it's the reason I have anything for you," Song replied. "First thing I looked for was serial numbers. The one that hit us? Fuck-all. The other two both have about sixty percent of an intact serial number.

"I don't have a full number for you, but two partials should be enough for LogDiv to flag which ship they're from," the engineer continued. "That's a phone-home job."

"But it's the most likely way to find out where these missiles came from," Henry agreed. "Any sign of tampering?"

"One of them had an active black-box protection system we had to disable," Song told him. "So, that actually says they *didn't* tamper. With these particular missiles, at least."

"How could they fire them, then?" he asked.

"Engine protocols are pretty universal," the engineer said. "Hand me any missile built on the Kenmiri design and I can make the engine fire. The penetrator warhead is initialized by the launcher tube and triggered by detecting a shear field."

"Guidance computers would be the only part they'd actually have to crack?" he asked.

"Exactly. And those are protected by the same black-box protection system as the penetrator system. When we bought Kenmiri missiles from other Vesheron, we just yanked the entire guidance computer system and installed a new one. With the protection system, they couldn't do that."

"Hence, straight-line fire at point-blank range," Henry concluded.

"Exactly. It's a great way to use a weapon you can't control. But ser? They couldn't know the warhead would engage."

"Another damn test?" he asked.

"It looks like," she confirmed. "Someone is playing with our stolen systems and gear they've built themselves to fuck with our grav-shielded units."

"It's nice to be feared, I suppose. I think I preferred being invincible."

"Sorry ser, but it looks like *somebody* is determined to pierce our magic armor," the engineer replied. "I can't tell you who from this. I can confirm what I'm sure you already guessed: the missiles and mines are Kenmiri design, if not necessarily Kenmiri construction. We have the same damn birds in our magazines, and while we don't *carry* mines, I could fabricate them in three days."

"And so could any other engineering department aboard the escorts gathered here, I presume?" Henry asked.

"Exactly. The rest of the weapons are going to be useless for tracking anything. We'll dig into these guys and see if there's *anything* else, but LogDiv should at least be able to identify which ship those two missiles were issued to."

"I'm impressed, Colonel Song," Henry told her. *"Raven's* crew has done me proud, I have to say."

She snorted.

"Say that again once this mess is over. I'm not in charge of it, but even *I* can see how this can blow up in our face."

"So long as my ship can get us back to Gathering Station in the same four hours we got here in, I'm happy, Colonel Song. I'll go talk to LogDiv.

"Let's see if the folks back home have an answer for us."

CHAPTER THIRTY-FIVE

ANY BUREAUCRACY IS INHERENTLY SPECIALIZED. THERE ARE things it does well and things it does poorly and slowly. Military bureaucracy is even more so. Getting missiles from point A to point B to make sure the ships on the sharp end had weapons? The UPSF had that down to a science.

Finding someone able to track down where a specific missile had ended up? That apparently took longer. Between Henry, Lauren Moon and half a dozen Chief Petty Officers, it still took them over two hours to finally track down someone who thought they could answer his question.

"This is Colonel Borghild Holst," the slim woman who finally ended up on the other side of the subspace channel introduced herself. "My team tells me that you're trying to track a specific pair of missiles, Captain Wong."

"I am, Colonel Holst," he confirmed. "They're ours. And someone fired them at me."

"That's not supposed to happen," she told him. "And you retrieved them intact?"

"That's also not supposed to happen," Henry agreed. "They were gravity-shield penetrator missiles, Colonel. My understanding is that we have multiple layers of safeguards to make sure those don't end up in unexpected hands."

"All safeguards can fail," the logistics officer said softly. "What do you have?"

"Partial serial numbers from the chassis of two missiles that we shot down before they impacted the gravity shield," he told her. "Scan data from their performance as well; we managed to break them down as being either Gen Two or Gen Three warheads."

"That suggests they've been in somebody else's hands for a long time," Holst said distantly. "I see the numbers here. Running the analysis now." She shook her head. "Even restricting it to Gen Two and Three gives me a thousand possibles for each missile, Captain Wong. Let me try something—"

For a moment, the connection disintegrated into static. Holst's voice was unintelligible, and static rippled through the image.

"Colonel?"

"I'm here," Holst replied. "Are you? That was strange. I've never seen distortion on a subspace channel before."

"Neither have I," he admitted. "That's a LogDiv problem, isn't it?"

"Not my departme—" She disintegrated into static.

"Colonel Holst?"

"That is very strange," the LogDiv officer said. "But I've got your source, Colonel Wong. Most likely, your missiles came from *Adelaide*. She was an escort destroyer backing up *Lynx* in the Ra-Nineteen System eight years ago. *Lynx* was the only ship to make it back out of a five-ship strike group. If one or more of the destroyers had a self-destruct failure, well...four destroyers could have given a salvage party the launchers they used against you."

"Eight years?" Henry considered. "I thought Ra-Nineteen was blockaded."

"I can't speak to that," Holst responded. "I'm a logistics officer,

Captain. The only time I've been in Kenmiri space was running the supply division on a LogDiv munitions collier. I don't—"

The entire transmission dissolved into static. Voice. Image. Everything suddenly cascaded into a distorted mess that got worse by the second. Henry winced back from the noise, reaching for the cutoff switch.

Then the distortion stopped...and someone *else* appeared.

Some*thing* else.

HENRY WONG HAD FOUGHT the Kenmiri for seventeen years. He could identify a Kenmiri Artisan on sight. The holographic creature now standing above his desk looked like an ant scaled to roughly six feet tall.

The creature's multipart torso was covered with a heavy carapace, bright red to mark its caste. Unlike an Earth ant, the Kenmiri only had four limbs with a clearly visible skeleton under the darker skin there.

"You are all fools," the Artisan said in flat Kem. "If you have stolen this frequency, you understand this tongue. You do not understand what you have done. You have thought this was yours to use, freely, without question or debate.

"It was not. This was the great artifice of the Empire, the subspace network *we* built to connect our worlds and those we saved. And you petty *children* thought you could steal it without consequence. Without consequence.

"When your rebellion was meaningless, we ignored your intrusion onto our network. Now our Mothers are dead. You have brought fire and death to our sacred crèches and destroyed our ancestors and our future.

"This intrusion will no longer be tolerated. Your lies, deception and violence will no longer be tolerated.

"We have abandoned the outer provinces. We no longer care what occurs there. But if you enter the stars where we remain, we will burn your ships to ashes. We will unleash arsenals like you have never seen and we will bring your stolen worlds and stolen stars down around you.

"And we will no longer permit your *violation* of our network. Scrabble in the dark like the primitives you are and understand what you threw aside."

The image vanished and a new icon appeared. It was an icon Henry hadn't even thought was programmed into the subspace communicators.

No Signal.

He was on his feet and heading for the bridge before the system finished powering down.

"COMMANDER MOON," he snapped as he entered the bridge. "Status report. What the hell happened to our subspace coms?"

"I don't know," she admitted. "They're just...gone. It's not just like we're not receiving a return signal from home. It's... It's like the transmission medium is gone. We're trying to send signals, but there's nothing to send them on."

"That's impossible," Henry replied, but a chill ran down his spine as he considered what the Kenmiri had said. Subspace communicators used an odd layer of space, one that defied most theories and acted like the hyperspace of fiction. Insufficiently stable for a vessel, it allowed instantaneous communication across the galaxy. "Unless..."

"I think that Kenmiri was telling the truth, ser," Moon said quietly. "We always knew that subspace was weird, but we assumed it was a natural phenomenon. I... I think it's possible it was artificial all along."

"And they just shut it down," he concluded. "How bad, Commander?"

"We don't have an alternative interstellar communication system, ser," she reminded him. "I mean...the USSF and the Imperatorskiy Flot both used automated skip drones, but that was a *security* measure since subspace coms were new and no one was sure how secure they were. The last time anyone used a courier or a drone was the Unity War."

"And that was a hundred years ago," Henry said. "I know there *are* couriers out there for high-speed physical deliveries, but that's not going to be enough. If we don't have subspace coms anymore..."

"The UPA itself is in danger," Moon finished for him. "Ser...what do we do?"

"We complete the mission," Henry told her. He stepped away from the communications console, moving around the screens to reach the center of the bridge, where Iyotake was currently in command.

He traded nods with his dark-haired XO, and Iyotake abandoned the Captain's seat for him.

The entire bridge was paying attention to him now, and Henry swallowed a grimace as he forced himself to calmly activate the all-hands channel.

"All hands, all hands, this is Captain Wong speaking," he announced. "Rumor travels faster than the speed of light, so I imagine many of you are already aware of the latest complication in matters.

"As of ten minutes ago, the subspace communication network is down. It appears to have been either disabled or jammed by the Kenmiri. We are not certain which, but what is important is that *we*, here in Resta, have no ability to communicate with the UPA."

He paused for a second to let that sink in. He could *feel* the concern of the bridge crew around him, and he knew he needed to head off real panic before it took hold.

"This does not change our mission," he told his crew. "It adds both complexity and urgency to our actions, but our mission remains the same: support Ambassador Todorovich's presence at the Gathering and bring her and her people home safely.

"We are four weeks from home. That has not changed. The ships that ply the trade lines back home haven't disappeared. The UPA will maintain communication and shipping links at home without us. They *cannot* shape the safe future of the former Kenmiri provinces from there.

"Ambassador Todorovich, with our help, can. She needs us here. *That* is our mission. And I have full confidence in the crew and officers of UPSV *Raven* to rise to these new challenges and overcome them.

"We have enemies here who just tried to kill us. The Ambassador is secure but arguably in danger. Our focus must be on the here and now. We must have faith in our comrades back home, that they will meet this challenge as we will meet ours.

"Now. Return to your duties. We will be setting out for Gathering Station in the next few minutes. Do so with the certainty that a communication failure does not mean that home is having any more problems than they were having fifteen minutes ago.

"Do so with the certainty that your Captain knows you are the best damn crew in the Space Force!"

CHAPTER THIRTY-SIX

HENRY'S SPEECH SEEMED TO HAVE SETTLED HIS BRIDGE CREW, AT least, but that seemed to be the *only* thing settled down in the entire star system.

"The Londu battle group just went to emergency deceleration," Ihejirika reported. Somehow, despite no one having officially called battle stations, all of Henry's senior officers were at their posts on the bridge.

"They don't have acceleration tanks," Bazzoli said. "That...means they're taking a good eight gees straight up."

"And *Rigid Candor* just brought her engines back up. Point three KPS^2," the tactical officer added. "Assuming they're going to match velocities...yeah."

"Tactical?" Henry demanded.

"They're leaving, ser," Ihejirika reported. "I'm guessing Saunt's already aboard the cruiser Intahlrahn is flying her flag from. Their vector is heading directly out-system toward Londu space."

"It's more than a coms failure," Henry realized aloud. "A lot of these ambassadors don't actually *have* the authority to act on their own. Todorovich had it out of tradition as much as anything else, but she has it.

"Saunt probably *does* have it, but..." He shook his head. "Someone just shot the shit out of their battleship. They're writing the whole mess off. They were prepared to take Isis by force...and if the Gathering is a mess, Saunt probably thinks it's easier to just activate that plan."

"What do we do, ser?" Ihejirika asked, echoing Bazzoli's earlier question.

"We complete the mission," Henry repeated. "If the Londu think they're fine, let's stop playing babysitter. Is our shuttle at Gathering Station yet?"

"Still half an hour out," the tactical officer reported. "Without the subspace link, I don't have decent data on what's going on there—and what I've got is a minute and a half old."

"Bazzoli, get us moving," Henry ordered. "Let's get at least four fighters out for perimeter escort and to expand our view. We're so damn used to live data, it's going to take some adjusting, but let's get as good a look as we can."

"What happens if they start shooting, ser?" Ihejirika asked. "Loss of the subspace network is going to leave a lot of those captains with itchy trigger fingers."

"We have the gravity shield," the Captain pointed out. "We can take someone else's sucker punch and we *will*, if needed. But no one shoots at us twice; am I clear, Commander?"

"Yes, ser." He paused. "What if they're shooting at each other?"

Henry nodded.

"We deal with that then, depending on who's shooting at whom," he told Ihejirika. "In a perfect world, we'll have the Ambassador aboard by then...because *that*, Commander, is a political decision."

And thank *God* he had an Ambassador nearby to dump it on!

HENRY HAD *TRAINED* for tactical analysis in a lightspeed sensor situation. He'd used that training to one degree or another in most of his battles, in fact. Subspace communicator–equipped drones were a handy tool, but you needed to get them closer than was usually practical to have real-time data.

Since over ninety-five percent of battles took place at less than a light-second, lightspeed sensors weren't that much of a limitation once battle was joined. It was the getting to the fight where it mattered, where learning of a maneuver two minutes after it happened could make it impossible to close to combat range or intercept an enemy.

Here in Resta, though, he'd left a probe behind at Gathering Station and had been relying on having real-time data on the fate of the Gathering the whole time.

Three and a half hours out, as the grav-shielded shuttle *finally* docked with the station, he was silently arguing with himself about the decision to sustain standard acceleration. Tanking up and going to maximum thrust would get him to the station in barely over an hour...but would inevitably be seen as a hostile maneuver.

"That's...not good," Moon said slowly. She was eavesdropping on the radio chatter coming back from Gathering Station.

"Commander?"

"One of the Set Sector factions is arguing with the Resta. They want to pick up their Ambassador aboard one of their escorts."

"And the Restan are insisting they use a shuttle," Henry guessed.

"Exactly, ser," Moon confirmed. "It's the Kron, ser. Are you familiar with them?"

"Yes," he confirmed, racking his memory of their tour in Set for the species. The Kron weren't Ashall. They were an odd race, four-legged creatures with thick rocky skin who could use tools only while sitting. That limitation made them...well, paranoid.

"That's not going to go over well," he said aloud. "If the Kron are feeling that twitchy, they're not shuttling their Ambassador around in a shuttle. They're going to..."

"I have engine light-up on two escorts," Ihejirika barked. "I *think* they're the Kron ships."

"That would be a very Kron thing to do," Henry agreed. "What are they doing?"

"Accelerating toward Gathering Station at half a KPS squared," the tactical officer said. "I can't tell from this distance if their weapons are online."

Henry didn't need to ask if the Restan battleship playing guard dog for the station had her weapons online. There was no way she didn't. The Restan wouldn't let their responsibility to protect the station lapse enough to leave the battleship cold as everything went to hell around them.

"I have multiple other ships bringing engines online, and our drone is telling me that there is a *lot* of targeting radar active in the area," Ihejirika reported.

"And no one actually respected the Restan's order to move to one light-second away from each other, did they?" *Raven's* Captain asked.

"Only a few, ser," Ihejirika confirmed. "The Trintar have moved well away from everyone else and sent a shuttle in to retrieve their Ambassador. Everyone is busy pointing targeting sensors and plasma cannon at each other." He shook his head. "What happens now, ser?"

"I don't know," Henry admitted. "Squadron-Voice Ta Callah is in command of the defenses. She's brave and competent, but her orders are what they are."

"She'll fire," Iyotake said, the XO's voice very soft. "A warning shot, but that might be enough."

Twenty-five minutes for the Kron to make rendezvous with the station, but it would only take five minutes for them to be in range to blast it to pieces with an escort's heavy lasers.

Ninety-second time delay. Everything Henry was seeing was out of date.

The entire Vesheron alliance might have already blown up, and all he was able to do was *watch*.

THE FIRST SHOT wasn't what anyone had been expecting. With every eye in the star system on the pair of escorts making their approach toward the Resta's red line, no one was watching the rest of the escort fleets.

It was one of the handful of Kenmiri dreadnoughts in the mess, one from a faction Henry had never interacted with in his life. Six heavy plasma guns targeted the Kron escorts and opened fire.

The range was still short, less than fifty thousand kilometers. No one had a chance to react before massive bursts of plasma tore into the ships heading toward the station. The expected next step had been a warning shot from the Restan, and the Kron ships' evasive maneuvers had been focused on the Restan battleship.

Both came apart into balls of fire that kept hurtling toward the station. Moments later, engines and weapons came alive across the collection of escorts, targeting scanners acquiring final lock as dozens of commanders tried to find the right answer.

The Drifter guardian and another dreadnought fired first, massive plasma cannon blasts lighting up Henry's scanners as they opened fire on the instigator.

With engines running at maximum power, it would still be several minutes before the ships were separated enough for *Raven* to sort out much now that the shooting had started.

Henry closed his eyes for one eternal second.

"Battle stations and acceleration stations," he ordered softly. "All hands to the acceleration tanks and hooked for juice. Emergency acceleration once all hands are in position, Commander Bazzoli."

"Are we respecting the Restan limit around Gathering Station, ser?" Bazzoli asked.

"No. The Gathering is over. We will retrieve Ambassador Todorovich and her staff by any means necessary."

HENRY'S harsh words hung in the air of the bridge as he could faintly hear klaxons sounding in the rest of the ship. Other icons flickered across both his seat and his internal network as his own acceleration-tank system activated.

A panel in the floor in front of his seat slid open. A stand with a mask and hose rose up from the ground, and softly glowing marks on the floor told him where to stand.

Similar panels were opening all around him as Henry stepped onto the footprints and took the mask. Taking one last breath of regular ship's air, he closed the mask over his face. His network flashed up a warning to close his eyes...and then the floor beneath him sank away as he dropped into the acceleration tank directly beneath his command seat.

Warm gel closed around him, viscosity increasing as he settled into it. He knew the space would be lit up, but at this point, he needed to run the ship through his internal network. He kept his eyes closed as he activated the virtual bridge software.

It wasn't a perfect facsimile of his bridge, but it would let him see what his people were doing just as well as if they were at their regular stations.

A display told him how many of his crew were in their battle-station acceleration tanks. It was already over sixty percent and skyrocketing. It hit a hundred and he checked the timer with a chuckle.

"Sixty-seven seconds," he said aloud. "Even *Panther* couldn't make it that fast."

"Everyone was basically *at* their stations," Iyotake told him. "They knew this was coming."

"Commander Bazzoli, final check, please," Henry ordered.

"All hands report in the acceleration tanks. System reports all crew secured. All animals secured. All items of record secure. We are prepared for full acceleration."

Henry took a deep breath and brought up the display of the space around Gathering Station. Multiple ships were dead or dying now, but they were no longer his concern. The consequences of the explosion would be his concern in the future, but *right now* he needed to get Sylvia Todorovich out.

"Message to Ambassador Todorovich," he dictated. "We are coming to you at maximum speed, ETA two point five hours. Get aboard the shuttle and be prepared to come out to meet us. It'll make life a lot easier if you can rendezvous with *Raven*, but I will do whatever is necessary to retrieve you.

"Captain Wong out."

He blinked the message away and turned his attention back to Bazzoli.

"Commander Bazzoli."

"Ser?"

"Engage."

CHAPTER THIRTY-SEVEN

THE TANKS WERE DESIGNED TO MAKE SURE A HUMAN COULD survive twenty pseudogravities of thrust. The gel itself had a carefully adjustable viscosity to help the fragile human at its core absorb the thrust without blood ending up in the wrong places. Drugs were fed in via the air coming down the hose. Even the air itself was pressurized specifically to allow function in this circumstance.

With all of that, the human would *survive*. They couldn't function or physically *act*. Control of the ship, the drones that moved around trying to keep it intact at this thrust, all of that was exerted via a virtual-reality space linked to the internal networks of *Raven's* nine hundred SpaceDiv crew.

This was the only way a starfighter pilot operated, so Henry was more used to it than most of his crew. The starfighters flying escort on his ship certainly weren't going to have any problems keeping up with his battlecruiser.

The ETA on his network changed the moment the acceleration hammered him into immobile uselessness. At 0.5 KPS^2, their ETA had been three hours and twenty minutes. Now it was two hours and thirty minutes.

It wasn't much. It might not even be enough—but it was all the time that Henry could gain by pushing his crew to their absolute limits.

"Most of the ships have now managed to get out of suicide range, at least," Ihejirika reported. "I'm still seeing multiple exchanges of fire going on, but it seems to be quieting down...for now."

"How bad, Commander?"

"At least fifteen ships are just gone," the tactical officer said grimly. "I'm not even sure *who*. Everyone is shifting IFF protocols. It's a damn mess over there, ser."

"We're flying right into it. What about Gathering Station?"

"So far, the Restan have managed to stay out of the mess and everyone is more than a light-second away. I guess the question *now* is, how long until someone starts ignoring that?"

"And whether anyone out there is still going to try and pick a fight with us," Henry said. "Where are the Kozun and the Drifters?"

New icons flickered across his network as Ihejirika tried to ID ships.

"I can't confirm the Kozun either way," he finally admitted. "They showed up with a dreadnought and a pair of escorts, and there's enough ships still in play that I can't confirm IDs until I've managed to flag more of the beacons.

"The Drifter guardian would stand out more...but she's gone."

Henry swallowed.

"Gone?"

"Two dreadnoughts and the guardian blew each other to dust bunnies before everyone got separated. *Somebody* is going to lose trade privileges when that report gets back to the convoys," the tactical officer noted. "But there's only four dreadnoughts *left* in this mess, and they're opening up distance from each other like there's no tomorrow."

"What about the Restan capital ships at Ost?" he asked.

"They've definitely gone active, but they aren't moving

anywhere. I guess their job is to make sure this doesn't spill over onto the planet."

"And they're doing a fine job," Henry noted with an attempt at a shake of his head. The motion *hurt* and he quickly stopped. He might be mostly living in his brain and network right now, but his body was still very much getting crushed.

"Watch those dreadnoughts, Ihejirika," he ordered. "Those vectors might be away from each other, but they look like they're going to come far too close to us for *my* comfort."

"I'll watch them and try to ID them, ser," his officer replied. "But...one thing I *can* be sure of?"

"Yes?"

"The Kozun's dreadnought wasn't one of the ones that got wrecked," Ihejirika warned him. "If, say, your assassin friend is looking to notch up a battlecruiser and has some of the anti-grav-shield weaponry that's been thrown around...they could be one of the ones heading our way."

IF THE DREADNOUGHT headed toward them *wasn't* trying to intercept them, they were doing an unusually poor job of it.

"Commander Moon, warn them off," Henry ordered grimly. "Though...are we getting any coms from anyone?"

"Most of our Vesheron com protocols were subspace-based," his coms officer told him. "We didn't have any radio protocols for the Londu. We just received a radio transmission from them, but my people are having a hard time deciphering it."

"Probably took Kahlmor that long to realize he didn't *have* a protocol," *Raven*'s Captain noted. "Well, hit that dreadnought with every Vesheron radio protocol we've got. If they don't break off before they enter one light-second of us, I will have no choice but to consider them hostile."

Enough people had died today that he couldn't risk *his* people.

"If they're Kozun, we *do* have a radio protocol," Moon said. "Same if they're Resta. We *should* have protocols loaded for anyone who had a dreadnought."

The massed Vesheron factions only had fourteen captured Kenmiri dreadnoughts, after all. Several of those were already debris today. An ignoble part of him hoped that Kal Rojan's dreadnought was one of them and that the assassin had been aboard.

The universe was never so helpful, in his experience.

"Ser, we have a transmission from the Ambassador," Moon reported. "No response so far from the dreadnought."

"Play me Todorovich's message," he ordered.

The video feed lit up his network a moment later, showing him Sylvia Todorovich in the cockpit of the heavy shuttle he'd sent in.

"Captain, be advised that the Restan are in full panic mode," she said bluntly. "They are refusing to let any shuttles leave Gathering Station until the 'situation among your escorts has calmed down.'

"Of course, this is going to actively make the situation among the escorts *worse*, I'm sure. This shuttle's sensors are giving me better data than the Restan are providing, and it does not look good out there."

She swallowed hard, a momentary break in the mask visible only to Henry himself.

"The Gathering is over," she said firmly. "Without subspace communications, none of these people can engage in useful negotiations. I... I am specifically not ordering you to use force to extract us from Gathering Station. If you believe you can calm the situation out there enough to ease the Restan's paranoia, that would be preferable.

"That said, you have the better eyes on the mess out there. I am authorizing you to do whatever you judge necessary to retrieve the diplomatic party from Gathering Station. I take full responsibility for whatever is required.

"Ambassador Sylvia Todorovich...out."

Apparently, he'd grown on the Ambassador even more than he'd thought. That was a blank check, one that would cover him up to and including boarding and taking Gathering Station by force.

He wasn't sure Thompson's people could pull that off, but it was something he'd have to keep in mind.

"Let me know the moment that dreadnought responds to us or crosses the five-hundred-thousand-kilometer mark," he ordered calmly. "Or if anyone else starts shooting or the Restan make a move."

"No response or course adjustment from the dreadnought," Ihejirika confirmed. "Range is one million kilometers and dropping rapidly. I am detecting charged capacitors."

An hour left before they reached Gathering Station. That was still over six million kilometers away, barely a factor in the current problem.

The dreadnought was closing at just over fifteen hundred kilometers per second, burning at one KPS^2. Their vector wasn't directly opposite to *Raven*'s identical deceleration, which meant the potential hostile had a net acceleration of about a tenth of a kilometer per second squared.

They were already *in* missile range. Of course, a multi-minute flight time didn't leave much opportunity for surprise.

"Bazzoli," he said softly. "Can we adjust our course to line the grav-driver up on that big bastard?"

"Not without cutting our deceleration, hugely increasing our intercept time with Gathering Station and being damn obvious," she replied. "We'd have to flip again, and I can only get maybe a twentieth of a KPS^2 without the main engines."

"And they know it," he murmured. "Maintain course, Commander Bazzoli," he ordered more clearly. "Commander Ihejirika?"

"Ser?"

"We still have to let them fire the first shot," Henry told the broad-shouldered black officer. "We need to look reasonable and rational, even after the situation has gone to pot."

"If I may ask, ser, *why*?" the tactical officer demanded. "There's a dreadnought headed for us. Without adjusting their course, they'll pass within a hundred thousand kilometers of us. The money is better than even that that dreadnought has already killed a ship today.

"Why are *we* playing nice when they've already killed people?"

The tactical officer was following his orders even as he asked. There was time for the question, unless the dreadnought started launching missiles. Henry could have shut the officer down...but tactical officers became XOs became Captains. Someday down the line, Okafor Ihejirika might have to face the same decision.

"We're playing to two audiences here, Commander Ihejirika, and neither of them is on that dreadnought," Henry told him. "One is back home. Every scrap of this day is going to be examined under a microscope, and how we react, what we do, will define how the UPSF's proposals on dealing with this new galaxy are treated.

"The second audience is the Restan. They're panicking and they're afraid. We need them to start letting the diplomats go, but right now, they're being too paranoid. Someone they *trust* has to make them do it...which, since the Londu ran and everyone else started shooting at each other, means us.

"Which means we *cannot* risk that trust, Commander Ihejirika. We *will* take these bastards' best hit to make us look reasonable and respectable. And then you are going to blow them into next fucking week. Understood?"

"Yes, ser. Thank you, ser."

The range was at six hundred thousand kilometers. It was a question of nerve now. Did Kal Rojan understand space battle well enough—or trust his captain well enough—to know that closing to a hundred thousand kilometers without changing his course gave him the best first shot?

And if he *did* understand that, would the terrorist turned assassin turned right-hand man of the Kozun's ruler have the nerve to hold that long?

"Bazzoli," Henry called his navigation officer's attention gently. "We're going to hold course until they fire, and then this is what we're going to do..."

CHAPTER THIRTY-EIGHT

THE SILENCE WAS EERIE. HENRY WAS USED TO SUBSPACE COMS flying all around during combat, the Vesheron communicating with each other and occasionally flinging insults back and forth with the Kenmiri.

Kenmiri Warriors were *not* known for being reticent and humble, after all.

With the subspace coms gone, everything was limited by light-speed and radio waves again, and the other ship wasn't bothering to respond to *Raven's* transmissions.

"I can't even get a handshake protocol," Moon admitted. "I *think* they're Kozun, but they've shut their radio transmitters down completely."

"They don't want to talk to us and they aren't aborting their intercept course," Henry concluded. "Range, Commander Ihejirika?"

"Three hundred thousand kilometers...*now*."

Henry caught himself holding his breath and released it. That was a *bad* idea when under twenty gravities, even if the drugs and the tank and the virtual reality made it possible to ignore his body to a point.

They were now in weapons range. *Raven* would take just over nine seconds to flip and bring the grav-driver to bear.

"Gravity shield?" Henry asked.

"Online," Song replied instantly. "Our capacitors are charged and we're pumping extra power into the shield to shore it up."

There was only so much the shield could *do* with extra power, but Henry figured his engineer knew what she was doing.

"Range is two hundred fifty thousand kilometers," Ihejirika noted.

"Should I commence evasive maneuvers, ser?" Bazzoli asked.

"Go ahead," Henry allowed. "Keep us on course to Gathering Sta—"

"Enemy firing!"

"Return fire!" Henry barked. It was an unnecessary order. They'd already gone over the plan, and the timing was far too critical to wait for the Captain to give the order.

Six heavy plasma guns had targeted his ship and opened fire. Each of the blasts of superheated gas hammered into his shield with enough force to vaporize his ship, only to find themselves torn apart by tidal forces.

Another eight heavy lasers fired along with them and suffered the same fate. The grav-shield wasn't invincible, but the odds were in *Raven*'s favor in any given salvo of energy-weapons fire.

Twenty missiles followed the beams and plasma bolts, and Henry had his suspicions about those missiles.

What he was certain his opponent had *not* realized was that *Raven*'s heavy lasers were multidirectional. They were roughly fifteen percent more powerful than the Kenmiri beams and could just as easily be fired *behind* the battlecruiser as forward.

And the energy screen was a power hog. Just like *Raven*, the dreadnought couldn't maintain the screen and fire all of its heavy energy weapons without dipping into capacitor banks. Knowing that *Raven* had to flip to fire her main weapons, the Kozun Captain had tried to steal a second salvo without draining their ship's capacitors.

The lasers smashed into the dreadnought before the screen came up. Armor could only do so much against the brute force of the energy transfer, and armor and hull splintered under the hit.

Then the thirty-six missiles, three full salvos, that Ihejirika had prepositioned under *Raven*'s wings came to life. They didn't have the thousand kilometers per second of the launchers, but the Kozun ship was already closing at over fifteen hundred KPS.

And they weren't targeted on the dreadnought, anyway. They weren't penetrators or conversion warheads. They were straight nukes, five-hundred-megaton fusion warheads that intercepted the hostile missiles and self-destructed.

"Second salvo on the shields, *we have a blowthrough*."

Raven lurched as she spun, her crew already in acceleration tanks against the thrust that had just vanished. Plasma seared along the lower hull, creating a mirror gouge to match the missile wound on the top of the ship.

"*Firing*."

"Their screen is up," Lieutenant Rao snapped, the assistant tactical officer focusing on the enemy vessel. "Two of their turrets are gone and they've stopped firing half their lasers. Not sure if that's damage or lack of power."

"We were expecting the screen," Ihejirika said calmly as *Raven*'s shields ate a third salvo of plasma bolts.

Henry's attention was with his tactical officer—focused on the single projectile flashing across space toward the dreadnought. A conversion round could overload the energy screen, opening the path for the lasers currently wasting their energy against it.

Raven hadn't fired a conversion round.

Just before it would have hit the screen, the heavy grav-driver round *skipped*, an icosaspatial kick that moved it out of realspace for a critical fraction of a second.

It returned to regular space *inside* the dreadnought, bypassing screen and armor alike to deliver a two-hundred-kilogram projectile traveling at seven percent of the speed of light.

A projectile including another five-hundred-megaton fusion bomb.

"Direct hit, direct *internal* hit," Rao barked. "Target is losing power and drifting off course."

"Your orders, Captain?" Ihejirika asked calmly.

Henry studied the dreadnought in silence. Her engines had stopped. Her weapons had stopped. Part of him wanted to finish the job...but he was still playing to those same two audiences.

"Commander O'Flannagain," he said flatly, linking to his starfighters with a thought. "Break off and match velocity with the hostile. Remove her turrets, if you please. Once that's done...leave her."

"Understood, Captain," O'Flannagain responded. "Adjusting vectors for disabling strike."

The virtual bridge was silent, and Henry smiled.

"Well done, people," he said aloud. "Let's get back on course for Gathering Station. This asshole wasn't the mission, after all."

Damage reports were showing up on his screen and he was glad no one could see into the tank to see his wince.

Raven had got off lucky on both of the hits she'd taken, but she was now basically unarmored over almost forty percent of her hull... and three lower decks were venting to space.

It was minor damage, easily fixed from onboard resources. The tanks had even protected his people from the loss of atmosphere...but seventeen of his people were now *stuck* in their acceleration tanks until someone could retrieve them.

CHAPTER THIRTY-NINE

"Drones will have the decks sealed in another twenty minutes," Song reported. "We've cleared paths to six of the acceleration tanks in the damaged zones, but we can't retrieve them until we stop accelerating."

"That's going to be soon enough," Henry replied. They were now inside missile range of the Restan battleship and the defenses of Gathering Station itself. "We're either going to be docking with Gathering Station or picking up a shuttle in the next ten minutes. After that, we should be sticking to standard acceleration."

"Oh, thank god," the engineer replied. "The ship is going to be a *mess*, ser."

"I know," he agreed. "It was necessary."

"I saw the same screens you did, ser," Song said. "What's the plan for the battleship in our way right now?"

"Waiting for them to talk to me, Colonel Song," Henry replied. A blinking icon appeared on his screen. "And Moon is informing me they've finally sorted out the radio protocols."

"Good luck, Captain Wong."

He snorted and dropped the channel.

"Link me up, Commander Moon," he ordered. He knew he'd be sending an avatar. There wasn't much need for the Restan to see him floating in viscous clear gel, after all. It did terrible things to his hair.

"Captain Wong, this is Squadron-Voice Ta Callah," his old comrade-in-arms greeted him, her Kem harsh. "If you do not break off your course, we will open fire."

"I will break off my course when you release my Ambassador," Henry replied. At this point, *Raven* was moving slowly enough that there was almost twenty minutes left in his flight time. He was two light-seconds from the station, well out of anything except missile range.

"My orders are clear. No one leaves the station until I am certain of the security and safety of my star system," Ta Callah snapped.

"So, you admit to holding the ambassadors hostage?" Henry asked. It took four seconds for him to see the response to his question, and Ta Callah may as well have physically recoiled, for all the success she had in concealing her emotions.

"Nothing of the sort," she replied. "But people barely stopped shooting twenty minutes ago, Captain. As *you* should know."

"I did not pick that fight, Ta Callah," Henry told her. "I did not start any of this. But if you do not start letting the ambassadors go, we will see an all-new fight here, my friend. I have no desire to destroy Restan ships or kill Restan officers. You are my allies; many of you are my friends.

"But if you hold my Ambassador hostage, you become my enemy. *My* orders, Squadron-Voice, are to do whatever is necessary to retrieve my diplomatic party. The situation out here is as stable as it is going to get. You can either let Ambassador Todorovich's shuttle leave—and I would suggest letting all of the ambassadors' shuttles leave—or you can fight me."

Seconds ticked by.

"I have my orders as well," Ta Callah said. She was trying to speak calmly, and the extra focus of speaking in a non-native tongue probably helped, but her eyes screamed her fear.

"You are the commanding officer of Gathering Station's defenses," he said gently. "That battleship answers to you. The station's fixed weapons report to you. Ost is seven light-minutes away. There is no time to ask permission, Squadron-Voice. You have to decide, right here, right now.

"Are you going to hold the diplomats who came here trusting *your people's honor* hostage? Or are you going to accept that the Kenmiri have struck one last blow and the Gathering is dead where it lies?

"I am leaving with my Ambassador, Squadron-Voice Ta Callah. I would far rather do so without having killed a friend."

Four seconds of transmission lag...and then the channel went dead.

"They cut the channel on their end, ser," Moon reported. "I think Ta Callah just hung up on you."

"Let her think," Henry ordered. "We're open to her calls right up until she starts shooting."

"And then, ser?" Ihejirika asked.

"Then we kill her battleship and hope she sees sense after that," he said grimly. "My patience with the Vesheron is running out."

A MINUTE. Two. Five. Six...

"We are entering weapons range of the Restan battleship, ser," Ihejirika reported. "Any change to your orders?"

"No," Henry said. "Moon? Stand by to trans—"

"Incoming message from Ta Callah, ser!" she interrupted.

She put it through to his network without asking.

"Captain Wong, please adjust your course to pass a minimum of fifty thousand kilometers from Gathering Station," Ta Callah instructed. "We are lifting the lockdown on the shuttles and transmitting holding orbits to all escort units while we arrange rendezvous for the ambassadors.

"Minimum distance of three hundred thousand kilometers will be required from all ships, but your vector will make that extremely difficult."

Henry exhaled in relief, then activated his own coms.

"Thank you, Squadron-Voice," he told her. "You made the right decision, you know."

A new green line appeared on his screen, *Raven*'s new adjusted course...a course set at point three KPS^2 as Bazzoli finally got to cut acceleration.

"I know," Ta Callah acknowledged. "I *request* that *Raven* remain in the orbit we are sending you to provide backup to my people until further Restan units are in position to secure the station." She held up a green-skinned hand.

"It is only a request, Captain Wong, but it would be appreciated."

"I am more than willing to honor a request from a friend," Henry replied. "We'll need the time to finish our repairs before we can skip, anyway."

She exhaled.

"Home then, for you?"

"Without subspace coms, the Vesheron are done," Henry told her, putting into words what everyone in the system had to have realized. "When we cannot even talk to you without a four-week turnaround, any alliance becomes difficult at best."

"Trade is possible and I'm sure the diplomats will return in time," Ta Callah countered. "But...you put it well before. The Kenmiri in their defeat have destroyed us in turn. We never knew they held that weapon, and they have ended our alliance with it."

"Without the Vesheron, it falls to each power to maintain order around it," he said. "I trust your people to be just. I can't say the same for others."

"Nor can I. But that is the future we face," the Restan told him. "I thank you, Captain Wong. Others might have been less patient."

"Enough blood was shed today," Henry replied. "I will not shed one drop more than needed."

RAVEN SLID into her assigned orbit, exactly three hundred thousand kilometers from Gathering Station, and Henry *finally* got out of his acceleration tank. His hair and uniform still slick from the gel, he met Todorovich in the shuttle bay.

"Somehow, seeing you like that makes me feel a lot better," Leitz said dryly as the diplomats left the shuttle.

"Felix, get our people settled back aboard the ship," Todorovich ordered. "Some of the juniors are stressed the fuck out. Get them settled."

Diplomats and analysts didn't usually see a lot of training on being crammed into a shuttle with a bunch of soldiers while a space battle raged outside. In Henry's opinion, they probably should.

The Ambassador gestured for him to join her away from the slow trickle of soldiers and diplomats leaving the shuttle.

"Do we even know whose dreadnought you wrecked?" she asked.

"Not yet," Henry admitted. "We probably will before we leave, but it's almost certainly the Kozun. The people we're going to have to deal with most, going forward."

"Because what we need when our government wants to stay the hell out of everything is an enemy," Todorovich said with a shake of her head. "How quickly can we get home, Henry?"

"I promised Ta Callah we'd stay here until her reinforcements arrived," he said. "That'll be about six hours. If we plan to stick around for ten, that will cover making sure all of the ambassadors get out safely and discharge any pretense of moral obligation here."

"And then four weeks?" she asked.

"Exactly. Same series of skips as it took us to get here to get back to Procyon...and then we need to sort out what exactly we're telling the UPA."

"The Vesheron as we knew it is dead," Todorovich replied. "There's not much else to say."

"They're going to want a recommendation from us, Sylvia," Henry pointed out. "They're going to look to you and me, as the leaders and the ones who dealt with this mess, to at least *suggest* what the UPA and UPSF should do next."

Every action he'd taken since the first mine went off had been keeping that moral authority in mind. He wasn't sure what he wanted to say, but he knew he needed to make sure that he got to speak.

"Do next?" The Ambassador shook her head. "We know what they want to do next, Henry. They're going to pull the UPA's head back into their shell and try and forget any of this ever happened while we quietly expand our own dominion."

"We helped bring things to this point," Henry replied. "I know what our government wants to do, Sylvia. But I can't help but feel that it's wrong. That we have an obligation out here to do *something*."

"To do *what*, Henry? We can't wage a war out here. We can't even afford to position ships on trade routes, let alone take on some quixotic mission of peace and justice."

"I don't know what we need to do yet," he admitted. "But a 'quixotic mission of peace and justice' sure as hell sounds better to me than writing off ten thousand star systems and everyone who lives in them, doesn't it?"

She was looking at him sharply, and despite all of his experience reading expressions, Henry really wasn't sure what was behind her gaze.

"You're a strange damn man, Henry Wong," she told him. "You know Don Quixote is a *tragedy*, right?"

"Yeah. But maybe I'm thinking a few minor tragedies to avoid a major one is a worthy trade."

"Think on it," she told him. "If you can come up with a plan, I can get you in front of the right people. But it's going to have to be you, Captain Wong. The man the Vesheron call 'the Destroyer'. The man who ended the Kenmorad and saved *my* life.

"I can put you in front of the right people, but you're the one who has to know what kind of mission you want and be able to sell it."

Henry inhaled deeply, met that strangely intense gaze of Sylvia Todorovich's, and nodded firmly.

"Then I'd better get thinking on that plan, shouldn't I?"

"I'd suggest a shower first," she told him with a laugh.

CHAPTER FORTY

"ALIGNING WITH ASSIGNED ORBIT...NOW," BAZZOLI REPORTED.

Every screen surrounding Henry on *Raven's* bridge was busy, full of icons and images as dozens—*hundreds*—of ships swarmed through Earth orbit.

The homeworld itself was central on most of the screens, its green and blue hues still calming for the descendants of her diaspora. A cleared zone had been established inside geostationary orbit for safety purposes, but above that, space stations were as close to each other as safety margins allowed.

"Well done, Commander," Henry told her, rising from his seat. "Lagrange Yards has a slot clearing for us in six hours. You feeling up to that navigation challenge?"

"Whether I am or not, Earth Traffic Control will feed me the course," Bazzoli replied. "Nobody picks their own course here."

He nodded his acknowledgement and turned to face Iyotake. His XO was standing behind his chair, waiting. The Native American man saluted crisply.

"You ready, ser?" he asked.

"No," Henry admitted as he returned the salute. "This is not my battlespace, Colonel Iyotake. But it's the battle I got called to. You'll take good care of her?"

"It's one meeting, ser," his XO pointed out with a grin. "I don't think they're planning on shooting you."

"You never know," Henry replied. "You have the conn, Lieutenant Colonel Iyotake. Once I'm in, my network will be cut off for security reasons. If you have any questions, get them to me before I hit the surface."

"*Raven* can take care of herself for twenty-four hours, Captain Wong," Iyotake assured him. "It's not the first time the Ambassador has hauled you away."

"You should be at Lagrange Yards by the time I'm free," Henry said. "Send me an update and I'll arrange a shuttle from there."

"We'll be waiting for you, ser," his XO confirmed, then offered his hand. They shook firmly and Henry gave his subordinate a nod.

He almost made it off the bridge before Iyotake's voice sounded one more time.

"Company! Atten-tion!"

Henry paused on his heel and turned around. The entire bridge crew was on their feet, facing him with perfect academy salutes.

He returned the salute, concealing a smile.

"I'll be back," he promised. "Don't break her while I'm gone, will you?"

TODOROVICH WAS WAITING by their shuttle. Most of her staff would be traveling separately—they were returning to the actual operational offices of the United Planets Alliance on the moon. Felix Leitz stood beside the sharp-edged Ambassador as they waited for him.

Their pilot stood by the shuttle door as well, and that was *not* right.

"Commander O'Flannagain," Henry greeted his CAG. "I don't believe you normally pilot shuttles."

"Nope," she confirmed. "But I know how and, well...*nobody* is flying my Captain into the cesspit that is New York but me."

At some point, he'd become *her* Captain. That was novel.

"All right, Commander. But *only* because we're in as safe an orbit as we possibly can be," he warned. "You have too much responsibility as CAG."

"But we're in Earth orbit, so *Raven* is safe...and you're flying into New York, which means you aren't," she said brightly. "The city is full of *politicians*."

Todorovich cleared her throat.

"You're a diplomat, Em Todorovich," O'Flannagain pointed out. "*Much* more useful breed."

"I think that might be the nicest thing a UPSF officer has ever said about us," Leitz replied. "Regardless of who is flying this bird, we need to get going." He tapped his ear to indicate he was getting data from his network.

"Updates are saying that the weather over New York is crap, but you do *not* miss an appointment with the Security Council!"

Only years of training prevented Henry from having a spike of panic at the thought as Todorovich ushered him onto the shuttle. It was one thing to be in a meeting with the Secretary-President, her subordinates and several admirals.

It was quite another to be speaking in front of the Security Council, the representatives of the member systems of the United Planets Alliance. They had no real power over the UPA, but they were also the people who'd go back to their governments and convince them to either support or deny new funding agreements.

"You'll be fine," Todorovich murmured in his ear as they took their seats.

"Feels like this should be anybody but me," Henry replied. "An Admiral or an undersecretary or somebody with authority."

"Even if we sent an Admiral or an undersecretary or, hell, me on my own, we'd still just be presenting the plan you put together," she reminded him.

Six weeks had been plenty of time to put the skeleton of a plan together, even given the resource limitations Henry knew the UPSF faced.

"Plus, if we were sending someone else, you'd have to sell the UPSF or UPA leadership on this in advance," she said with a chuckle. "This way, we only have to sell the plan to one hostile audience."

"I'm not sure that helps," Henry replied. "One shot, with a starship captain as the only one to speak to the plan."

"You're the Destroyer, the man who landed the final blow against the Kenmorad," Todorovich pointed out. "I know that's a nightmare for you, but it gives you weight. But more than that...it means you understand *why* this has to be done."

She squeezed his shoulder.

"You know what you need to do, Colonel Henry Wong," she told him, her hand lingering on his shoulder to reinforce her message. "Make your battle plan, and when you meet the enemy, toss it aside and improvise."

THE COMPLEX HAD STARTED in the twentieth century as the United Nations building. That organization had waxed and waned in influence over the years until the final three-way conflict between the United States Colonial Administration, the Novaya Imperiya and the Terran Alliance of the rest of the colonies had consumed human space in fire for eleven years.

When the peace conferences had severed *all* the colonies from their mother nations, a new structure had been needed to keep humanity at least nominally unified. The United Planets Alliance had been born, absorbing chunks of the interstellar administration of the Terran Alliance powers alongside all of what was left of the UN.

The UPA operated primarily out of offices on the Moon under the watchful guns of UPSF Base Mario, but tradition said that the General Assembly met on Earth: in the old UN building, now the central structure of the UPA complex.

The guards who met their party at the shuttle pad were overtly decorative, in dark red uniforms that were cut in the style of the old French Foreign Legion. The way the Assembly Security Force soldiers moved, though, told Henry they were far less decorative than they looked.

The fact that they carried fully functional energy weapons, still a rarity in human space outside of elite UPSF GroundDiv assault companies, finished the story. Dressed up or not, the ASF were real soldiers doing a very real job.

"We need to scan everyone before you leave the pad, please," the woman leading the team told them. "No weapons are permitted in the UPA Complex except with ASF personnel."

Henry shrugged and unbelted the sword and gun from his dress uniform.

"I have these," he told her. "I presume you have safe storage for them?"

The officer eyed the platinum energy pistol—a third of the size and three-quarters of the power of her rifle, as befitted the former personal weapon of a Kenmorad—with cautious respect.

"Of course, Colonel Wong," she said. "We're used to the requirements of UPSF dress uniform. At some point, we'll even convince your superiors to *tell* people they need to leave those behind when they come here."

"Military tradition grinds slowly, Em...?"

"Lieutenant Cole, ser," she replied as her team finished scanning them. Henry winced as his network threw up an alert informing him that its external scan protocols had been activated. "Sergeant?"

"No weapons, and networks are clear of intrusion worms," the ASF noncom replied. "They are clear. IDs match the appointment."

"Good." Cole shook her head. "If we had to run anything more intrusive, you'd be at risk of being late. And even *we*, Colonel Wong, do not want to waste the Secretary-President's time."

Let alone the Security Council's went unspoken.

"Come," she instructed. "I'll show you the way."

From the way Cole's team fell in around Henry and his companions, strangers in this place were kept under escort. *Show you the way* made for a solid excuse for doing so without offense, though.

It was all very smooth and friendly and diplomatic...and still probably more effective than a harsher approach might have been.

"ARE YOU READY?" Todorovich repeated as they approached a large set of double doors. She was whispering. Their networks were now truly internal, wireless-suppression nodes throughout this section of the building keeping them from linking to anything else.

"No more than I was earlier," Henry told her.

"Remember who you are and why you're here," she suggested. "Everything else is logistics, Colonel."

"We're here," Cole told them, stopping beside the door. She tapped a hand against a panel, presumably checking data with her network—she probably had a specialty system that let her network connect despite the suppression field. "You are one minute early, but they're ready for you.

"Go on in." She held up a hand to Leitz. "Just the Ambassador and the Colonel, Em Leitz."

The chief of staff nodded his acknowledgement and faded back against a wall as the doors slid open. Henry swallowed hard, years of training failing to control the instinct this time, and then stepped forward into the belly of the beast.

Said belly was surprisingly familiar. It was a midsized conference room, the same as would have been attached to any Admiral's suite on a space station or planetside base. It had been arranged slightly differently, with a single table facing the rest of the room to allow for witnesses to be questioned, but the furniture and the room itself were identical.

He recognized Secretary-President Vasudha Patil at the back of the room. The lighting had been rearranged at some point to keep the dark-skinned woman from blending into the shadow. Instead, she was highlighted like she was sitting in a halo of divine light.

Henry doubted that the symbolism was unintentional.

Admiral Lee Saren sat at Patil's right hand, but the back of the conference room was otherwise unoccupied.

The middle row was the key. Thirteen people occupied those seats, each with a nameplate stating their name and who they represented. One Councilor for each of the UPA's eight star systems, plus five for the Earth powers that weren't considered part of the Sol Councilor's area of authority.

The United States, Russia, China, the European Union and the African Union were all powerful enough to equal the economic weight of entire star systems. It was telling that of the thirteen Councilors, only the American, Russian and Chinese Councilors represented truly single-bloc nations in the old sense.

"Take a seat, Colonel Wong, Ambassador Todorovich," Patil instructed, gesturing toward the table facing the Security Council. "The Security Council is waiting."

The Security Council, Henry figured, could probably speak for themselves. They almost certainly would before this was over.

Nonetheless, he took his seat and faced the fifteen people who would decide whether his quixotic quest was going to crash and burn or be the flag that led humanity into a new era.

"Ambassador Todorovich has called in more favors than I thought she was owed and has probably blackmailed at least one person to get this meeting, Colonel Wong," Patil told him once they were seated. "You understand, I'm sure, that the United Planets Alliance is in a state of flux, dealing with an all-new environment now that the subspace network is gone."

"I presume the Kenmiri's message made it this far," Henry said softly.

"It did," Admiral Saren confirmed. "Fortunately for us, we had the schematics and automated construction templates for the skip-drive courier drones used prior to the Unity War. They were even modernized, as aspects of that technology are key in our grav-shield penetrator weapons."

"We are back in regular communication with all of the UPA's stars and outposts," Patil continued. "It will take time for us to get used to a two-week to four-week communication turnaround, but humanity has run governments with that before. We will meet this challenge, as we have met the challenges that faced us in the past."

That was directed at the Security Council rather than him, Henry suspected.

"But this calls for much of the focus and funding of the UPA," the Keid Councilor said in accented English, the massive black man's Nigerian heritage still coming through. "And you would have Secretary-President Patil expand that focus—an expansion that would require new funding agreements. More money from a population that has not seen a practical increase in their safety from their investment in a decade."

"Em Kariuki summarizes the situation well, I think," the American Councilor said crisply. Em Kennedy was a redheaded woman in an old-fashioned suit, glaring at Henry with cold eyes.

He'd hoped for at least some support from his countrywoman, but it seemed he was going to have to start from the beginning.

"I think the proposal is quite straightforward," he said slowly. "Beginning with long cruises to survey stars and locate potential trouble spots, we would locate systems in need of our assistance and provide that assistance. We would secure alliances, friends and trade routes, starting in the Ra Sector and expanding as rapidly as practically possible.

"In the long run, the expanded trade routes should make the increased strength of the UPSF required for this operation self-supporting. In the short term, as Em Kariuki notes, the UPA would require new funding agreements with the member nations to support expanded operations of our battlecruisers and an expansion of our destroyer strength."

He studied the Security Council and laid his hands flat on the table in front of him.

"All of the details of the logistics, the trade routes we know we should be able to open, the potential threats we know are out there... all of those details are in the download you have all been provided," he reminded them. "Ambassador Todorovich's analysts and my own crew aboard *Raven* have calculated cost-benefit ratios under a dozen scenarios, done Monte Carlo analyses, and projected the long-term economic benefits of this plan to the United Planets Alliance and our member stars.

"But that is not what you are questioning, and that is not why we need to do this," Henry told them. He'd stood up. When had he stood up?

"We can argue the costs and the benefits of becoming peace-keepers to the galaxy, but they are entirely secondary," he continued. "We need to do this. Because if we don't, if you decide you would rather spend a piddling amount of money at home than outside our borders, millions are going to die.

"We *broke* the galactic order. We shattered the peace the Kenmiri enforced. *We committed genocide.*

"There is blood on your soldiers' hands. We are *drowning* in the blood of a species, and we keep denying it," Henry said fiercely, hoping that his words would have *some* impact. "We set into motion the fall of the greatest civilization we have ever known. It needed to fall. It needed to be broken, but ours are the hands that broke it.

"The consequences of that now fall upon the galaxy. Ten thousand stars face an uncertain future, and a million greedy potential warlords look to their neighbors as prey. *We* caused that. *We* made their predation possible.

"We can let that stand. We can let *ten thousand stars* fall into anarchy and fire and death. You can watch your soldiers fall, one by one, to the ancient curse of our kind as our very *souls* rebel against what we did.

"Or we can do what humanity always does when our back is to the wall. We can *fight*."

He realized he couldn't even see the Councilors, and he brushed angry tears from his eyes.

"It was *my* hand that finished the Kenmorad," he told them, forcing his voice to calm. "My hand that set into motion the final doom of a race of a trillion sentient beings. Therapy can give me the ability to live with that, but it can never give me peace.

"We have damned ten thousand stars. Let us reach out our hands and help as many of them as we can reach."

He ran out of words, standing there, staring at fourteen politicians and hoping that enough of them understood. That enough of them could hear the truth.

"Breathe, Colonel Wong," Kariuki told him, the big man's voice very soft. He glanced around at his compatriots. "If you and the Ambassador could give us a few minutes?" he asked. "I believe we should discuss this in private."

THE DISADVANTAGE of having a computer network embedded in your body was a perfect sense of time. It was seventeen minutes and forty-two seconds from the moment the door closed to the moment it opened again.

"Come in, Colonel, Ambassador," Saren told them, the Admiral holding the door with her own hands. She led them back to the table at the front and stood next to them.

"We have discussed your proposal and your...assessment of its necessity," Councilor Tzu told him. The androgynous Chinese councilor looked at him gently. "Some of us pretend to have hearts of iron, Colonel, but we are all human. Most of us have, in fact, been soldiers.

"Your points ring true, but I must remind you that it is not the Security Council's task to authorize new funding agreements. It is, in truth, our task to say no to the UPA's leadership when we believe that the nations we represent have no chance of saying yes."

"We are not saying no this time," Kariuki said loudly and clearly, as if shutting down any last scraps of argument. "I will take your proposal—and, I think, a recording of your presentation—to Keid. I believe I can convince the Grand Council to authorize a funding agreement to keep your peacekeepers in operation."

"We will all take your proposal home," Kennedy confirmed. "And we will do all we can. For now, though, to begin this operation calls for the UPA to take on the risk that our governments will *not* choose to fund it."

"Then we will take that risk," Saren said flatly. "Too many of my officers came back from Golden Lancelot looking for an answer. They don't know the question yet, and therapy helps them put it aside, but they are still looking for an answer. I do believe that Colonel Wong has finally helped me understand the question:

"We have committed a great evil. However necessary, the destruction of a species can be described no other way. How, then, do we make up for that? How do we balance our accounts with God?

"To be peacekeepers is only a beginning, but the need is there, and we have the strength to act. While you convince your governments that the funding will be required, I and the rest of UPSF command will go over Colonel Wong's proposals in detail.

"By the time your ship is ready to return to action, Captain Wong, we will have a peacekeeping fleet to send you to."

Henry bowed his head in relief. He'd done it. Somehow, he'd done it.

He knew the task he'd set before himself and his comrades wasn't an easy one. It was, in many ways, an impossible one. They couldn't save everyone.

But to balance their accounts, they would save everyone they could.

JOIN THE MAILING LIST

Love Glynn Stewart's books? To know as soon as new books are released, special announcements, and a chance to win free paperbacks, join the mailing list at:

glynnstewart.com/mailing-list/

ABOUT THE AUTHOR

Glynn Stewart is the author of *Starship's Mage*, a bestselling science fiction and fantasy series where faster-than-light travel is possible–but only because of magic. His other works include science fiction series *Duchy of Terra, Castle Federation* and *Vigilante,* as well as the urban fantasy series *ONSET* and *Changeling Blood.*

Writing managed to liberate Glynn from a bleak future as an accountant. With his personality and hope for a high-tech future intact, he lives in Southern Ontario with his partner, their cats, and an unstoppable writing habit.

VISIT GLYNNSTEWART.COM FOR NEW RELEASE UPDATES

📘 facebook.com/glynnstewartauthor

OTHER BOOKS
BY GLYNN STEWART

For release announcements join the mailing list or visit **GlynnStewart.com**

STARSHIP'S MAGE

Starship's Mage
Hand of Mars
Voice of Mars
Alien Arcana
Judgment of Mars
UnArcana Stars
Sword of Mars
Mountain of Mars
The Service of Mars
A Darker Magic
Mage-Commander
Beyond the Eyes of Mars
Nemesis of Mars (*upcoming*)

Starship's Mage: Red Falcon
Interstellar Mage
Mage-Provocateur
Agents of Mars

Pulsar Race: A Starship's Mage Universe Novella

DUCHY OF TERRA

The Terran Privateer
Duchess of Terra
Terra and Imperium
Darkness Beyond
Shield of Terra
Imperium Defiant
Relics of Eternity
Shadows of the Fall
Eyes of Tomorrow

SCATTERED STARS

Scattered Stars: Conviction
Conviction
Deception
Equilibrium
Fortitude
Huntress
Prodigal *(upcoming)*

Scattered Stars: Evasion
Evasion
Discretion
Absolution *(upcoming)*

PEACEKEEPERS OF SOL

Raven's Peace
The Peacekeeper Initiative
Raven's Course
Drifter's Folly
Remnant Faction
Raven's Flag *(upcoming)*

EXILE

Exile
Refuge
Crusade
Ashen Stars: An Exile Novella

CASTLE FEDERATION

Space Carrier Avalon
Stellar Fox
Battle Group Avalon
Q-Ship Chameleon
Rimward Stars
Operation Medusa
A Question of Faith: A Castle Federation Novella

Dakotan Confederacy
Admiral's Oath
To Stand Defiant *(upcoming)*

VIGILANTE
(WITH TERRY MIXON)
Heart of Vengeance
Oath of Vengeance

**Bound By Stars: A Vigilante Series
(With Terry Mixon)**
Bound By Law
Bound by Honor
Bound by Blood

TEER AND KARD
Wardtown
Blood Ward

CHANGELING BLOOD
Changeling's Fealty
Hunter's Oath
Noble's Honor
Fae, Flames & Fedoras: A Changeling Blood Novella

ONSET
ONSET: To Serve and Protect
ONSET: My Enemy's Enemy
ONSET: Blood of the Innocent
ONSET: Stay of Execution
Murder by Magic: An ONSET Novella

STAND ALONE NOVELS & NOVELLAS
Children of Prophecy
City in the Sky
Excalibur Lost: A Space Opera Novella
Balefire: A Dark Fantasy Novella

Made in United States
North Haven, CT
28 October 2023

43307833R00190